KARLEE BERRIOS

Albatross

Contents

Trigger/ Content Warnings

- Mentions of past assault
- Anxiety Attacks/ PTSD
- Violence & Gore
- Torture
- Alcohol Use
- Sexual Harrassment (mild)
- Misogyny (Religious in nature)

A special trigger warning for people like me:

I have spent years deconstructing my own religious trauma. Writing this story has been a part of that. If you are triggered by religious themes, including the rampant misogyny and violence against women due to it, maybe pick another book. I mention this not to deter you, but because I love you and want to protect your peace.

Content Shopping List

Okay, we all know what we're here for. Here's your kink list, you sick freaks. I love you.

- MFM & MMF content
- Voyeurism
- Primal Play
- Orgasm Denial
- Praise & Degradation
- Squirting
- Public Play
- Sex Toys

Dedication

This book is for you.
Whether you're here because you're a romantic at heart, a spice fanatic, or just someone who likes Venom a little more than they should. Trust me, *I get it.*

This book is also for the survivors. I see you. I love you.

1

This is Why I Don't Leave The House

Bel

"Oh fuck- yes, yes, right there!" *Wow, really?* "Oh, don't stop, I'm coming!" *No one comes that quickly, and from penetration only? Please.*

"He groans loud and long in my ear, filling me to the brim with his spend." *Oh, that didn't last long. At least she got to come first, I guess.*

Ring* *Ring

Is that my phone?

I can't even greet my caller before she begins to shout, "You better be dressed cuz we are going out!"

"I'm on a deadline, I."

"That you gave yourself," based on the rustling on the other side, Isla is scrambling to get herself ready, too.

Before I can dignify that with a response, she blurts, "Do they fuck in this one?"

"Yes, Isla. You called right in the middle of the climax, and now I'll have to re-record the entire scene."

"I have a better idea. Instead of reading and talking about getting railed, you actually *experience* it."

I try and fail to keep from sighing. It seems like we talk about this constantly. She believes in trying everything at least once, while I think things can be experienced safely from a distance. My job gives me what I need without the risk. "My book and a toy can get me off better than any man could."

"Do you get off listening to your own voice recordings? I totally would."

Stifling a laugh, I ask, "Mine? Or your own?"

"Both. Now I'll give you 20 minutes to *finish*," Isla cackles, "then I'm showing up and you better be dressed and ready to go."

"Where are we go—"

"You know exactly where we're going," she tells me, "Put on your littlest dress and those killer heels, right fucking now."

* * *

45 minutes later, Isla is dragging me out the door to a taxi, where the driver looks as happy to be there as I do.

"Ladies, we gotta get a move on. Unfortunately, I don't get paid to sit here and idle."

"I'm so sorry," she tells him. "I'll leave a good tip and a five star review, I swear."

"Alright, alright. But we gotta get goin'. You've got two minutes, then I'm outta here, with or without you."

Last chance. I open my mouth to protest again, but the look on Isla's face has me snapping it shut. She's usually pretty go-with-the-flow, but right now, she's on a mission.

Once we get settled into the backseat, she nudges me with her shoulder and says, "Tonight is the night, Bel. I can feel it in my bones."

"The night for what? To get frostbite? It's colder than Santa's tits right now."

"Babes, we live in the desert. It's still 70 degrees," she laughs. "No, tonight is the night we both find the loves of our lives." I hold back an eye roll.

Don't get me wrong, I adore her enthusiasm and positivity. She's seen more loss and heartache than anyone I know, yet nothing seems to hold her back. She gets her heart broken at least once a month, but every time she gets back on her feet, ready to try again.

Meanwhile, I've resigned myself to the fact that I'll never let another man touch me again. My therapist calls it "avoidance," but I think it's just self-preservation. If they can't get close to me, they can't hurt me. If I have to be a bitch them first to keep them at a distance, I'll do that too. And honestly, I'm comfortable this way. I like my life, my solitude, my freedom. I like living my life however I want, without restrictions.

Of course, I can't say any of that to her. She'll just give me some platitude about how we can't give up and that there's someone out there for everyone. I keep hoping some of her glass-half-full thinking will rub off on me, but sometimes I worry her heartaches cripple me more than they do her. If she needs me to take the brunt of the pain of each of her breakups so she can keep her sunny disposition, I'll do it.

Tuning back into her monologue about *seizing the moment,* I stop her and ask, "Wait. I thought you were seeing someone," and that was the wrong fucking thing to say. Maybe someday I'll learn to keep my mouth shut, but I guess it's not today.

For a split second, I see the gut-wrenching look I've come to know so well. Then she waves a hand in front of herself as if dispelling the bad vibes and gives me her best *I'm not bothered at all* tone, "Yeah, well it didn't work out. She said that I need to choose a side. *Pick a team,*" she emphasizes with air quotes.

Now that I've taken the wind out of her sails, she redirects to another conversation we've had before. "People just don't get it, Bel. It's not about teams or sides or any of that. I just want to find a person. *My* person. He, she, they, does it really matter?"

"It shouldn't matter, no. You'll find someone who gets it eventually," I repeat back the words she's tried to tell me a thousand fucking times. Even if I don't believe in true love, I know that if anyone deserves it, it's her.

"Alright, ladies, we're here. Have a good night," our driver announces.

"Ahh, I'm so pumped!" Isla pulls a wad of cash from her handbag and counts it out, handing it up to him before giving him her friendliest smile and wave, shouting, "Thank you so much, sir, have a good one!" as we step towards the bar.

It smells like Vegas in here. I stifle a gag at the stench of cigarette smoke, booze, and sweaty bodies. I might have more faith in the whole *finding the one* plan if we had somewhere to go nearby that wasn't so run-down. I shouldn't have such a crappy attitude, especially since I know that once I get settled in, something about this place feels like home. We know all the bartenders, we can usually guess what songs are going to play, and we can always sense which group is going to start a fight.

But with that same knowledge comes the wisdom that we will have met 99% of the patrons, too. I don't think Chad, who drives home half-drunk every weekend, is going to be the love of my life. And I'll be damned before he gets his grabby hands on my friend.

Glancing around, I do see a couple faces I've never seen before, and as Isla drags me towards the bar, I get a whiff of a familiar cologne and freeze. Every inch of my body suddenly feels cold, there's a ten-ton weight on my chest, and I have the urge to puke all over my shoes.

It's not him. He's two states away. That stupid cologne is like catnip for douchebags like him.

I try to take stock of the world around me to help calm my racing thoughts. I find one thing I can see: that god-awful neon Corona sign above the bar. Then something I can hear: coincidentally, also that fucking sign. Something I can smell: the sharp citrusy scent of the bar cleanser. Something I can feel: my toes squished into these heels Isla insisted I wear. And finally, something I can taste: our favorite bartender, Char, slides me a sparkly pink mystery cocktail with a wink. I take a small sip, and all the tension bleeds out of me.

If I got one good thing out of therapy, it's that single exercise.

* * *

After an hour or so, I'm actually having a great time. Neither of us has found anyone who piques our interest, but that's not *really* why we're here. Whether she'll admit it or not, Isla just needed a night out. If she needs to make every outing a clandestine affair to ensure she doesn't get discouraged, I'll happily play along.

But then there's the more difficult part of being out with her. I always find myself envious of Isla when we're in public. Even just in sweatpants, she's beautiful. But when we do go out, it's harrowing to stand next to her. From her wavy, dark hair, always sun-kissed and freckled face, to her eyes that can best be described as storm cloud gray, she's the kind of beauty that strikes fear into the heart of every man.

If her looks weren't enough, there's the effortless way she seems to float through the world. Every person we meet becomes charmed by her, like she always knows the right thing to say. When she speaks to you, she makes you feel like her entire world revolves around you; Like there's nowhere she'd rather be. While I find it safe to assume every conversation I have with a stranger is tainted with an expression that says *Get me the fuck out of here.*

Getting drunk and waxing poetic about my friends' beauty? This is what Friday nights have become? Maybe I should try to get laid or something. With that, I think I've had enough liquor and get a beer instead.

We're sitting at the bar, snacking on cheese fries and chatting with Ash when they have a break between customers. When someone loudly plops onto the chair beside me and snaps their fingers at them, I'm hit with a whiff of that horrible cologne.

Before Ash can fully get to the snap-happy asshole, he blurts, "Top-shelf vodka tonic."

I shoot Isla and look, and she gives me the same one. Women's universal code for *Can you believe this prick?*

Completely unaware of our silent conversation, he leans our way and slurs over the music, "*Heyyy.* Buy you a drink?"

"Which one of us are you talking to?" Isla asks, masking her laughter. This guy is so drunk he can't focus on either of us. I grab her arm in an attempt to keep my cackling at bay.

His eyes make their way lasciviously over both of us, pausing to keep eye contact with both of our tits before proudly proclaiming, "Both. I'll buy you both a drink."

Listen. If some dickhead wants to ogle the girls for a second and buy me a drink for the privilege, who am I to say no?

"Sure." Ash is watching us, an amused grin on their face, and I ask, "Can we please get two more of these?"

"Of course. On this guy?"

"On that guy," Isla answers, wiggling all her fingers in his general direction.

Once Ash places the drinks in front of us, we look at each other, mutter a small thanks to the buyer, then grab our goodies and stand to walk away.

"Hey, hey, hey wait!" Drunk-guy holds up a hand to stop us. "You can't just take the drinks an-and just *go*."

"Well, why not?" Isla begins.

"You didn't say there were any conditions to buying us drinks." I add.

"What is it that you were expecting?" She finishes.

He firmly grabs my arm and forces me to plop in the seat next to him, "You're *supposed* to sit and drink with me." His face is turning beet red, and I'm beginning to wonder if this guy is drunk enough to make a scene. Honestly, I've been keeping calm about his proximity thus far, but there's only so much I can take.

"Hey buddy, keep your hands to your self," I vaguely register Ash saying. From the rough treatment and the awful stench, it's like I'm hearing it all through a wind tunnel, thanks the roaring in my ears. The room starts to spin again, and I fight for balance.

I push off my chair, slam my beer on the bar top, and lurch toward the bathroom. Fortunately, it's not a busy enough night that there's a line, so I beeline to a stall and barely make it in time before the food and all the beer force their way back up.

Within seconds, Isla kneels beside me and holds my hair back as I retch again and again. It's not the first time she's witnessed a panic attack, but it is the first time it's been accompanied by bar music and a symphony of drunk idiots.

"Hey babes," she soothes, "Ash is calling us a cab, okay?" All I can do is nod my head. "I can't believe that guy put his hands on you like that. But don't you worry, he gets to wear half a vodka tonic and an entire pint of beer for the rest of the night."

"Ohhh god, don't make me laugh, I'm gonna vom again," I do not want to spend any more time on my knees in a public restroom. She gently helps me to my feet, then wets a paper towel and hands it to me.

"You good to walk? I bet the cab's here by now." *She's rubbing my back like I'm a child. God, this is humiliating.* As we make our way outside, I keep my head down. I don't even want to chance a glimpse of that asshole.

When we get to the taxi, I duck inside, lay my head against the seat and try not to let my mind wander back to why that man had such an overwhelming effect on me. He's definitely not the first dickhead to think he had a right to my body, but usually, I can deal with it. Could something as insignificant as cologne really send me back to that place so quickly? I guess so.

* * *

Pulling up to my house, Isla hops out first and gives our driver her signature, ultra-friendly send-off before linking her arm in mine and carting me inside.

"Since your stomach is totally empty now, we should order a pizza!" she gushes.

"Sure. Just give me a minute to change and brush my fuckin teeth," I just *know* that I smell rank right now. "Do you need some sweats?"

"Please!" she nods, "I'll order while you go do your thing."

I make my way toward my en-suite bathroom and pull my hair up out of my face. After brushing my teeth and changing into my designated home sweats, I grab a fresh pair from the dryer for Isla.

Her and I being nearly the same clothing size has been a godsend. We both grew up being the only girls bigger than a size two, so when we found each other and could finally experience the glory of sharing clothes, it was nothing short of life-changing.

I hand her the clothes, and as she walks down the hall, she shouts back to me, "I'm going to just use Charlies room tonight, okay?" She should just start calling it her room since she stays in there every time she's here.

She returns, having changed into the unofficial uniform for pizza and movies. We turn on whatever some new rom-com for background noise and spend a few minutes unwinding by playing on our phones.

I'm reading, of course. Prepping for the new book I need to start tomorrow. *Demon summoning? And there's no spice? Just a plain old horror book. That'll be a good break from all the fake moaning and noisemakers.* And I'm pretty sure Isla is prepping for her presentation next week.

When the pizza finally arrives we dive in, not bothering with plates. We have this routine down so much it's nearly clockwork now. Bar, home, sweats, pizza. There's nowhere I'd rather be than right here with my best friend, but I know she dreams of so much more. Love, kids, the whole happily ever after thing. I just want to enjoy a quiet life, left to my own devices. *Lots of devices.*

Isla gives me the respect of not trying to ask about the events earlier in the night. She knows by now that I won't talk about it, not about tonight or why it was so triggering. Anytime my past comes up, she gives me this look so full of pity it makes me sick. I don't need her feeling bad for me. What I went through wasn't even a big deal. Everyone's first time having sex is a disaster, so why should I— or anyone else, for that matter— feel sorry about it?

After we are both stuffed and sleepy, I pour myself into bed, and she does the same. She's a morning person— *ew*— so she'll be up and out of here long before I'm ready to drag my ass out of bed.

In my still half-drunk state, I do my best not to let tonight's events tear me back years in time, but *fuck*, it's so difficult sometimes. Try as I might, the last thing I remember before falling into a fitful sleep is memories of wild, hateful blue eyes and unwelcome hands.

2

The Prude and The Papercut

Bel

After the disaster that was Friday night, the only thing I want to do is focus on my next project. Dragging myself out of bed, I go about my morning— *okay, late morning—* routine. After brushing my teeth and smoothing my hair into a braid down my back, I brew my coffee in one of my best punny mugs and make myself a bagel and some eggs. I take my breakfast and set it on the kitchen table next to my computer.

The best part of working from home is being able to do it in my pajamas. I just have to change from my *sleeping* jammies to my *working* ones. Neither set are acceptable for others to see, but at least these ones don't have tears in the seams from years of usage.

Glancing at my phone halfway through breakfast I see a few texts I've missed.

Isla: Hey, I'm thinking this year we go on vacation for Christmas.

Isla: Somewhere with snow!

Isla: Do you have a passport? I forget.

Isla: Maybe just Colorado for some skiing?

Absofuckinglutely not. I respond with a gif of a disgusted face, followed up by, **You're not gonna catch me dead in the snow.**

For the last few years, we've been each other's family. We go on vacation for the holidays, so she doesn't get pressured into going home. Yet again, another reason I have no interest in getting tied down to a man. What man is going to support me and my best friend gallivanting off across the states just to hide from her fucked up family?

As I sip my coffee she doesn't respond, and I message her again, **Hey, I'm plugging in to do some work, so we'll have to figure it all out later.**

I look through my email and respond to a few, hoping to land a couple more jobs so I can be ready for the upcoming holiday season. Studying my calendar, I find empty spaces where I can squeeze in a few hours here and there. If all goes to plan, I can still fit another three jobs before Thanksgiving.

I'm not super close with my family, but I still want to be able to get them something. Doing all that this year will be extra tough since Charlie moved out, leaving me without a roommate in this massive, *expensive* apartment. I can manage, but it sucks having to.

Of course, I'm so glad Charlie found his happily ever after, and I would never suggest he hold himself back from moving forward. But it's thrown a wrench in my plans for a big fat savings account. I look towards his room down the hall and wonder what he's doing right now. Probably almost exactly what I'm doing. Late breakfast and beginning to work.

With my emails all caught up, I close the computer and start cleaning up after myself. I start a second cup of coffee, and while it brews, I quickly rinse my other dishes and throw them in the dishwasher.

Glancing around my kitchen and living room I think, not for the first time, that I need to get some decor in here. Since Charlie and I both worked from home we needed an apartment with enough room for two offices and two bedrooms. He had converted the living room into a makeshift office for himself, and now that he's not there, it's a mere skeleton of what it used to be.

Shit, it looks like someone died, and all their stuff just got tossed in the dumpster.

With that terribly morbid thought, I grab my drug of choice off the coffeepot and head upstairs. Both of our rooms are up here, as is the third bedroom he helped me transform into the beauty it is. Because I'm a glutton for punishment, I poke my head into his room. *Maybe it's time for me to find a new roommate.* Or, maybe I should just sell what's left of the lease and find somewhere smaller.

Continuing on, I open the door to my little sanctuary. *God, I love this room.* My entire book collection is here, as are the fan art and maps to go with them all. I blow a kiss to my favorites on my way toward my desk and glance at the closed cabinet, smiling to myself. I love what's in there, too. But I can only partake once I get some work done. Whenever I finish with a long day of reading smut and feigning sex noises, I find myself in desperate need of release.

I have fake cocks and toys of all kinds in there. I mean… how could I talk about different shapes of dicks if I don't have intimate experience with them, right? The large human-looking ones are fun, but the best are the most depraved. The ones with extra ribbing, the *tentacles*, and especially the one that mimics knotting. Why would I want to fuck a real man when I can stay home and guarantee as many orgasms as I want?

Bel, you horndog, focus. Put in your hours, then go fuck yourself.

I laugh at myself and try to get my head in the game. Today won't be a horny work day anyway. I need to do a quick read-through of today's content before I turn on the equipment, so I grab the manuscript and head over to my cozy corner chair.

I paid more for this chair than all the furniture in my living room but it was worth every fucking penny. It's nearly wide enough for two people, made of the softest dark green velvet, with the top tufted to look like a scallop seashell. It's accented with coppery gold and has a matching ottoman. Kicking my feet up on it, I set my drink on the table beside the chair and begin my reading.

If I can keep myself on track, I can probably get through 25% of the book today. I'll read for an hour, then take a break before I begin recording. I try to set reminders to take a break every 90 minutes or so, otherwise I'll get so sucked into the work that I'll go the whole day without eating or drinking anything. More often than not, I even forget to get up to pee unless my phone yells at me to do so.

As happens so often, I lose track of time and get lost in the story before me. Three teenagers have decided to summon a demon to enact revenge on their abusive parents but it doesn't exactly do as told. Rather than eliminate the parents, it sets seemingly innocent tasks in front of the teens, threatening their lives should they fail. But from what I can tell, those tasks bring the kids closer and closer to their worst nightmare.

Ring* *Ring

There's Siri telling me to take a piss again.

I take care of business in my en-suite and run down the stairs to grab a water bottle. Long hours of talking, moaning, and sometimes even fake crying mean I need constant hydration.

As I set up to finally get to work at my station, I find myself really excited about today's work. Horror isn't my usual genre, but getting to try something new and stretch my limits a little bit will be incredible. This book seems like it'll require screams of terror rather than the type I'm used to.

I trudge through the first few chapters, which include the intro to each character and the reasons they've decided to off their parents. *Honestly, I get it.* The parents are truly horrific and deserve whatever demise they'll find at the end of the book. *But I don't trust this bookseller lady.* I mean she just happened to have a book of exactly the type of spell they're looking for? No way, it's too easy. She's in cahoots with the forces of darkness, I'm telling ya.

I decide that's a good enough place to stop and take a break. But the plot is so compelling that I practically inhale my lunch so I can get back to work.

I return to my studio and continue well into the evening. Realizing that I'm now in the unfortunate position of reading the sacrifice and summoning long after the sun has gone down has my skin pebbling. Pushing through the discomfort, I proceed.

The kids make their way to the local deserted church house, ready to call upon a demon fresh from the pits. Each of them takes turns slicing their palms open, spilling it into a white marble mortar they stole from their kitchen. *Gross.* Then they all snip a lock of hair from themselves, and the oldest tosses in the horrifically fresh jawbone of their mother's prize-winning cat. *Poor Flannery.*

The youngest starts reciting some obscure Latin that I don't understand. I had the good sense to research Latin pronunciation, so I know I'm at least getting that right. I think I recognize the word for warrior and another that I'm pretty sure has something to do with protection.

As I turn the page to continue their incantation, I slice my middle finger on the corner of the page. *Motherfucker!* Trying to ignore the burning in my finger, I continue through the summoning spell. As they finish, black smoke begins to rise from the floor of the church they've broken into.

For the first time since they started all this, the middle sibling is actually scared. This whole time she didn't believe anything would come of this and that they were just kids being kids. While I'm not sure killing cats and slicing and dicing your palms is kids' stuff, I get the sentiment. Nothing could convince me that shit was real, apart from seeing it with my own two eyes.

As I finish the page, I realize my blood is seeping a little bit heavier than I'd like it to be, so I stop the recording to search for a bandaid. *No wonder it hurt so much; it's bleeding like crazy.* I stick my finger in my mouth in some primal instinct to stop the bleeding.

Then I hear it.

Someone is in my house.

"Charlie?" *Maybe he came by to surprise me and grab the last of his things.* "Isla?" No answer. Both of them would have texted before coming over, so I check my phone.

Nothing.

Okay, think, Bel. Maybe they think no one is home. I shouldn't make myself known quite yet. First things first, I dial 911.

"Dispatch, what's the address of your emergency?" I rattle off my address, trying to keep my voice low but clear. "And what is the emergency, ma'am?"

"Someone's in my house. I live alone, I don't have any pets. I was working and there was this terrible ruckus downstairs like someone broke through a fucking wall or something and now they're rummaging around down there. Please, please send help."

"I have officers en route, they're about ten minutes out. Would you like me to stay on the phone with you until they arrive?" *How is she so fucking calm right now??? She's about to listen to me get murdered!*

"Y-yes please," I stutter.

"Do you have anything to defend yourself with?" she asks.

I think for a minute, responding, "I have a little pistol thing my dad got me when I moved out on my own."

"Can you get to it without drawing attention to yourself?"

"Uhhh yes I think so." As quietly as I can, I sneak across the hall into my bedroom, open the drawer of my bedside table and grab the little thing that I swore up and down I would never touch. "Okay I got it. How do I use it?"

"Check that the safety is off. Check for ammo. Point and shoot." *What the fuck is a safety? Oh, right there.*

There's another pounding sound coming from downstairs, and for just a split second, all the lights go out. I drop my phone and cover my mouth to keep from screaming.

Once I manage to calm down, I decide using both hands on the gun makes more sense than holding a phone to my ear. What's she gonna do? Tell me to not die?

Gathering all the courage I have, I sneak down the stairs, deciding that going after them on my own terms is better than waiting for them to find me.

I move slowly and silently, or at least I try. The lights downstairs are all off, so it's creepy as fuck. But if I can't see, neither can they, and I know my home better than they do.

I think I hear heavy breathing, but the pounding and movement have stopped. I hold my breath for fear of being too loud. Whoever it is doesn't seem to know they've been made yet, so at least I have a small advantage.

There! A slight movement in the corner gives me somewhere to point my gun, but it doesn't look like there's a person there. It just looks like layers of shadows dancing in the moonlight coming from the half-open blinds. Two white reflectors show from far above my head, and I wonder if the person is wearing a helmet. *Who wears headgear to a home invasion?* The only thing I can figure is that maybe they're wearing night vision goggles.

The figure moves again, and without even thinking, I pull the trigger. I hear the worst, wet thunk and watch what looks like someone half falling over. My whole body begs me to bend over and puke all over the floor. My only saving grace is the elation I feel over actually hitting my intruder.

Keeping my voice even to hide my fear, I shout, "Ha! Got you, fucker. The police are on their way. So you better jus-just stay down until they get here or I *will* shoot you again." Then I flip the light switch, planning to get a better lock on them while they're temporarily blinded by the goggles. But instead, what I see has me cursing and dropping my only defense to the floor, "Oh, Jesus Christ."

What the fuck is that thing?!

3

Sweet Rutting Freedom

Caspian

What foolish mortal dared to unleash me? The first coherent thought I've had in what feels like eons. *How long have I been trapped within the Prison Realm?*

Something smells delicious. It's faint but unmistakable, the sweetest blood of a pure soul spilled, and in the name of what? Avarice? Vengeance? Pride? These mortals are always so willing to sacrifice another but never to pay the price themselves.

No matter, I'll remove their heads from their bodies before they realize their mistake. I begin to move towards the only thing I can sense, a wonderful, slightly sweet scent, bathed in the endorphins of fear. My eyes have not yet adjusted to being open again, but I could find my prey blindfolded.

A horrible pop ricochets through my head moments before I feel a burning sensation in my thigh. *What in the Gods name is that?! That hurts.* I drop down to one knee before I can stop myself, the pain and smoky scent of a firearm momentarily overpowering everything else. I've been shot before, but this is far more powerful than I've faced. This creature must have heard tales of me and come prepared for a fight.

"Ha! Got you, fucker. The police are on their way so you better just stay down until they get here or I will shoot you again." *Brave words for someone shaking and nearly pissing themselves in fear— Did she say police? Why would*

16

someone summon me just to call upon the Watchmen? Something is not right here.

A flicking noise followed by overwhelming light surrounds me as I reel from the agony in my leg. I look down to find the painful area pulsing blood in time with my heart. Growling, I quickly dig my claws into the gaping wound, finding the tiny piece of metal and tossing it aside to the floor.

Once the offending chunk of ammunition has been removed and my healing process begins, I attempt to stand to my full height. Though before I can do so, I'm stopped by the short ceiling. I have to slightly duck so as to not get my antlers stuck in the material. Blinking my eyes rapidly to get my bearings, I hear a gasp.

"Oh, Jesus Christ." The terrified woman mutters. Finally, my eyes adjust, and I spot my next meal. It's rare for a woman to be responsible for sacrificing a virgin. A shame, too, because she is quite lovely. Big blue eyes filled with tears, long hair the darkest shade of red, and the kind of luscious curves to write sonnets about.

Though her clothing is very strange and wildly inappropriate. Even brothel women wouldn't allow themselves to be seen in such a state of undress in civilized society. She's clothed in some form of silky pants that do not even come close to covering her knees and a matching top, barely held up by tiny little strings. They look more akin to underthings than to actual clothing, baring every inch of her smooth, pale pink flesh.

But her weaponry is what I find most concerning. How could something so small cause such pain? And so quickly? The firearms I remember took minutes to prepare and could hardly be carried by someone so tiny. Dropping her weapon, she lifts her hands to cover her mouth, holding back a scream. Her eyes meet mine, and the terror within them is so vibrant I can't stop myself from grinning.

Faster than she can react, I launch at her, slamming us against the wall, wrapping a black-clawed hand around her throat, ready to tear it out. Her blood dripping down my hands will be the sweetest warmth, the ripping of her flesh the most exquisite symphony, and her tainted soul— *Why am I not killing her?*— She should be dead by now. I'm using all of my strength to try to tear at her neck— *WHY IS SHE NOT DYING?* I flex my claws around her throat, trying to ignore her desperate pleas and sobs.

"Why are you not dying?"

A small sniffle, then she croaks, "What?"

"You are not dying. Why?"

"I mean... well, you're not squeezing very hard." I try with every fiber of my being to squeeze the life out of this tiny, wicked human but cannot. "Please don't kill me," she begs as I watch the tears stream down her face. She smells intoxicating. Those who summon me never smell this delightful.

"What witchcraft is this? I should be removing your spinal cord from your body right now." She sobs again, *loudly.* "Stop crying, witch. This is your penance for summoning me." I lean down to get a better look at her face.

"What?! No! I didn't... it wasn't real. I didn't mean to," then quietly, more to herself than me, "This cannot be real." Even with fat tears and mucus streaming down her face, she's a vision. But she summoned me with the blood of a virgin, and I will not allow her beauty to deter me. The most wicked are often the most enchanting.

"Oh, goodness me, this is all just a big misunderstanding then," I run a free claw across her cheek, collecting a tear as she shudders. "You did not *mean* to utter my summoning incantation, and you did not *mean* to murder a virgin, my mistake." The derision in my voice pales her further.

"*Murder?* I didn't kill anyone! I was just minding my business, doing my job, ya know— reading a book, when suddenly I hear a loud-ass-fucking sound. I thought I was getting fucking robbed! So I grabbed my gun, called the cops and ran down here! The only person— fuck, or uhhh being I've hurt was you." She releases a laugh bordering on unhinged, "And myself, but that was just a paper cut, so nothing to worry about there. *I'm* not the one holding five huge knife-like *things* at someone's throat." She looks down pointedly to where my hand cradles her neck, "There's no one else here! No one, I swear."

A papercut? She couldn't possibly have- "Are you a virgin?"

"What?" she stammers. "That's a little personal. Are *you* a virgin?"

"No," I barely hold back my amusement.

"Really? Wow, do you fuck humans or just like other monster people? Cuz it seems like it might get pretty complicated. You're *very* large, do you know that? And it's probably proportionate," she gestures toward my lower region, where my member is safely concealed in the tattered remains of my pants. "So you couldn't really make the beast with two backs with someone too much smaller than you are, just— ya know, logistically." I slam my palm over her mouth, unable to listen to another vulgar word. That alone would have her whipped were anyone else to witness it. Not to mention her clothing.

Despite it all, she smells so heavenly I can't stop myself from burying my nose in the crook of her neck and inhaling. The sweet aroma of fear, sweat, and what must be her washing oils have me dizzy with a hunger of a different nature than I'm accustomed to with my summoners. My palm almost completely covers her face, making her seem so small and delicate, and I nearly groan at the sight before me.

I realize I'm also covering her nose and instinctively remove my hand from her face, instead running it down her arm, then tracing it down the outside of her thigh, reveling in every inch of exposed skin. *She's so soft, so warm.*

At my exploration, her sobs return in full force, but I can't make myself pull back yet, so I squeeze her throat enough to quiet her and run the tip of my tongue along the juncture of her neck and shoulder, just for a taste of her sweet perspiration. She whimpers in fear and grips my forearm with her tiny hands. Though she isn't pushing me away, just holding onto me as if to ground herself.

"Hush," I say against her ear. She called me a monster. She truly hasn't the faintest idea what manner of death is staring her in the face. I lean back enough to look at her face, but she's squeezing her eyes closed with her head leaning against the wall. "I am not a *monster person*. I am born of Vankhala. A demon, if you will."

I loosen my hold enough to allow her full breath, and as she takes a heaving inhalation, my eyes wander of their own volition to her barely concealed breasts.

Instantly, I release her and take a step back. I cannot be having those kinds of thoughts for someone who could still very well be responsible for witchcraft and murder. Although by the looks of it, she seems to believe she's about to be the sacrifice. If my body would cease its betrayal, she likely would be. A sacrificial little offering at my altar. The thought causes me to nearly shudder in pleasure. She would be so pretty strung up for me, begging for mercy.

Crossing my arms over my chest, I ask, "What is your name, Little Dove?"

She scoffs as if I am the one in offensive attire and speaking with such vulgarity, "I go by Bel."

"But it is not your name?" All I asked for was a name, and instead, she was giving me an attitude. "Will you not just tell me your name?"

"Bel is close enough. It's the name everyone calls me." I internally chuckle, feeling properly invigorated by her ire. *By the Gods, this woman is stubborn. And she shot me.*

I release a false sigh, "It will do for now. Bel, do you still have your *purity*?" I say the word that the mortals use for virginity. She narrows her eyes at me, refusing to answer, so I ask another way, "Have you felt the touch of a man?"

She cringes and answers through gritted teeth, "Yes, I have. Okay?"

Narrowing my eyes in confusion, I counter, "That is impossible. Only the spilling of virgin blood while reciting my summoning spell could have released the bonds holding me in Vankhala."

She shrugs indignantly, "Well, I don't know what to tell you, buddy."

Did she claim she was cut by paper? "Give me your injured hand." She tentatively urges her hand my way, and I snatch it, cradling it. Based on how she stumbled closer to me, I realize I may have pulled her a bit too hard.

Every instinct in my body has me longing to reach and steady her lest she falls. *Why am I feeling so... protective?* This makes no sense. I clench my hand and keep it to my side to keep myself from wrapping it around her waist.

Her middle finger has the smallest sliver of a cut I've seen in all my years, and I fight the urge to tongue the wound, searching for a drop of her. I catch myself staring at it like it holds all the answers. "And the incantation?" She tries to pull her hand from mine, but her strength is nowhere near enough. I'll release her when I've decided to, not a second before.

She answers so quietly I hardly hear her response, "I was just narrating an audio book."

"Audio... book. I do not understand." Only then do I realize what I should have been asking all along, "What is the year?"

After another tug, I begrudgingly allow her to remove her hand from mine and she crosses her arms across her chest, mirroring my posture. Only now is she realizing her state of undress, but it's a bit late for that, as I've already cataloged every curve and soft angle of her perfect body. She's got a constellation of freckles across her chest that I long to trace with my tongue. It would certainly only frighten her further, but this sad, scared little offering is difficult to resist.

"It's 2022. Come on I'll... I'll show you the book," the girl tells me reluctantly, still debating whether she's done fighting me or not. It's clear that, for some reason, I can't harm her. Nor do I want to, now that my head is clearing from my tumultuous journey from the prison realm.

Something in the back of my mind is shouting that I must protect her at all costs, and it's exhausting. If she's as innocent as she claims and it's all just a strange occurrence, there's no reason to hurt her. Though the delicious scent of terror seeping from her stops me from assuaging her fears.

Shoving away those tumultuous thoughts, I catch up to what she's just revealed. *2022. For nearly 300 years, I've been locked away.* What have I missed all this time? Firearms are much more harmful, women more prone to nudity— *a welcome development, truly*— and the homes are strange. She pushes herself from the wall and heads toward the hallway she emerged from.

Knock knock knock "Miss Hart?" comes a muffled voice from down the hall she's walking towards.

Once again, I find my palm covering her mouth. Then I'm dragging her back, placing my free hand against her soft stomach to keep her secured to me. If those at the door have weaponry like the gun she used on me, I do not want them entering her domain and possibly harming her. I hold her tightly, feeling every inch of her warmth against me.

"Is that law enforcement?" I whisper so only she will hear me, voice full of mirth at the promise of violence. She nods as best she can while trapped in my hold.

They knock again, "Miss Hart? You called dispatch about an intruder? And one of your neighbors reported hearing a gunshot."

"You'll have to get rid of them, my dove," I'm walking slowly and quietly towards the voices, forcing her legs to move with mine, "If you do not, then I will. And you will not like how I choose to do so."

I release her mouth only to find she's completely frozen, unable to breathe, much less speak. I smooth her hair, willing her to relax. "Breathe, Bel," I command and her answering inhale pleases me thoroughly.

Though before she can find her voice, the man outside yells again, "Miss Hart, we are coming in." *Too late for that then.* She's shaking in my arms now, unable to stop the tremors—*though at least she is breathing*— as loud, almost rhythmic pounding sounds from the hallway. I narrow my eyes, wondering what could be making that sound.

When the door bursts open, she uses the momentary distraction to rip my hand from her mouth and run towards her would-be saviors. *She truly believes she could escape me so easily?*

I give her three steps before snatching her around her waist and yanking her back to me, lifting her off the ground slightly as she attempts to scream. I grip her throat hard enough to keep any sound from escaping but not tight enough to cause harm, before tsking at her, "Oh, Little Dove. You shouldn't have done that."

4

Hell On Earth

Bel

"It would appear that I can't hurt you, but what have you done to your would-be protectors?" I can feel as much as I hear his throaty rumble. He sighs against my hair, almost enraptured by the promise of bloodshed, and whispers, "Pardon me for a moment, won't you?"

"What the fuck is that?!" One of the police shouts at the others as he draws his gun. I guess they like my new houseguest about as much as I do. *What did he even mean he would get rid of them? He couldn't possibly mean—*

Whatever thought I was going to have gets cut off by several gunshots. Quicker than I can see, the large demon from... whatever he called it shoves me behind himself to protect me from the projectiles. He takes one step forward, using a hand to push me toward the couch while remaining in front of me.

I hear the wet thunk of a bullet hitting flesh, and he grunts and then growls like the kind of thing that only exists in nightmares. As I scream and duck, there's a whooshing of air and an agonized scream, followed by several thuds. I don't want to look, but I have to; I have to see the reality of the shitstorm I'm in.

I peek over the back of the couch, spotting something I'd rather I didn't recognize so quickly. "Is that his fucking *spine?!*" I scream at no one in particular. The monster moves far quicker than any man could. He's almost entirely just a swift mass of black dropping assorted body parts along the way, followed by black smoke that seems to devour the officers weaponry, sucking it into oblivion. I barely catch a glimpse of those massive claws he had draped around my neck and the sharp white teeth dripping with blood.

All the while, my living room is bathed in his terrifying, haunting laughter. Okay, maybe *bathed* isn't the right word, but I'm using it because this is a god-damn blood bath.

I duck back down and sit with my head buried between my knees, breathing deeply. Each wet thud and splattering sound has me flinching, waiting to be struck by a wayward organ or something. There's the unmistakable sound of teeth crunching through something hard, followed by a swallow, and— *Jesus Christ, he's eating them.*

I try to swallow down the bile threatening to escape, using both hands to grip my hair until just this side of painful, trying to keep myself centered. *I have to get out of here.* For a single moment, I'm thinking clearly. I don't want to leave the cops behind; it feels like the cowardly thing to do.

But what else could I possibly do? They're *dead*, and I'm not, and I'd really like to keep it that way. He may have said he can't hurt me, but who knows how long that'll last. *I have to go find help.*

As quietly as I can, I crawl to the wall near my demolished front door, avoiding the puddles and paintings of red scattered throughout the room. Flattening myself against it, ignoring the squelch and crunch of my new *friend's* snack, I slowly scootch towards the door.

I consider closing my eyes so I don't have to hear *and* see the horror, but I need to avoid the blood. I've only got my socks on, and if I step in any, I'll lose my shit, and my puke will be added to the gruesome artistry.

Every second of this is torture, moving as quickly and quietly as I can. Each little scoot is accompanied by the sound of blood dripping from the ceiling and the quiet groans of someone enjoying their first meal in a *very long* time. The only thing I don't hear is the sound of dying men, so at least it was over quickly, I guess. Idly I wonder how much this giant monster can eat at one time, then decide I'd rather not find out.

I've almost made it. Just a few more steps and I'll be out in the hall. Once I'm in the hall, I can run. Where the fuck am I supposed to run to? It doesn't matter, I can figure that out in a few seconds once I'm outside the do— ***thud*** something hits the wall and slides down to the floor inches from my head, and I squeeze my eyes shut so I don't have to watch my death coming.

"I asked you to pardon me for a moment. You do not want to tempt the hunter inside me again, *Miss Hart,*" he says my name like it's some inside joke between him and his banquet. "As you can see, it will not end well for those around you. I am almost finished, then we can resume our discussion." Looking down, I see a foot still inside its boot on the ground. My gaze travels from its spot up the trail of blood to where it had first struck the wall.

I look to where he's standing, thankfully empty-handed for the moment, "You almost hit me with that," I say indignantly. I cannot believe that's the part of this I'm choosing to complain about, but it's the only thing I can think of without collapsing.

At that, he gives me a cruel smirk, mouth dripping red, "I have impeccable aim. Notice you do not even have so much as a spot of their filthy blood on you." I don't believe him for a second. I give myself a thorough once-over, and he's right. Not a single drop. *Huh.*

"Th-th-there's going to be more coming, you know," I warn him, hoping that's incentive enough for him to get the fuck out of here.

"More?" his eyes light up as he licks his fingers. *This sick fuck really isn't full yet?*

"Yes. More cops. But you can't eat them all. When, um, these ones," I vaguely gesture around the room, "don't check in with their higher-ups, a lot fucking more will show up. They'll have bigger weapons and—"

"Why do you use such language?" he interrupts me.

"Excuse me?"

"Your vulgarity is off-putting and indecent." *Is this guy for real?*

"You just slaughtered a trio of police, but the word *fuck* is where you draw the line?" I honestly cannot believe what I'm hearing right now. This asshole has blood and sinew clinging to the tips of his claws, and he thinks he gets to have an opinion about my language?

"It is unbecoming of a lady to use such words," he says as if it's obvious.

"It is *unbecoming* of a demon to crunch his way through all the people in someones fucking living room." The grin he shoots my way seems almost giddy, like it's all so fucking funny that he's killed three people in a matter of minutes.

"Forgive me," he begs with barely contained humor, "It's been centuries since I've fed and they did offer themselves up by trying to shoot us." *Us?*

"First of all, they were shooting at you. Second—"

"They did not even attempt to avoid hitting you. In fact, had I not stepped in the way, you'd have a hole through your body, right here," he points at his rib cage, protruding slightly as he breathes.

"*Secondly*," I ignore him, "My neighbors probably heard everything and you've left a crime scene in my home. I'm going to be arrested for this." My voice raises with every word as I realize the ramifications of what he's done.

He freezes, "No one would ever believe you did this, don't be ridiculous." He justifies, "How could they possibly think someone so small and harmless could be responsible for this... carnage?" *Now that's a fitting word for this.*

"You believed not five minutes ago that I *slaughtered a virgin,*" I argue. *Why am I fighting with him?*

"That was before I saw how innocuous you are. No one will think a little half naked woman did this," he laughs.

"Who is going to believe that a *demon* broke into my home and killed them? Are *you* going to stick around and explain it to them?"

"No. I will simply clean up the mess. I am not uncivilized," he states with such conviction that I can't help myself anymore. I start to laugh. Full belly laughs that nearly have me on my knees.

"*I am not uncivilized.*" My attempt to mock his old-timey accent falls flat between my cackles.

He tosses an unrecognizable look my way before he starts to pick up the pieces of police on the floor, "Does your home have an ice box?"

"You are not putting your leftovers in my freezer."

"Where am I to put them then? Do not forget that this is your doing," he uses a mystery limb to point at me for emphasis. "You ran and I hunted. I cannot harm you and I don't think you'd appreciate my other, *more creative* forms of torture, so I made do with what I had."

Other forms of torture? Based on the smug grin still gracing his haunting and beautiful face, he wants me to ask. But I'm not going to. Nope. I'm not.

"Why can't you just poof them away like you did the guns?" I ask, trying to steer us away from the dark thoughts plaguing me.

"It's not cold enough there to keep them from rotting. It would be wasteful," he says with humor lacing his voice. *Cold enough where?* "Now ask me what you're really wondering, Little Dove," he taunts, walking towards me. He's seemingly forgotten all about his clean-up job for the moment, focused entirely on me. He lowers his voice and adds, "Ask me from what delicious torment I would have you screaming. I'll gladly tell you."

I have to stop this little game right now. He's playing chicken, and I'll happily lose if it stops *whatever* this is, "Okay! You can use it, but first, you need to fix my fucking door so no one else comes in." I can't have any more blood on my hands.

"Fine," he mutters. It's hard to tell with them being pure white, but I think this asshole just rolled his eyes at me. He waves his free hand toward the empty space where my door should be and within seconds, the door lifts off the wall and rights itself, the wood loudly snapping back together as if it never happened. "There. Repaired."

"Thank you," I gesture around us, trying to avoid looking too closely at the mess around us. "What about the rest of the room? Can you Bippity-Boppity-Boo all the blood away?" I'm barely restraining the awe and fear rising inside me.

"Bippity-boppity-boo?" Narrowing his eyes, he turns to face me, "Is that the witchcraft you mortals use now?"

"I... No. It's a— It's a joke," I explain.

"Oh. I do like jokes. I'll tell you one of my own. What's red," he looks pointedly at my hair, "the palest pink," his eyes drip slowly down my frame, "and utterly delicious?" I'm too scared to say anything, so I just stare as he rumbles, "Little doves who tempted the wrong devil." Then he goes on doing his magic. He returns himself and my plain little living room to its former, goreless glory, gathering his bloody prizes along the way.

* * *

Five minutes later, here I am, showing a fucking demon my fridge. *May as well get a drink while I'm at it.* I snatch the bottle of whiskey Isla got me for my birthday last month. Popping it open, I watch as the demon rearranges my freezer to make room for— *oh, God, that's gotta be a femur.* I quickly avert my gaze to halt my growing nausea.

As I gulp down as much as I can in one go and let it burn down my throat, I take a moment to actually look at my new... well, not friend, but I still don't know what to call him. What I originally thought were horns on his head look to be more like the antlers of a deer. But the color is the deepest blue-black, matching his dark, shiny skin, and— *why do they look so soft?* I'm nearly touching one of the velvety smooth tips before I realize and drop my hand to my side. "What is your name?" I ask tentatively.

Without deterring from his task, he responds, "I am Caspian. Do not touch those, they are sensitive."

Sensitive?? Now I'm even more curious. Keeping my hands to myself and my booze, I continue my perusal, appreciating how long and lithe his limbs are. I watch each muscle and vein dancing beneath his skin while he works, wholly enchanted by him. Thin black smoke wafts from his shoulders and forearms as if some power inside him is restlessly trying to escape.

Distantly, I wonder what's hiding underneath the scraps of pants hanging from his lower half. *Bel, what the fuck?*

I realize now that I've definitely read too many monster romances. This isn't like those. This is a nightmare come to life, and I have to get rid of him. I should not be letting him use my freezer right now, but I think telling him no might be more dangerous. He'll need to leave eventually. He'll have to like... I don't know, go find more humans to eat? What do demons do when they're not wreaking havoc? Do they get jobs? Do they have communes where they all live together? Do the—

"This is quite the invention you have. How does it remain so cold?" His abrupt question pulls me from my thoughts.

Fighting the blush rising on my cheeks, I answer, but I suppose just the word electricity might not mean much to someone who called it an ice box.

"Oh yes," he snaps his fingers at me in understanding, apparently finished with his task. "The Queen mentioned something about that! Then there was a fellow with a key! My, my, you mortals have come a long way in the centuries I slumbered."

Grabbing his arm and gently removing him from the freezer to close it, I watch as he stands to his full height. *Jesus, that's a big dude.* He has to be at least seven and a half feet tall. I'm watching him, completely unaware that I haven't removed my hand from his arm until he glances down at it. I pull away, asking, "When did you... fall asleep?"

His answering laugh holds no humor, and I have to fight a tremor at his grim tone. "I was sent to sleep in the Prison Realm during the year 1760. Enough questions, show me this book you claim holds all the answers."

"Okay. I'll show you. Then you'll take your... this stuff and leave?" I ask hopefully.

He pauses, looking at the freezer, then me and back again, "Once I have the answers I seek, I will leave your home, yes." His reluctant tone leads me to believe there's a hidden meaning in what he's said, but I ignore it for the moment, deciding to face this one problem at a time.

5

A Vulgar Virgin

Caspian

Stalking behind my Bel, she leads me up the stairs to something she called a *studio*. The doorway is so short I'm forced to duck to enter it. *Perhaps I should take on my smaller form.* I shake off the thought, enjoying the power in my long strides and the pervasive scent of fear it causes to waft from my sweet little dove.

Strange contraptions surround me, one of which is a small circular net floating behind a black cylindrical shape, and in front of it lies a music stand. The lighting in here is quite dim, and I'm not sure how she can use it to do much of anything.

"Your walls are very odd. How can this material protect you from the elements?" It appears to be a dark, spongy material, hardly fit for a domain. I begin to poke at one of the walls, and my claw sinks right in. She doesn't seem to notice, so I retrieve my hand and clasp them both behind my back, lest I destroy anything else.

Now that the thrill of the hunt and the bloodlust have subsided, I realize I may have gone a bit far. I do not want to harm or scare her. *Maybe a little.* Only because her fear smells so good that it's dizzying. If I didn't know any better, I'd think she *likes* being afraid, and that's why it smells so godsdamn sweet. *Maybe she craves the hunt, too.*

"Oh. It doesn't, it's just an extra layer. It makes for good acoustics," at my quizzical look, she clarifies, "keeps the sound clear and makes it so my neighbors can't hear me." Her lovely, soft cheeks fill with blood again, and I fear I'm missing something of great importance. Looking closer at the contents of the shelving, I'm appalled by what I find. Countless depictions of nude men and women in positions of copulation, even more of shirtless males, both decidedly human and some only vaguely humanoid.

She catches me staring, my jaw nearly to the floor, and her blush deepens to the sweetest red. Stammering out apologies, she explains she obviously wasn't expecting company.

"A young lady should not have such... artwork." I try to say, mouth suddenly feeling dry, "It is distasteful. What is it that you do here? I do not see this tome of witchcraft that you speak of."

"Well basically, I read books out loud and that," she points to the cylinder, "records my voice. Then people who enjoy books but prefer to listen to them, or have trouble reading, can still partake of the joys of it."

"That is a spectacular innovation!" Humans are ingenious when they aren't too busy fighting wars and killing innocents, "But it does not explain the crude artwork."

"Oh. Well... I specialize in narrating books that have... sex in them," she eeks out, trying to hide behind the sheets of scarlet cascading down from her head.

I had heard of books containing romance, but it was only spoken of in whispers among the filthiest of mortals. It appears much has changed in my time away. I grab a book from her shelf and thumb through the pages. The words within are so crass I cannot look away. I stumble upon a passage containing the phrase *her hungry cunt,* and despite myself, a warmth begins to grow low in my belly.

I slam the book back into its space, unable to bear more, turning to face her again. With barely restrained laughter, I tell her, "This is filth. You read filth aloud so others may consume it."

At this, her face lights up with fury, "Okay, asshole, you do not get to come into my home, create a maelstrom of corpses, stuff them into my freezer, and then lecture me about *filth*." She shoves a handful of loose pages into my chest and spouts, "Here's your fucking spell. Take it and get the Hell out of my home."

As much as I'd love to punish her for her crude language, her boldness actually has me holding back a smile. No one else would dare speak to me that way, and I find her bravery refreshing. My mind wars between drawing her fear and her ire, both equally enthralling. *Perhaps I can have both.*

With one hand holding the papers to my chest, I reach my free hand out and gently rake a claw down her jawline, down the middle of her flushed throat, and pause it just above her thundering heart, "Make no mistake, Little Dove. I may not be able to harm you, but I've already mentioned once how thoroughly I'd love to make you suffer, so I suggest you watch," I tap her with my clawed finger to punctuate my words, "your," tap, "tone." Tap.

If I'm being honest with myself, the only suffering I'd want to put her through is the kind where she'd be very, *very* naked and begging for the mercy of release. She'd be so stunning, strapped to an altar for my own personal unholy rite, praying to me for the rapture just out of reach.

Fortunately for her, she's stunned into silence for the moment and I can now focus on the task at hand. Flipping through the loose sheets, I see a superfluous amount of steps for summoning a demon, followed by *Princeps inferorum— prince of hell.* There are a few more meaningless honorifics and poorly written Latin, then *Adiuro nos ad tuam tutelam— I bind us together for your protection.*

Oh, my poor little sacrifice. She has bound us for *my* protection? The most wicked laughter escapes me as I turn to her. It doesn't explain why I can't harm her or why a non-virgin could free me, but it's clear she did, in fact, accidentally summon a prince of Vankhala. *What could I possibly need protecting from that she could provide?* Such a tiny mortal does not stand a chance against anything that would be a threat to me.

Why should I care that I can't kill her? I *should* just leave and never have to hear her utter another vulgar, inviting word. It is wholly uncomfortable that the idea of never seeing her again has me clutching the spell in my hand hard enough to wrinkle all the paper.

My laughter slows as I watch her pick at the skin around her nail beds. "Goodbye, Bel." Even as I say it, I know it's a lie. She will never be rid of me now. But if I do not put some distance between us, I'm going to have this human screaming for a different reason, and I'm not sure she'd survive it. The pages in my hand catch flame and turn to ashes, and I make my way down the hallway toward the main entrance to her home.

"That's it? You're leaving?" She chases behind me, and the relief in her voice has me considering staying if only to vex her as she does me. She must feel this strange pull, too, or she would be far more fearful of me. I am a monster, for the Gods' sake. She must be two feet shorter than me, yet now that I've ceased killing those intruders, her terror has all but vanished, replaced by wicked curiosity.

"Yes. This spell is completely vague so I may do whatever I please," she doesn't need to know the details in the wording; it wouldn't mean anything to her.

"Except kill me. Why? Can you not harm your summoners?" *Stop asking questions I do not have answers for.* I can practically feel her adventurous nature fighting against her need to be rid of me.

"I have killed every mortal who has dared to summon me. I do not enjoy being at the mercy of another," I answer without meaning to.

A flash of sorrow crosses her face before she responds, "I can understand that. I- I'm sorry you were brought here against your will like this." *Sorry? She's feeling sorry for me? What an odd little mortal girl.*

Before I can contemplate that, she rants, "You can't go out there like that, you know. Everyone here carries guns and even though mine barely made a scratch, I don't think it would feel super great to be hit with 100 of those at a time. Plus my gun is really small, some have way bigger bullets and can make, like, a *ton* of shots in just a few seconds. If you walk out there right now, looking like that, you're going to be torn to shreds before you can smoke yourself or whatever."

"Are you *concerned* about me?" I ask, chuckling. Apologies and warnings no more than five minutes after calling me names and ordering me out of her home. *She wants me gone but not harmed. How adorable.*

Looking down, I surmise she's right. This form will draw too much attention, even though the other one is such a drag to wear. I absolutely have no desire to find out how many of those projectiles it would take to put me on the ground. I'd recover, of course, but it would be terribly painful.

As I force myself to shrink to my smaller, far less powerful size, she spins around to shield herself from looking at me.

"Most mortals find this version of me far more appealing, and yet this is the first time you've looked away since I've arrived." Riling her up is the most entertainment I've had in centuries, and I can't resist pushing her a bit farther. Sneaking up until my breath tickles her hair, I ask, "Do you prefer the monster, my little sacrifice, like those in your novels?"

The overwhelming scent of her fear fills my nostrils, accompanied by the unmistakable sweetness of something else altogether. The combination of terror and arousal has me groaning, burying my nose in her hair. *She smells so divine.* I barely resist the urge to grab her scarlet locks, wrap them around my fist, and yank her head back so I may witness the expression that matches her scent.

"I just–" she begins, "I just wanted to give you a little privacy while you... changed."

"Mmm, so very thoughtful of you, Little Dove." I hook underneath one of her tiny straps with my forefinger and run it up and down, teasing her warm skin. "Though I think it would be only fair of you to steal a peek seeing how we are now in nearly the same state of undress."

Surely sensing the danger she's in, she slowly steps out of reach, pulling her hair to one side with both hands, not daring to look at me. "I'll grab you some clothes," she tells me before disappearing up the stairway momentarily.

When she returns, she keeps her eyes carefully downcast and hands me a bundle that smells of soap but not of her. I step into the strange undergarments, followed by pants and a short-sleeved shirt of the softest cotton. She refuses to look in my direction lest she accidentally catches a glimpse of my nude form. *How strange for a mortal to be so open about sexuality in theory, yet so afraid of the human body.*

"Whose clothes are these?" I ask. Surely if there was a male she shared a home with, they would have made themselves known.

"Roommate. Moved out a few months ago, left a few things behind." She can't hide the sadness in her voice.

"You miss him deeply?" If there's anything more to her history with this man, I may have to pay him a visit. There's a sour feeling in my gut at the thought of any man being too close to her. A *roommate*, she said. If he's the reason for her sorrow and fear of the human form, I'll—

"I do, very much. Him and his husband saved me in more ways than I can count." *They may live, then.*

"I deeply appreciate your willingness to part with these so that I may be clothed. I'll be on my way now," I tell her.

"Where will you go?" she asks, prolonging this conversation the same way I long to. The last thing I want is to leave her presence, but needs must.

With a sigh, I partially explain, "That spell was entirely unhelpful, so I must go in search of answers elsewhere." She chews on her thumbnail and nods, still avoiding looking directly at me. "Hopefully, another of my kind with answers will not be too hard to find."

I don't bother telling her that if I stay any longer, she'll be splayed out like the finest feast across her dining room table. I gather that even though she's curious about the tension between us, she's not quite ready to accept it yet. I need to give her space and find answers.

She walks beside me and opens her front entry, leaning out to ensure no more peacekeepers are waiting. Then she points down the hallway to her left to a large gray metal door, "That's the stairwell. Take those all the way down and you'll enter right onto the street."

With a small bow, I leave her home, ready to rediscover the world I've been locked away from for centuries.

6

Leftovers

Bel

The moment he leaves, I realize my mistake.

His fucking leftovers.

I grab some sweats and a jacket, throw on my designated mailbox slippers and sprint out my door. There's no way I can just leave them there, and what can I do with them? Nothing. I was so glad to be rid of him that I didn't even think about the consequences. *And I don't even really know what he looks like!*

I couldn't bring myself to look at him while he was nude, and seeing someone else in Charlie's clothes would have gutted me. But if how he smelled was anything to go by, he's probably gorgeous. *Christ, what is wrong with me?* He smelled like snowy nights; like chimney smoke, balsam, and like... fucking roasted marshmallows or something, making my head spin.

Ignoring that alarming train of thought, I burst out the doors and onto the sidewalk, the chilled Fall air smacking me in the face. "Caspian!" I'm shouting, running down the sidewalk, looking for all to see like an idiot running after a man. Yelling it again, praying I find him before the police come back and find *me* with dismembered officers in my freezer.

"Missing me already?" he laughs from the shadows a neighboring building casts in the moonlight. With mock pity, he adds, "Come now, darling sacrifice, I've only been gone a moment."

Panting, I manage to choke out, "You left something in my freezer." I rest my hands on my knees, catching my breath.

"I believe you mean I left some*one* in your freezer." Laughing again at my scowl, he begins to emerge from his hiding place.

God damn it all to Hell, he is hot. As if reading my mind, he gives me a small smile and allows my perusal as he strides closer. Probably six feet tall, maybe a bit more, and *definitely* at least six inches taller than me. Inky black hair that falls into gentle waves around his ears and nape. *That haircut is terrible.* Even that doesn't detract from how gorgeous he is, with eyes so green they nearly glow, full black brows, and a strong, straight nose. *You could cut glass on that jawline, fuck.* And I'm waxing poetic about a monster. I definitely need to stop reading so much smut.

"I *did* warn you that many enjoyed this form." *Asshole.* Snickering, he continues, "You needn't worry, I have every intention of returning for a midnight snack." For a moment, I forget what we were talking about and picture a *very* different kind of late-night treat he could enjoy. "You're blushing again. You and your filthy imagination. I was only talking about the contents in your kitchen." He takes a step closer, and I take one back. The predatory look in his eyes has me considering fleeing again. Maybe in a crowded city like this, he couldn't find me.

"I wouldn't try to fly away, Little Dove. I will *always* catch you, and you won't like the consequences when I do."

"But you can't hurt me," I taunt, literally flirting with the devil. Our little dance continues until I'm nearly backed into the street.

He doesn't say anything, only takes another large step toward me, reminding me of those fucking videos of a panther stalking its prey. *He's too close. God, he smells so good.* Keeping his eyes locked on mine, he twists one of his fingers around a strand of my hair and tugs before releasing it. Leaning down, he mutters quietly, "Go straight home, Bel. I'll be back for you and my *treats* shortly," his eyes light up with mischief.

Wait, no. He's supposed to take his shit and *go.* "That's not what I meant. I meant that you should just like take it all with you, wherever you're going. I don't want it, or *you*, in my home. No offense."

He grins, "No offense taken, I assure you. However, unfortunately for you, I'll be remaining close by." I feel my jaw drop in dejection, only causing him to smile wider. "For now, I must reacquaint myself with this world, and hopefully find one of my kind wandering around who may have the answers I seek."

"I— no, I—"

"You're cold," he remarks suddenly, "You can argue with me about leaving you alone later. *Go inside and get warm.*"

I'd like nothing more than to stand here on this street and tell him that he can't fucking tell me what to do, but I am, in fact, freezing my toes off, and if I look at him any longer, I'm going to go insane. *He's so hot it's blasphemous. The fucker.*

"Fine," I mutter eventually, storming away.

"See you soon," he yells to me in a downright cheery voice as I leave him behind.

* * *

As I walk around the corner toward my apartment, I see the door ajar. *Shit, I thought I closed it behind me.* Voices waft out into the hall.

"There's no one here."

"They radioed in that this is where they were going." *Radioed?? The police are in my apartment with the remnants of Caspian's meal.*

"Hello?" I announce my arrival, fighting to keep my voice as calm as possible, "Can I help you, officers?"

"Are you Belissenda Hart?" one of the four asks me.

"Yeah. What's going on?"

"Well, Miss Hart," my name doesn't sound the same off his tongue as it did Caspian's. *Where did that thought come from?* "After your 911 call, we received several reports from this building. Strange sounds, screams, gunshots, and now we're missing three officers who were coming to investigate.

These officers are already in my home, and if I just kick them out, I'm going to look so guilty. But what am I supposed to do? Give them free rein to poke around and hope Caspian's magic was enough to hide all the evidence?

"Oh." *How did I already forget that I called the police?* "Well, my intruder turned out to just be a T.V. show I left on. Uhhhh... Criminal Minds reboot, you know how it goes." I try to laugh, but it sounds false even to my own ears.

"And you haven't heard from or seen any officers? They never came to check in on you?" another questions me, genuine bafflement coloring his features.

"No, sir." *Yeah, lay the honorific's on thick. They eat that shit up.* "But, I mean... you're already he-here, so you're welcome to look around." And then the lightbulb goes off, "Actually, I think I may have an explanation for all the, uhhh, screams and strange noises."

I explain that I have a home office for my work before asking them to follow me so I can show them. If they're all near me, they're nowhere near the freezer and its horrific contents. They give me a once over, and one of them gives me a quick pat down, checking for weapons. I try to keep my breathing calm as his hands graze my body. Fortunately for me, he uses a professional, if somewhat embarrassed, touch. I'm thankful that he's as uncomfortable with this as I am.

This is going to be humiliating, I think to myself as we wander toward my office. I open the door and hope that maybe they'll overlook the photos and just see the equipment in the middle of the room. At this point, even if they look at the pictures, I'll get over it. Better this than exploring the rest of my apartment. The blood might be gone, but *I* still see it on every inch of the place.

The youngest of the bunch looks around in wonder, "Oh! Are you a singer?!" I think to myself that if they were subjected to my singing, they would arrest me on the spot.

Trying to smother my laughter, I answer, "No. I narrate audiobooks, and sometimes that requires props." Gesturing around the room to my assorted goodies, I add, "and those props sometimes make interesting sounds."

A loud, breathy moan wrenches the air, and everyone jumps. "Oh fuck, that's so good." Loud, wet slaps punctuate each word, "Please don't stop. Pplease, fuck- please don't stop," followed by a series of cries and masculine groans getting louder. I scramble to hit the pause button on the playback before they have to hear me fake a screaming climax.

The one who pushed the playback button looks properly chagrined, and an uncomfortable silence settles over us. I am mortified that four grown-ass men are standing here, having just listened to me pretend to be in the throes of passion.

They look like they're searching the room, either avoiding eye contact or wondering which of these objects I had to utilize to mimic skin meeting skin. They seem more embarrassed than I am until the seemingly oldest one howls out his laughter, momentarily forgetting the reason they're here.

I clear my throat and explain, "There's only so much that can be done to block the noises sometimes. I'm sure this isn't the first time my neighbors have wondered if I was being murdered in here." I can feel the heat rising in my cheeks, and I swear to myself that when Caspian comes back, I'm going to stab him just for making me embarrass myself this way. It won't hurt him, apparently, but it'll sure make me feel better.

With the tension seemingly cleared, one officer who seems close to my age gives me a slow once over that makes my skin crawl. "I'm sure it's all just a misunderstanding, miss. Thanks for the show," he says. *Smarmy asshole.*

The walk back to my front door is sprinkled with laughter. Whilst exiting into the hall, one of the officers says, "We appreciate your cooperation ma'am, and we'll, uh, let you get back to work." And this time, even I can't help but giggle along.

Closing the door behind them, I take the first deep breath I've managed all night, breathing out a little "Fuck".

I don't really want to brave going into the kitchen, but I *do* want to continue the drinking I started earlier. Deciding it's worth it, I slowly make my way toward the fridge, pretending the freezer does not exist at all and quickly grab my prize. Out of the corner of my eye, I notice my kitchen knives and decide, if nothing else, it'll give me a sense of security to have one with me.

There's no chance of getting any sleep tonight, no matter how much I go swimming in this bottle, so I may as well get caught up on some T.V. *And where is my phone?* After turning on something just for background noise, I hunt for my elusive phone, remembering it's probably still in my bedroom from earlier.

When I finally get my hands on it, it lights up, showing three missed calls and at least a dozen texts from Isla. *She's going to kill me.* Just as I think those words, my phone starts ringing again.

"Hiiii," I sing out tentatively.

"Ugh *finally!* I've been calling you all night! Did you get sucked into a book again?"

Well, yes, but like literally. "Uhhh, yeah, you know how I get. I need to get through this manuscript by the end of the week." Hopefully, that'll be enough for her, and she can begin to tell me why she really called. I start meandering back to my drink and T.V. show while waiting for her to take over the conversation.

"You need to take a break from time to time, Bel. I worry about you," she sighs before a long pause. "So," she perks up, ready to launch into whatever has caught her attention this week, "I met someone special."

"I just saw you the day before yesterday. How did you meet someone already?"

"Well, sometimes you meet someone and you just *know* they're going to change your life!" she gushes, "You're going to love him, I just know it. When can you meet him?"

I'm always hesitant to meet her paramours, as often as they come and go. Isla is the best person I know, just... with the absolute worst judgment. Every person she meets is someone special, and every time, it ends in heartbreak. "Well..."

"Belissenda, you will not ditch me on this," she orders.

"I'm not... ditching. I'm just... Maybe you should get to know him before introducing him to your life, you know?" I aim for nonchalance, no doubt falling flat.

"Ugh *fine!* Two weeks, then I'll expect you to meet us for brunch," I can almost see her pouting from here.

"Two weeks. Brunch. It's a deal. I gotta go, babes. I'm exhausted." Not technically a lie, even though I won't be getting any sleep.

"Okay, love you!"

"Love you, too."

All I want to do is bundle up under a blanket and zone out for a bit. So that's exactly what I do. The laugh track of some rerun is my background music. It must work because eventually, I find myself dreaming of green eyes and golden skin with bulging veins, whispering filthy promises, calling me his *Little Dove.*

7

Those Are New

Caspian

Words cannot describe this new world I have entered. Though the closest ones might be *smelly, loud,* and *bright.* I hate to admit, even to myself, that I am unsure how to navigate this strange place. So much has changed in the past few centuries.

It would appear that mortals have certainly gotten over their fear of technology. Every person I see has a tiny, glowing box they seem to be glued to. They hardly even register that a monster is walking amongst them, and I idly wonder how those of my kind have acclimated to the 21st century.

As I walk and try to take in my new surroundings, I relish the memories of the night thus far. *Bel.* The way she said it has me thinking it must be a shortened version of her real name. Bel alone is so fitting; from the delightful bell shape of her hips to her tinkling, musical voice, everything about her sings to me.

But how did she summon me, and why couldn't I harm her? She had even hurt me! The last time a simple mortal drew blood from me was ages ago, and they didn't live to see their next breath. But this tiny little woman did. *Why?*

Although, if I'm being honest with myself, her living has made my return far more interesting.

Surely, someone has the answers. I just need to locate another demon who has lived all these years. As I walk, I wonder if an old friend is still around and where he might be. In the meantime, I'll need to stay close to Bel. She won't like it— well, if her body language was any indication, she'll love it. But she won't *like* that she loves it.

No, my sweet little sacrifice feels betrayed that her body gravitates toward me. She nearly grazed my antlers before she realized what she was doing. Had she stroked them, I could not have resisted her pull. Just being in her proximity, I couldn't help but imagine how she'd clutch onto them as I buried my tongue between her full, soft thighs. I had no business thinking those wicked things about her. She was a vulgar, uncouth woman, and the last time I felt even a fraction of this aching need, it ended disastrously.

She allowed me to use her freezer for my spoils, though, truly, they were her own fault. I *had* warned her not to run. But, oh, how I loved watching the shock and horror on her face, her big blue eyes filling with tears, that mouth dropping into a silent scream. And then she thought she could just slink away, but I couldn't have that.

I was pleasantly surprised by how quickly she calmed herself when the damage was done. Even dripping blood, holding onto the fruits of my labor, she defied all logic and *scolded* me for making a mess. Her quick temper and disallowance of disrespect had me nearly on my knees, begging for another taste of her ire. Perhaps all modern women were as fiery as this one, though I doubt it.

She seemed less afraid of my monstrous form than my mortal one, and that was a conundrum as well. Were those filthy tomes in her home responsible for that? Some of the... artwork was only vaguely humanoid. The crass language used within made it clear that this woman and those like her were only too willing to speak openly about such private things. In my time, women were not permitted to use such vulgarity or discuss the manner in which they chose to fornicate.

While I much prefer openness about the wonder of sexuality, it still may take some... adjusting. All of Bel's bare, soft skin on display had me searching for any excuse to touch her. The smallest invitation would have sent the beast inside me into a frenzy, begging to feel her warm body wrapped around me.

I shake off the debased thoughts, focusing again on my goal. *I've been wandering for nearly an hour now with no sign of another demon.* Surely, they could not have been eradicated, but perhaps, in this modern world, it's easier for them to hide. I wonder if the mortals would even look up long enough to notice a demon walking around their city.

That's when I hear them. *Sanctus Sculutis. That was fast.* Rather than draw more attention to myself with so many witnesses around, I keep my stride steady, aiming for an alley up ahead.

Demon hunters' life force is invisible to demons, so if they can hide from our other, more heightened senses, they can find us unprepared. These must be novices; their movements are heavy, and their talking is far too loud. I almost feel bad for them, being sent after me when they're so clearly out of their depth.

Turning the corner, one of them whispers, "Could you be wrong? He just looks like a normal dude."

The other answers, "No way. As soon as it landed in the city, all the alarms started going off. We couldn't get a read on it until about an hour ago, when the compass finally stopped spinning and pointed in one direction."

A compass? It would appear the mortals *and* the warlocks have come a long way in just a few centuries. If Bel's was any indication, firearms have developed a lot while I was away too. She mentioned that everyone carries one now. I'd rather not be hit with one if I can help it, especially one that's possibly been enhanced by magic.

I hide within the shadows and watch them saunter down the alleyway. *So much confidence for only being two of them.* I notice too that they're wearing badges with their names on them, along with clothing similar to the law enforcement I just tore to pieces. *Parker* and *Harrison.* Wearing badges on a stealth mission seems counterintuitive to me, but perhaps masquerading as officers allows them more freedom with their movements and weaponry.

I step into the light behind them, standing in the way of their only exit, "Hello, friends. Can I do something for you?" They spin around, and sure enough, two terribly large firearms snap up and point vaguely in my direction.

One of them instantly starts firing wildly, shattering a nearby window, while the other tells him to *calm the fuck down and aim, dumbass!*

I have to stifle a laugh. It's as if they sent children after me. Have the demons become so docile in the centuries that the hunters are so complacent? These imbeciles don't stand a chance—

FUCK! One of them actually managed to hit my shoulder, and the monster inside me fights to escape. Another shot buries in my thigh before I can even think to run. I sink down on one knee. *What is in those bullets?* I can feel myself becoming sluggish, hit with the realization that they must have laced their weapons with some kind of intoxicant.

They cannot catch me. I won't go back.

Letting the demon loose is as natural as breathing, and within seconds I've shredded through the clothes given to me. *I have to kill them both and get away from here before I'm too addled.* Trying to fight off the fatigue, I leap and rip an arm off the one with the terrible aim, letting his agonized screams pierce the night. The surrounding city is so loud it'll only add to the cacophony of sound around us. The other one is shouting for him but doesn't have the sense to stop shooting as I grab what's left of his whimpering friend.

I am a resourceful demon, so I'll happily use a human as a shield, and I do. Once the man realizes that he's killed his comrade and slows his shots, I throw the corpse at him, shaking some of the blood from my hands as I do so. *Hunters' blood smells vile.*

He drops his firearm while attempting to catch his fallen friend, and they both topple to the ground. As they collide with the terrain beneath them, the still-breathing one ricochets off the ground with a satisfying ***thunk* *thunk***.

As I stalk over and peer down at them, the smell of urine soaks the air. *Is that from the corpse or from the soon-to-be corpse? Likely both.* I laugh while I watch him attempt to push what's left of his buddy off so he may flee.

I take a step back and lean against the wall, feigning nonchalance and hoping it's believable. I'm not entirely sure I could chase him in my current state, "If you run, your death will be far more painful. Tell me what I wish to know, and I'll make it quick." Nonetheless, he attempts to escape on a very clearly broken ankle. It takes nearly all my effort to take a few steps, grab him around the neck and turn him towards me, "How did you find me?"

He spits in my face, followed by some sputtering of an old prayer in Latin. I sigh and squeeze his neck a bit tighter, knowing I'm nearly out of time to deal with this, "You said something about a compass? Hmm? Sound familiar?"

With great struggle, he responds, "You should be in Vankhala, foul demon."

"Perhaps, but that doesn't answer any of my questions," I do not have the patience for this, "I will give you one more chance to earn a swift death. You could not locate me when I first arrived. Why?"

"Don't know," he chokes out, so I loosen my grip, "Every alarm in the compound went off and the compass started spinning like crazy."

"Where is this compound?" I ask.

"I don't know, man. They blindfold us going in and out, can't risk shit like this happening," he sputters, the fear finally overtaking him. Keeping my eyes trained on him when I feel this drowsy is difficult, but I don't think he notices.

"Tell me more about the compass," I demand.

"It spun like fucking *crazy* when all the alarms went off, okay? About an hour ago, it stopped spinning and pointed in one direction. Then it started spinning again and we were like *fuck man*, then it gave us a heading again," he takes a heaving breath, "So we had to scramble to get out of there before we lost the advantage we had. The big guys strapped us up, blindfolded us and dropped us off like 20 minutes later, saying *good luck!*"

"Your superiors just dropped you off and left you here?" he nods. *They're just throwing these children to the dogs.* Usually, I'd hate to kill someone so young, but this little fuck shot me first, so I tell him, "Thank you," and snap his neck.

I'm a demon of my word, after all.

Digging through their belongings, I find the compass of which they spoke and stuff it in my pocket. They can keep their weapons and their silly outfits. *I could use those boots, though. They'll need a good cleaning, but that's nothing.* I collect my prizes, knowing I'll need to eat and rest before I can repair or clean any of them. Part of me dreads entering Bel's home covered in blood again, both mine, the color of my skin, as well as the deep scarlet of theirs, but needs must.

Wondering to myself what to do with their bodies as I lean against the wall, I notice what I'm almost certain is a trash receptacle. I carefully lift them into it, refusing to breathe in lest I inhale some of the disgusting smells emanating from it. I wish I could have just eaten them; it would make things easier, but hunters taste horrible, and it wouldn't help anyway.

As I shrink into my human body, I can't help but think maybe Bel is the reason for their tool's malfunction. We are bound for protection, and while these hunters hadn't been much of a threat, their magic-laden bullets are still working to slow me down. Having a human that masks me from hunters could certainly come in handy.

Throwing my new boots on, I use the wall as a support, hiding in the shadows of each building, slowly making my way back to her. I'll just have a snack and get some rest, then I'll be good as new. I'm able to blend into the walls, going completely unnoticed. If nothing else, humankind's reliance on technology makes it easy to move around them. The constant beeps and buzzing tell me exactly where every being is and helps me avoid them.

What feels like an eternity later, I use the last dregs of my power to let myself into Bel's home, ready to collapse. As I enter, I spot my little sacrifice sound asleep, snoring *very* loudly. The bottle on the table in front of her smells similar to the humans wandering around outside. I spot something small and silver in her loose grip— *is that a— darling girl, that sharp little thing will not protect you from me.* I give her a mock pout, though she's not conscious to see it. Gently, I extract the knife from her grip to ensure she does not accidentally harm herself with it.

Looking at her strange positioning, I can't imagine this is her usual sleeping chamber. How could anyone sleep with that terrible light and sound blaring from the monstrosity across from her? *Something to revisit once the room stops spinning.*

Leaving her there for the moment, I quietly enter the kitchen and pull the compass from my pocket. I understand what the hunter meant now; my re-entering Bel's proximity caused the compass to spin in rapid circles. Setting it on the table, I turn to where I'll find what I'm looking for.

Opening the door, the scent of meat makes my mouth water. *It's better fresh, but this will do.* I generally don't need to eat, but it helps restore me. I'll need every bit of power I can hold while I relearn how to survive in this world. Two measly hunters already found me. Had there been many more, they may have even overpowered me with their new weaponry.

After having devoured a tattooed hand, tasting slightly *off* due to the ink, I'm feeling more like myself. I glance back at my snoring hostess, struck by her beauty, even deep in her drunken slumber. I think to myself again that she can't possibly sleep there. She's nearly falling off.

Making my decision, I go in search of her rooms on the upper level of her home. I peek into the first room, the one she grabbed the clothing from, *her housemates,* then proceed down the hallway. The next room must be a water closet, though I don't recognize anything inside of it. Continuing on, I remember which room was her studio. After she's settled, I'll have to return and continue my research.

The final room I find is filled with her sweet scent. The bed is unmade and rumpled, but it looks and smells so inviting that I'd give anything to sleep there, surrounded by her scent. Some lacy things lie scattered around the room, and based on their exquisite scent, these must be her underthings. Ideally, I would spend some time investigating her room, but it'll have to wait. I turn around to leave and—

Okay, maybe I'll just take one. I slip a pair of her strappy underwear into a pocket in my pants and make my way back downstairs to her.

Returning to my sweet, sleepy offering, I gently slide an arm under her back and my other beneath her knees, lifting her to my chest. She lets out the smallest sigh and snuggles into me, all but nuzzling where my neck meets my shoulder.

"Mmmmm, you smell good," she mumbles at me.

"You smell drunk, Little Dove." The sleepy, shut-eyed smile she graces me with makes my heart momentarily cease beating. Even with the messy black streaks running down her face from all the crying, she's the most beautiful thing I've ever seen. The short walk to her room will not be nearly enough time to bask in the gift that she is. But it'll have to do for now.

As I lay her down and pull the blanket to cover her body, she mutters something unintelligible. Leaning down I ask her to repeat it so I may understand.

"M' name... 's Belissenda," she slurs before turning over to bury herself in a mountain of pillows.

Belissenda. Brave warrior.

"Goodnight, Belissenda," I whisper, fingering her red locks one last time before retiring to the spare room for the night.

8

Where Do We Go From Here?

Bel

The first thing I register is my pounding headache. *Did I get hit by a fucking train?* Wracking my brain, trying to remember what happened last night, the second thing I register is that somehow I made it to bed. *No, that's not right. Someone put me here.*

Caspian.

I didn't actually expect him to come back. I naively thought he was messing with me, or he'd change his mind when he found some other demons or something. I wonder if he's still here and decide to investigate. *Oof, maybe after I brush my teeth.* After I use the restroom and pull my rat's nest of hair into a scrunchie, I try to sneak toward the stairs.

"Good morning, Belissenda," he calls to me, the humor in his voice giving it a musical lilt. "Come along now, you needn't be shy."

Bracing myself with a deep breath, I walk downstairs and come face to face with the man who haunted my dreams all night, leaning against my kitchen counter like he owns the place. "Morning," I manage to squeak out.

"I would assume you are famished after all the excitement last night," he begins. "I had planned to make you something to break your fast, but alas, nothing is familiar to me."

"Oh, that's alright. I get the feeling we have different tastes in food," I tease. *If I make jokes, this will be easier, right?*

"You mean you do not have a hankering for peacekeeper flesh?" He tsks, "Such a pity. Here I thought we might have something in common."

I only allow myself a small smile, even though that *was* funny. I'm not telling him that. He doesn't get to be hot *and* powerful, *and* also funnier than me. Absolutely fucking not.

Walking closer and gesturing for him to move, I say, "I really just want coffee, which you happen to be blocking."

Rather than move, he just stares down at me, a slight smile pulling at his perfect mouth— *don't think shit like that; he can probably hear you.* At the obvious blush rising to my cheeks, his smile widens. "What are you feeling right now?" he asks lowly, and at my obvious displeasure, he lightens his tone, adding, "You seem to have imbibed a bit after my departure, are you feeling alright?" as if he's completely unaware of how his first question came across.

"I'm very hungover, hence, the coffee." Finally, he steps aside, only enough for me to squeeze in next to him and start up my Keurig. "Ummm. Do you want some?"

His eyes slowly raze over every inch of me before he answers, "Absolutely, I do." *God damn him.* More earnestly, he asks, "Will you teach me how to make it?" At my answering nod, he moves off the counter and angles his body to be slightly behind me without blocking his view of the machine. The way he's standing causes his arm to barely graze my back, making it impossible to breathe without inhaling his incredible scent.

"It's re-really easy, actually. They made these coffee machines idiot proof," I tell him.

"And yet, I could not figure the damned thing out," he chuckles to himself.

Continuing, I point to the reservoir, "This just needs to be full of clean water. Then you hit this button here to turn it on." Leaning over the counter, I grab a k-cup off the little decorative tree, open the holder and plop it in before remembering, "Oh. I didn't grab a mug. They're in that cupboard right there if you wanna get me one."

If I wasn't nervously clenching every muscle in my body, I would be in hysterics over the mug he chose. One of my personal favorites; it's a simplistic cartoon rendition of a gargoyle covered in chocolate and the phrase "Monster Fudger" beneath it. The smirk on his face gives him away. *He picked that one on purpose.* I glare up at him, once again caught in the wonder of how his eyes could possibly be so vibrantly green.

"Bares a bit of a resemblance to me, I think," he grins, holding it out to me.

"He's much more handsome," I respond, but we both know I'm lying. As monstrous as his larger form is, it is equally beautiful. I place the mug in the drip tray and press the brew button. "Then we wait."

Once it's finished, I hand him the mug, and he takes a sip. He makes a pinched face, and I laugh as I turn to make my own cup, "Is it not good?" I ask.

"It is... different, I suppose. You mortals used to make it far less potent," he tries to force down another small sip.

"I'll grab you some creamer," I pause, looking at the fridge. Do I really want to get any closer to that thing than I have to? My throbbing head answers with a resounding yes.

As I pour creamer into both of our mugs, he watches his coffee with trepidation. But when he finds the courage to try it, his eyes light up, "That's delicious!" he nearly shouts. As I grab my coffee and begin to walk towards my coffee table, he halts me, "But still, you must eat. This is not sustenance enough for a human."

"I'm really not hungry," I may have been a minute ago, but the reminder of what is currently sharing space with my hash browns has my stomach ready to revolt.

He steps his giant body in front of me, "You need to eat, Little Dove."

"Buddy, *you* need to back the fuck up," before I spontaneously combust.

Leaning down, he says, "If you recall, I have warned you once about your atrocious language. It is unwise to speak to me that way, and I might have to punish you for it."

I've had just about enough of his policing, so instead of thinking clearly, I double down. "Listen. In your time, maybe you got away with bossing women around, but now you don't get to. So if I want to say fuck, or asshole," I give him a pointed look, so he knows I mean him, "or even *cunt*, I will."

The growl coming from his chest should probably scare the shit out of me, but it only emboldens me to continue, "You do not get to let yourself into my home, and then think you get to have a *fucking* opinion about my *fucking* language. Are we clear?"

Oh shit, he is seething. "We are. You are a terribly vulgar woman who doesn't know when to leave well enough alone." He looks like he's ready to say something else, then the tension leaks out of him, and he snickers, "but also one who requires food immediately, if the grumbling in your stomach is any indication."

Fucker.

"I'll just order something. I'm not getting into," I tip my chin towards the freezer, "that."

I grab my phone out of my pocket, and he stares at it in wonder. I quickly put in my usual order for the cafe around the corner. I get caught up in my job more often than I care to admit, and might even be on a first-name basis with their delivery girl.

"Will you teach me about your little box, too?" I start choking on the sip of coffee, trying to tamp down the ideas the double meaning in his words gives me. *No, I will not be teaching him* anything *about my box.*

Calming my racing thoughts, I hand my phone to him. "It's a phone. It basically contains all the knowledge in the known universe, but mostly we use it to send each other funny videos and nudes." *Why did I say that? I've never even taken a naked picture, much less sent one.*

"What is a video?" Realizing this man is going to need an entire lesson on the history of television, I guide him over to my TV and turn it on.

"These moving pictures are videos. They can be watched on this," I point to the tv, "that," I gesture to Caspian's hand that's dwarfing my phone, "or a computer," he opens his mouth, and I stop him with a raised hand, "which I will show you later."

Seemingly pleased with that answer, he asks, "May I sit there?"

"Be my guest." He gives me the brightest smile I've seen from him yet, and I have to tamp down on the butterflies attempting to take flight inside me.

After a moment, he says, "We have much to discuss, Bel. But I prefer you be fed first, so I will wait. Did you use your little box to summon food?" Again with that phrasing.

"Please don't call it that," I'm barely containing the laughter now. Before he can ask why, I spit out, "Little box is like- colloquial for vagina."

"Oh." For a second, he seems chagrined, then his grin is back before he states, "I prefer cunt," halfway through the sip I'm taking, making me choke again.

"Now who's being vulgar?" I sputter between coughs. *He definitely did that on purpose.*

"Well, if I live in the modern world now, I must adjust to its customs," he responds in a comically dramatic voice, still holding back the smile on his face.

"Fair enough." Debating what to watch, I figure he might want to watch something to help him catch up to the now, "I'm going to turn on the news. It'll discuss some current events, wars, crime, shit like that." And I plop down on the couch, as far from him as I can possibly plant myself.

* * *

After roughly 20 minutes, there's a knock at my door. Instantly, Caspian darts up ready to attack. Looking at me, he says, "Do not move. I will retrieve your sustenance."

"Do you think I'll try to bolt again?" I ask.

Narrowing his eyes, he simply states, "Yes," before turning on his heel and strutting towards my door. Swinging it open, I can see the moment Darcy gets an eyeful of my new housepet, and her jaw nearly unhinges. To break her from her spell, Caspian greets her, "Good morning. You are here to deliver food, yes?"

"Uh-huh. For Bel?" she nervously tries to lean around him to find me, but he blocks her view. Rolling my eyes, I stalk towards them and not so gently push Caspian away from my poor, entranced friend.

"Hey Darcy, how are you?" She barely registers me, too petrified by the giant beast of a man in my living room.

"Oh. Uhhh, I'm good. Here's your food. Bye!" and she takes off before I can say anything else. Generally, Darcy likes to chat for a minute, but I guess seeing a strange guy in my apartment has kicked her into high gear.

"Good job, you scared the poor girl," I smack his arm with the back of my free hand.

"Yes, well that is the proper reaction to meeting one of Hell's warriors. *You're* the one who reacted to me without the appropriate amount of fear," he removes the package from my hand and gestures me back to the couch.

He follows behind me, places the take-out bag on the coffee table, and begins to open it, the smell of fresh bagels permeating the air. I sit and watch as he takes a deep breath, and I wonder again what it's like to be experiencing this new world for the first time.

"This smells marvelous," he states in awe. "Oh! I remember these. They were fairly new to the world in my time, but they were very good." His excitement over bagels is absolutely understandable. They are the food of the gods, I swear. "But what is this container?"

"Oh, it's just like toppings you can put on the bagels. Do you eat? Food? I figured it was just..." I grimace, trying to block out the memories of the night before.

He glances at the kitchen, showing that cheeky fucking grin again. "I do not need to consume mortal food, or mortals usually, but I *thoroughly* enjoy both."

Slathering cream cheese on my bagel, I look up at him incredulously, waving my knife around for emphasis, "Sooooo you just ate those cops for what, fun?"

"It was fun, wasn't it?" His eyes light up, "Especially when you attempted to fly away and I had to remind you to be a good little dove."

That nickname has got to go. I feel the need to remind my silly body that we do not want to be Caspian's little anything, but I don't think she's listening to me. "But no," he continues, "They had seen me, thus they could not be permitted to leave. Call it.... damage control. A necessary evil. One that I relished," he finishes with a wicked smile.

I can't talk about it for another second, so I ask the question I've been dreading all morning, "Why are you really still here?"

"I told you that I would return, did I not?" Before I can answer, he adds, "It is as I said, we have much to discuss. *After* you eat."

"I'm *eating* right now," I say around a mouthful. Every instinct in my body tells me I should stop goading him, so I try to have some manners, "You can have one if you want. I always order extras, just in case I forget to go to the grocery store or whatever when I'm in the middle of a project."

"Thank you," he grabs a bagel out of the bag and bites straight into it, tearing the chunk off, not unlike how he ate the— *don't go there.* He sits down, leaving only a couple inches between our legs, and I feel like I can't breathe. Trying to be subtle, I scoot to give myself a little room. He peers at me from the corner of his eye, smirking, "You are attempting to escape me again."

"No, I'm not." But he's not convinced, so I continue, "I'm just getting comfy."

I'm full of shit. He knows it. I know it. But, thankfully, he shows me the mercy of not saying anything about it.

When he's finished scarfing down his bagel, he turns fully to me, "I have discovered what is meant by protection in the summoning spell. You protect me from being detected."

"Detected by what?" *What could possibly be a threat to him?*

"Demon Hunters. They call themselves *Sanctus Scultis*, but in my time they weren't much more than spineless holy men with spells." He pulls an ancient-looking compass from his pocket, and that's when I notice he's no longer wearing Charlie's clothes. Noting the surprise on my face, he gestures down, "I saw a few articles of modern clothing in a storefront on my walk last night, so this morning I snuck back and acquired them."

"Demon Hunters?" *Now I'm the one with a thousand questions. Wait—* "What do you mean *acquired*?"

He shrugs and says, "Simply that. They were unattended so I assumed no one would miss them. I returned those you lent me to the room just there." He gestures up the stairs with his chin, "They got a bit tattered and bloody last night, but don't fret, I managed to undo the damage."

Bloody? Oh, fuck. "You killed someone else?"

"Some*ones*. Demon Hunters. Weren't you listening? They cornered me, so I did what must be done. But I did not bring them home," he continues, pleased with himself for his restraint, "I left them and their weaponry in a trash receptacle."

Did he just call my house home? I know that's not the part of that sentence I should be most shaken by, but he keeps acting like he's going to be staying here. The coffee maker, the breakfast, saying I protect him. "How did they find you if I keep you from being detected?"

He shows me the face of the compass. It's spinning uncontrollably, round and round.

"I think your compass is busted."

"No, no. It is not mine. It was *theirs*. And it could not sense me until I was away from you. It has continued this incessant spinning since I entered your building," he explains.

"Huh."

"So you see. I must stay with you." At the very apparent fear on my face, he amends, "Only temporarily. Once I learn how to maneuver in this new world, and find some of my own kind, I *might* leave you be."

I panic, spouting, "No. You can't stay here."

"And why not?" His indignation is palpable, "You have an unused room, and I have already proven to be an excellent house guest. I repaired the damage those men did to your home, I carried you to bed so you could have restful sleep, and I ensured that you were properly nourished."

"*You* damaged my home," I remind him.

"I did not," he replies, clearly exasperated, "those men did. I just got a little blood on the walls, which I cleaned."

While I'm sure I look like a fish with my mouth opening and closing, I guess technically I can't argue with that. Eventually, I choose to follow the only lead I have on getting him out of my home, "How can we find more of... you?"

"And why are you so eager to be rid of me already, Little Dove?" at my lack of answer, he sighs, "My brethren gravitate towards places overwhelmed with sin. Large cities that are full of debauchery and the like. Where do your people go to indulge in their darkest fantasies?"

"Vegas," the answer is out of my mouth before I can stop it. Las Vegas would be perfect for him to go to. Tons of people, all partaking in their sins of choice, and more importantly, far away from me.

"What is Vegas?" he asks.

"Las Vegas is a city full of places where people gather to gamble, drink, smoke, dance, and fuck." Obviously, there are countless other things to do in Vegas, but if sin is what he's looking for, that's where he'll find it.

"Sounds dreadful *and* delightful," he perks up. "We must go there at once."

"Whoa, slow down," at the surprised look on his face, I go on, "I'm not going to Vegas. I'll get you on a train or plane or a fucking taxi if I have to, but I'm not going anywhere."

"Have I not already been clear that I cannot leave your presence?" he asks, "I'll not go without you."

"Caspian, I can't just pick up and go out of town. I have a job, it would take us probably five hours to drive there, we would have to find somewhere to stay there since we couldn't just turn around and drive right back, we would have to figure out what to do with the mess in my freezer, find places to eat along the way, you need clothes, we need—"

He cuts me off with both hands on my jaw, facing me towards him, "Breathe, Belissenda," he soothes, "all will be well." *My name sounds like a sonnet falling from his lips.* I nod and breathe in his dizzying winter scent. "If it is inconvenient, we do not have to leave immediately. So long as you remain by my side, the hunters cannot find me. I shall give you three days to make the arrangements needed, then we will be off, yes?" I give him another nod, incapable of much else with him cradling my face this way.

He releases me and stands, picking up the trash from our breakfast. "Where is your waste receptacle?"

9

Very Serious Business Props

Caspian

Bel informs me that she must dedicate a few hours to her work so we can begin our search in three days' time. After briefly teaching me how to use the television controller, she excuses herself to her studio.

She didn't quite take the news of our required proximity well. But she must feel this overwhelming pull between us. Even when we've had our... disagreements, and she's spitting venom my way, her body reacts to me. It's impossible to ignore, and I'm sure my intensity has her believing I'm equally angry. Truthfully, I'm just trying to resist the urge to lay her on the floor and rut into her like the feral beast she makes me.

But the way her cheeks constantly flush the deepest pink, her heaving breaths every time I come too close, it all points to her feeling this as viscerally as I do. Along with all those reactions, there was an undercurrent of fear, too.

Fear from mortals is something to be expected, but hers smells different. I was not only teasing when I asked if she preferred my true form over the mortal mask. She seemed less afraid of me when I was dripping blood than when I was wearing my more appealing face.

Stewing in my thoughts and watching the news has gotten *so* boring. Truly, mortals haven't changed all that much. Cowards still run everything, hiding behind the bravery of those they deem less than them. Their methods are the only things that have changed. The weapons are larger and more advanced. But the people behind them are just the same.

I *do* appreciate that many places do not punish same-sex attraction as they used to. It would appear that there are still those who choose hate, as there always have been. But many humans have created more spaces for their brothers, sisters, and siblings to live authentically.

If the media she's shown me is any indication, nearly everyone in this new world is similar to Bel. She called the crassness *sentence enhancers* and, begrudgingly, I understood. It will take a slight adjustment period, but finally saying whatever I please without judgment will be freeing.

I spend a small eternity- *okay, perhaps only an hour-* perusing the many channels and ways to consume modern media, but my patience is wearing thin. I want to spend more time with my Little Dove and show her that there is an unmistakable magnetism between us. I must show her that it's nothing to fear, even if those around her have led her to believe my kind is inherently evil.

The last time I felt attraction for anyone, it ended with me trapped for centuries. Thoughts of Tasha and her betrayal plague me. I have to shake them off, reminding myself that it was a different time, and a vastly different situation. I have no way to know for sure, but Bel doesn't seem like the type to crack under pressure and destroy someone to save her own skin. Things are different enough now that she wouldn't be put in the same position either. Women have fought for freedoms they never had before.

Just thinking of my past pushes me to my feet. I've had enough television, and I've been away from Bel long enough. Perhaps I'll just quietly step in and read while she works. I could probably learn more about her there than I ever could from here. She seemed to have a lot more personal effects in her studio. Her entry area holds barely more than a few impersonal pieces of art and her furniture. *I'll take her a cup of coffee. She couldn't possibly turn me away if I come bearing a gift.*

I head into the kitchen to prepare her beverage. Her collection of coffee mugs gives me a brief glimpse into her sense of humor, but I need to know much more. Everything. I want to know *everything* about her. I know how she takes her coffee, but I have to know her favorite food, which media program she enjoys the most, how she looks when she finds release; all of it. I need it. And I need to start now.

Grabbing the finished product and adding some sweetened cream, I walk towards her studio. I can hear her working through the wall, though I'm sure she thinks her noise-reducing walls protect her from me.

I crack the door as quietly as I can, inserting the coffee through the slight opening to show her my peace offering before I fully enter. When I finally slide through, I'm met with her beaming eyes for a split second before she continues her next sentence. I'm not sure exactly what it is that she's reading, but it sounds as if the characters in her novel are discussing sexual boundaries.

She pauses and takes a moment to play back the last few sentences, and as she does, she points at me, shakes her head, and points back at the door. So I walk a few steps closer and go to hand her the coffee. When she reaches for it, I snatch it back and raise an eyebrow. *Come on, Little Dove. Play along with me.*

Rolling her eyes, she mouths the word *fine.* I reward her with her caffeinated goodness and a smile before I mime zipping my lips closed like I saw on one of her programs earlier. She sips the coffee before making the smallest moan of contentment, and I feel that tiny sound all the way through my body, instantly needing to hear more of it.

But right now, she's working. I will show her and her profession respect. Fighting every instinct in my body, I turn away from her to peruse her studio. This room holds so much more personality than the rest of her home. A soft rug covers most of the floor, bookshelves line nearly half the walls, with maps and paintings covering every inch of wall space left over.

The open shelves hold a plethora of artwork, both lude and tame. They feature all kinds of bodies, ranging from regular men to half-spider males, each embracing human women. *I think I might love the modern world.* This room is a celebration of sensuality, and I want to thoroughly celebrate with her.

Picking up a book that looks interesting, I hold it up towards her with my brows raised in silent question. She begins to blush and seems to hold back a laugh but nods her head and points towards a dark velvet chair in the corner. I take the seat she directed me to, the perfect place to enjoy my find while I also take in the sight of Bel.

As she proceeds with her work for a while, I open the novel I've chosen.

I thumb through until I find what I'm looking for. *This is utterly vile and delicious.* Every detail is included in the sex scene and it's *incredibly* descriptive. The longer I read, the more I understand the appeal. I have to cross my legs to try to hide the effect the novel has on me, but if Bel's growing smirk is any indication, I've been caught.

My Little Dove has no idea the game she's just started. She knew exactly what I would find in that tome and *encouraged* me. As I rise from my seat, her face drops. I gesture for her to continue and go towards the closed cabinet opposite me. If she keeps sexual art out in the open, what does she keep behind closed doors? The startled expression on her face morphs into pure terror, and I wonder what could possibly be causing such fear. Opening the doors, I look around and—

By the Gods. Are these... all sex items?

Some clearly are, the phallic shape being entirely obvious. But others are less so. I don't recognize half the things in here, and I can't help but wonder if Bel has used these with others. I'm caught between being dangerously jealous and incredibly aroused at the thought.

I can work with some of these items. A bundle of ultra-soft feathers sits in a clear vase, a blindfold and some silk ribbons drape across the shelf, and what appears to be a riding crop is propped against the wall. Choosing one of the feathers to enhance our little game, I close the cabinet and turn towards Bel.

Finally, she hits a button and speaks to me, "Wh-what are you doing?" Her nervous little voice has the creature inside of me banging against the cage I've built around it.

"Exploring," I point the feather in her direction. "You're supposed to be working," I remind her.

Her eyes zero in on my hand holding the feather, and rather than back down, she challenges me, "I am working. *You* are interrupting."

I suppose she's not wrong, but I needed to see her. Before I can explain that, my curiosity gets the best of me. "Have you used all of these?" I gesture back to the treasure trove with my feather.

"No," her cheeks are positively scarlet, and *Christ*, I need to know if the rest of her body flushes that deeply. "I just... You can't really talk about sex and the toys if you haven't played around a bit." *Toys*, she calls them. *I wanna play so bad.*

"So you experiment for the sake of authenticity?" I taunt, planting the seeds for how we'll play. I'm nearly shaking from the effort of holding myself back from her.

"I guess so, yeah. But only by myself so half that stuff hasn't been touched." Based on the way she closes her eyes and heaves out a breath, it would appear she did not want to share that with me. I distantly wonder why she hasn't, while also feeling grateful because this entire collection might be burnt to a crisp if anyone else had used these with her.

"Well," I drawl as I stroll toward her, "In the spirit of giving an authentic narration, allow me to help." I step behind her workstation where she's sitting on her little bench.

She's practically panting, but she hasn't said anything, so I wrap her hair around my fist and gently tug until she's looking up at me. I lean down until we are breathing the same air, using my free hand to run the feather down the middle of her neck, stopping just above where her chest heaves with every breath. I whisper against her lips, "Tell me to leave." She says nothing. "Or resume your work, and allow me to aid your performance."

I release her hair and wait for her to decide.

After a quick moment, she leans forward to hit a button. *Oh, good fucking girl.* I nearly groan in relief. As she proceeds to read, I lower myself to my knees directly behind her and set the feather on her seat. I put my hands on the bench to each side of her and lean in to get another smell of her sweet hair, causing her breath to hitch. I gather her gorgeous strands, drape them over one shoulder, and rest my chin on the other so I may watch what she's reading.

Thus far, I hadn't bothered paying attention to the words she read, but now I'm fully invested, for authenticity's sake, of course.

"He ran his calloused hands along my skin, learning my every curve," she begins. My hands reach for where she's hiding hers in her lap, and I place them on the bench to the sides and slightly behind her, the position forcing her to arch her spine and put those perfect breasts in my line of sight. The hard points poking through her shirt, begging to be tasted, have my mouth watering.

Sliding my palms up her arms, I notice her words become shaky and strained, but she continues, "As his mouth skimmed my neck, I let out a breathy moan." I turn into the crook of her neck, running my open mouth back and forth, not quite a kiss, just a torturous tease, letting my breath warm her neck. She breaks out in gooseflesh and shivers, causing me to smile against her soft skin.

"The possessive hold he had on me, with his hand around my throat, left me dizzy with desire." I let one hand drift to her hip while the other drapes around her slender neck, pulling her into me. At the feel of my hard length against her, she gasps and both of my hands flex against her.

"Shhhh. Keep going, my Dove." I whisper against her ear and give it a little warning nip.

"I felt every inch of his hard cock as he rocked his hips against mine, only a few layers of clothes left between us." I grind myself into her soft, plush ass, and a small groan escapes me. When she whimpers, I can't hold back any longer. I have to taste her luscious, panting mouth. Using my grip on her neck, I pull her head back, forcing her to back and up at me.

Her eyes drift to my lips, and I watch, full of aching need, as she licks her pouty lower lip. Trepidation and excitement war on her face, a beautiful agony written across her features as she gives in, knowing where this will inevitably lead.

Ring

Ring

Ring

Please don't answer that, I beg internally, our eyes still locked on each other.

She gasps and pulls away, hitting the stop button on her machinery, "I have to get that. It could be important." She tries to stand, nearly toppling over in her lust-drunk state. Though I'm certain I'd fare no better right now.

"Hi, Isla! What? No, I'm not out of breath. No, no, I'm just- uhhh, working." She looks at me, still down on my knees, ready to worship her. For a moment, indecision crosses her face, but she proceeds, "No, it's not a bad time. I can take a break. What's going on?" She mouths *Sorry* to me and all but runs from the room. I tilt my head back and let out a breath, trying to release the tension from my body.

Taking advantage of her absence, I stand and meander back to the cabinet of *toys*, as she called them. There are so many, but the one I find myself gravitating towards again and again is the riding crop. Based on her reaction to being held by the throat, my little offering craves pain and fear with her pleasure. I slap the crop across my palm a couple times, then return it to its rightful place before continuing my exploration.

When Bel returns to the room, all the heat in her expression is gone, replaced by an apologetic smile. "That was my friend, Isla. She- ummm... she doesn't have a great relationship with her parents and they are trying to force themselves back into her life," she explains.

"Why does she not have a healthy relationship with them?" As someone without a family, I don't understand not clinging to them if you have one.

She takes a moment to answer, "It's a very long story, involving years of trauma and abuse. It's really not my story to tell, so you'll have to forgive me for not telling you more."

"I see. I can imagine that's very hurtful for her," I pause, "But she's very fortunate to have you as support."

"Thank you," she says with a small smile, then becomes more reserved and proceeds, "Look. I really have to get these scenes finished. Without any further distractions."

"Of course." Even though it's the last thing I want to do, I'll leave her to her work. "I'll take my book and be gone. I'll be in the main living area should you need me."

With a quick bow, I grab my reading material, walk out the door and allow her some privacy.

For now, anyway.

10

A Very Active Imagination

Bel

Yesterday was a disaster. Okay, well, maybe that's a bit dramatic. But I definitely did not stay on schedule with my work, between Caspian's little game and Isla calling about her latest issue with her parents. Both require more thought than I was able to give them before, but now that I'm lying in bed, avoiding getting up, my mind is running in circles between the two.

Since Isla went no contact with her parents last year, things have gotten much better for her. She doesn't talk about it much anymore, and I don't know everything, but I do know they were not supportive, to say the least, about her *lifestyle.* They had decided a long time ago that she was going to live the life they deemed fit, even if that life made her miserable.

Usually, they keep their distance. But like clockwork, every few months, once she has recovered from their last unexpected visit, they appear in the form of gifts or random suitors with her phone number. This time, they emailed her a round-trip ticket home for Thanksgiving, along with a message about meeting her mom's hairdresser's son when she comes to visit.

Every time a *gift* like this appears, she has to grieve for them all over again. She grieves for the parents she needed, she grieves for the life she deserved, and she grieves for the little girl she should have been. And every time, Isla feels the unbearable guilt of cutting off family members who *love* her. But love isn't real if it comes with terms and conditions.

I wish I had had more time to talk about it with her, to reassure her that she's doing the right thing by protecting herself and denying them control over her. But unfortunately, real life can't just pause when we need a minute. We both had too much work to get through yesterday. But I promised to meet her for lunch in a couple days so she could vent.

It'll push back my road trip with Caspian a day, but he'll be fine. If I'm being honest, I think he needs the extra day to acclimate before I spring the chaos that is Las Vegas on him.

That's another nightmare I'm trying not to think about. I'm supposed to be getting rid of him, not... whatever this is that I've been doing. His advances yesterday had me absolutely soaked through my pajama shorts. *And he barely touched me.* I can only imagine the mess I'd be if he actually made good on the promises his lingering touches were making.

The way his large, smooth hands mapped my skin and his rumbling whisper in my ear had me melting into him. When he cradled my neck in his palm and rocked against me, I thought I was already going to combust into a million pieces. I had tried so hard to keep my cool, but the desperation in his filthy groan had me pushing my ass back against him, begging him to release another sound.

I had no idea anything could be so... primal and intense. We didn't even get close to fucking, yet I became nothing but a mindless beast at the mercy of my stupid vagina's needs. *God damn it, I'm getting all wet just thinking about it.*

I could probably take care of it really quickly. I've been worked up since yesterday afternoon with no time to deal with it. I haven't heard Caspian moving around yet, so maybe he won't know. I can't use any of my toys since they're all in my studio cabinet. I might get a little loud being this frustrated. *Do demons have super hearing?* I meant to ask more about his abilities yesterday, but I kept getting distracted. *I could just bury my face into a pillow.*

Decision made, I gently run my finger down my neck, imagining it's that stupid feather. Behind my eyelids, a figure wafting shadows dances around my peripherals. As he climbs over me, I feel Caspian's palm grazing down the center of my chest, continuing down my stomach before pausing between my legs, over my pajama shorts. *He would never go straight for the kill. He would spend as much time as possible working me up and teasing me before allowing me release.*

Following that train of thought, I pause the hand between my thighs and use my other hand to gently thumb one of my nipples through my shirt. I work it again and again, before giving it a slight pinch and rolling it between my thumb and finger. Repeating the same action on my other breast, I start rubbing my pussy against my palm. *Christ, am I so needy I'm dry-humping my own hand?*

I shake off the unwelcome shame and continue my fantasy. The hand I've been using to play with my tits slides slowly up to my throat, and I finally let my other hand drift underneath my shorts. I find my center unbearably wet and let my fingers gently trace over my opening, dragging the wetness up to my clit.

A moan escapes me before I can help myself, and I bite into my lip to try to stifle the sound. I need to grab a pillow like I originally planned, but both hands are busy doing more important things. I tighten my grip on my throat as I start to rub small circles against my throbbing clit. With each pass, my hips move of their own accord, my back arches, and if my hand wasn't cutting off all sound, I'd be moaning like a wanton whore.

I picture his bright green gaze staring down at me, watching me fuck myself. There's so much hunger written all over his face and his darkening eyes as he watches me slide a finger into my center, hands gripping my thighs wide open so he doesn't miss a single second. "Oh, my Little Sacrifice, you're dripping onto the sheets."

I slide in another finger, nearly crying out at the stretch, moving my hand faster and faster, grinding my clit against my palm as my fingers work that sweet spot inside. *Fuck, I'm so close.* The imaginary Caspian moans with me, moving his hand from my throat to cover my mouth, and orders, "Come on, my Dove. Let me see you come all over those fingers."

I'm fucking *gone.* I come so hard stars burst behind my eyes, and my whole body clenches, each wave of bliss causing me to bite into my hand. I try working myself through it, but I've long since lost control of my body, and my fingers' movements become sloppy. Slowly I come back down to earth, the little pulses turn into aftershocks, and all the tension finally drains from my body.

I probably shouldn't have done that. There's really no way he didn't hear me, but it's his fucking fault, so he can suffer through hearing it without being able to be a part of it. Plus, I'm sure there's a special place in Hell for people who fuck actual demons, so maybe getting myself off just thinking about it is safer. *Yeah, that's what I'm going with.*

His being a demon should bother me more than it does. *A lot more.* But honestly, could he really be any worse than the human men I've known?

I mean he *did* try to kill me. Then succeeded in killing those officers. He didn't even act remorseful about it either. Those were men with families, people with their whole lives ahead of them and now they just... don't. And yet I'm laying here in bed, practically swimming in my own cum because of him.

If he's a monster, then what does that make me?

Disregarding that unhelpful thought, I roll over and look at my phone. 10:30. I really can't justify staying in bed any longer, so I drag myself to the edge and put my feet on the floor. I look towards the door, wondering what kind of shit show today will be.

After I brush my teeth and shower, I pull on some sweatpants and the biggest hoodie I can find. There will be zero skin on display for Caspian to tease today. Not a single. Fucking. Inch. I comb through my hair and put the top layer in rollers. *Now he won't be able to grab that either.*

I head down the stairs and pause at the foot of them. My new house guest is standing in the kitchen. Shirtless. His perfectly cut body, practically glowing golden in the morning light makes my mouth dry and my pussy decidedly *not.* I use every ounce of my willpower not to let my eyes drift to the V pointing down to what I'm sure could be considered a deadly weapon.

I fail.

Snapping myself out of my stupor, I look back up. Caspian has two cups of coffee in his hands, holding one out in my direction. The smug smile on his face, accompanied by the slow, mirthful, "Good morning, Belissenda. Did you sleep well?" he drawls tells me he knows exactly what I've been up to.

Grabbing my favorite addiction from his outstretched hand, I try to play it off, "I slept as well as can be expected for someone with a stranger sleeping in their home."

"We are most definitely not strangers anymore, Little Dove." His eyes sparkle with mischief, "In fact, I'd say we are well on our way to being *very* good friends." *Motherfucker.*

He's too happy about how this is going. He thinks he's holding all the cards right now. And while that might be absolutely true, I can't let him know that. We have to get him into the company of his own kind. Get him the fuck away from me before I do something really stupid.

"You need a haircut." *Really? That's the first thing you come up with?* "And you need... clothes." I look pointedly at his bare torso.

His smirk grows, and he replies, "Do I?" running his hand over his wet hair, slicking it all back before smoothing that same hand down his chest and abdomen. "I would require your assistance for both of those quests. If you recall, I cannot travel far from you without exposing myself."

"You are nearly *exposing yourself* right now, Demon," I spout before I can think better of it.

His smirk grows into a full, beaming grin. "Not yet, I'm not. Would you like me to? It seems only fair after your beautiful performance this morning."

I narrow my eyes at him, refusing to dignify that with a response, and turn toward the toaster, which already has perfectly toasted bread sticking out of it. "Is that for me?" I ask.

"Yes!" he beams, "I managed to prepare the bread *and* the coffee." *God damn him, he's so adorable when he's not being an insufferable flirt.*

"Thank you," I say curtly. I'm still peeved, but I have fucking manners. I grab the toast and smear some butter on it before turning to him to say, "Put on some clothes, Caspian. We're going to get you acquainted with modern life." I have to keep some of my dignity here. He can't catch me ogling him again, so he needs to be... more covered.

"Yes, ma'am," he winks at me, and I storm away.

I'm fully aware that I'm pouting and probably being ridiculous, but he's just shown up, torn apart my belief system, and invited himself into my life and home. In less than two days, he's completely destroyed any notion I had that I could be happy just masturbating and reading smut for the rest of my life. I'm supposed to be trying to rid myself of him, and instead, I want to tackle him in the kitchen and ride him into oblivion.

How fucking dare he come in here and do this, then act completely unaffected?

If all the romcoms I've read have taught me anything, it's that dressing for revenge is not the smartest move. But I never said I was smart. What I am is desperate. I need to make him as stupid as he's made me.

It's cold as all hell today, so I can't go around in summer clothes, but I can still make a statement. I slap on winged eyeliner and mascara, play up the arches of my brows, and smear on a little lip gloss. While I love a full face of makeup, I do not have the presence of mind for that today.

I opt with a little black high-waisted midi skirt with a slit up one leg and a slouchy, ultra-soft pink sweater that hangs off one shoulder, tucking in the sweater to show off my narrow waist and curvy hips. I stand for a long while debating between my sets of tights, but settle on my favorite set of floral fishnets. The idea of walking around town in heels makes me want to die, so I grab my tried and true knee-high boots and call it good.

As I leave my room, Caspian exits the spare across the hall and freezes. His eyes drop first to the bit of skin between my boots and skirt, licking his lower lip and pulling it into his mouth. Then his eyes slowly rise back up, landing on my bare collarbone and shoulder before meeting my eyes. "I love the modern world," he says to himself, and I internally pat myself on the back for that one.

"You ready?" I ask, feigning nonchalance. He looks so goddamn fine I have to hold back from giving him the same indecent perusal he gave me. For not being from this time, he has great taste. Black henley rolled up to his elbows, dark jeans, and a pair of gnarly-looking combat boots.

"I am. You look lovely," he pauses, then continues, "It occurred to me that I do not have any currency for the services we will be needing while I am here."

"Well, yeah. You'll probably eventually want to get a job. But for now, I can take care of it." A job? Do demons need jobs? I mean they'd probably have to, right?

"You would use your own money to help me? Why?" he seems genuinely confused.

"Because the other option is you stealing again," I tease and raise one brow.

He smiles at me, the look laced with teasing condescension, "Let's not kid ourselves. I absolutely will be using my abilities to acquire things. I will not allow you to spend an exorbitant amount on me, and it would appear that clothing is far more expensive than it ought be."

"No. You can't just go around stealing from people," I can't believe I have to explain this.

"And why not?" he laughs.

"Because it's... it's wrong." I start walking away from him down the stairs.

"Wrong? I have body parts in your freezer but *stealing* goes against your morals?" I gag at the reminder.

"No. That's wrong too. I just..." I don't know why this seems worse. "I can't prevent what's already happened, but maybe I can stop you from doing... more bad stuff." Gathering my bag, I start towards the door with him only steps behind me.

"You are attempting to impose your mortal ethics on me." He gently grabs my elbow, turning me towards him. Gaze locked on mine, he continues, "Do not make the mistake of thinking me like you. I am not mortal, and your treatment and expectation of me as such will only be to your own detriment."

That's very ominous. All I can do in response is nod.

His serious expression instantly lifts, "Splendid. Let's go rob some mortals."

11

Welcome to the 21st Century

Caspian

Bel can deny our connection all she likes; her actions prove otherwise.

There I was in the room she allowed me to reside in, using the shower she had shown me. I knew she was awake, but with everything that has happened to her in the last couple of days, I wanted to grant her a reprieve to think through all she's witnessed.

Imagine my surprise when through the walls a muffled moan escapes my little dove. She tried so hard to keep herself quiet, but there was no denying what she was doing. I'm certain that if my shower had not been so loud, I would have been able to hear the lewd sounds of her fingers working her to rapture. As it was, I had to fill in the blanks between her sighs and moans, followed by little cries of relief when she finally reached her peak.

Initially, I cursed her timing. Had she waited five more minutes, I could have stood in the hallway and soaked up every blissful second. But, upon further thinking, being in a place where I could easily take care of my rapidly growing erection worked in my favor.

As soon as she started making those exquisite sounds in earnest, I wrapped my lathered hand around myself and stroked to the rhythm she set for us. The desperate sounds she made urged me to fuck my hand faster and harder, squeezing until it was nearly painful.

After yesterday's teasing and now this, it did not take long for me to paint the shower walls with my spend, allowing myself one small groan. Finally having the release I had been craving, I quickly rinsed myself, threw on a pair of pants, and headed down the stairs, hoping to prepare Bel's food and coffee before she finished her own shower.

When she pranced down the stairs with her cosmetic-free face and curling rods atop her head, she looked so cute and flushed with pleasure I could not help but tease her. Perhaps I pushed too far if her ire is any indication, but it was worth it. The pink that bloomed across her cheeks, turning her freckles into stars, will be burned into my head for all eternity.

Then she dared to walk out in clothing seemingly designed to make me weak. She's not playing fair, and there will be consequences for that. Later. For now, she's showing me the utmost kindness by taking me out into the world to retrieve the items I require.

Walking a few steps behind her, her swaying hips acting like magnets for my eyes, I nearly run into another person in the hallway. I mutter a quick apology and speed up so I may walk side by side with her.

"What will we do first, Belissenda?" I resist the urge to tug on her soft hair again, then I wonder aloud before I can stop myself, "Does your hair grow that way naturally?"

"No," she blesses me with a bashful smile, "I color it this way. Our first stop will be to fix *your* ridiculous hair." I smooth back the waves in question, humming to myself in agreement. She leads me to some kind of enclosed box she calls an elevator. It begins to move, and her eyes are full of humor as she gestures all around her, explaining its usage.

"We had something similar," I tell her, "but it was pulled by animals and rarely used for transporting humans due to the unstable nature of it." She nods, expression alight with curiosity and fascination. As the doors slide open again, she walks into a very large dark room with black terrain, gray walls, and vehicles as far as the eye can see.

A sharp chirping noise sounds, and I grab her arm to push her behind me, but she brushes me off, "That's just my car, Caspian." Pulling me by the hand, she leads me toward a very small gray steel *car.* "You sit here," she opens the door for me and gestures me inside.

"I know how to sit in a cart," I tell her indignantly.

"Apparently, you don't," she grins and leans slightly inside the car, grabbing a strange strap from beside me. "This is your seatbelt. You wear this any time you are in a car so that if the car crashes, you don't die."

"Your little mortal inventions could not kill me, silly girl." She brings the belt across my body, and it clicks into place.

"I wouldn't be so sure. Have you ever been hit by 2 tons of steel traveling at 90 miles an hour?" *Well, no.* My silence gives her the answer she was looking for, and she gives me a look that screams, *I didn't fucking think so,* before pulling away from me and shutting the door in my face.

She moves around the front of the vehicle, and I get to watch her every step through the windows. When she climbs into her own seat, I can't help myself, "You will also wear a safety belt, yes?" I've never worried for anyone this way before, and I can't help but wonder if the bond has created this overbearing nature in me or if it's just Bel.

"Yes, mother hen, I will wear a seatbelt. I always do." She twists to set her bag on the floor behind our seats, and the position brings her so close to me I can smell her sweet perfume where it sits on her skin. *By the Gods, do not sniff her like a feral animal again.* With the marriage of sweet vanilla, marzipan, and almost spicy warmth, she smells like a God's damned dessert, and I want to devour every inch of her.

Shaking the thought away, I watch as she uses a button to power on the vehicle, moves the little stick about, then we slowly start moving backward. The rumble of the engine feels so incredibly powerful beneath me, and I know instantly this will be my favorite part of the day.

"I'd like to drive this vessel," I announce.

"Uhhh, well probably not today. I'd have to teach you how," she moves the stick thing again, and we are suddenly passing all the other parked cars, heading towards what must be the exit, based on the bright light coming from it.

"How difficult could it be?" I ask.

"It's not super hard. It just takes a lot of patience and practice to do it safely. We start learning how to drive when we're like 15." That makes sense, I suppose. Commanding a beast this powerful without harming others would require precision.

"But you will teach me?" I'll observe her for now, and when the time comes, I will be her most enthusiastic student.

"When we have time, yeah, I'd be happy to," she shrugs, not realizing the gift her words have given me. She'd be *happy* to. She wants to keep me as surely as I am desperate to have her, even if she does not see it yet.

As we make our way into the sunshine, she turns a couple knobs and soft music begins to play. I can only imagine how sick of all my questions she is, so I don't pester her with them anymore as we drive to our destination, even though I am fascinated by her motor vehicle being able to project music.

Bel begins to hum along to the tune playing, and I realize I would commit every atrocity known to man if she asked, just for a moment of her song. I lean my head back against the seat, basking in the magic that is her.

When the car begins to slow again, she's directing it between two others of similar size in front of a building mostly made of glass. She presses a button to release my seatbelt, then her own, opening the door and climbing out. Following her lead, I exit the vehicle and trail closely behind her.

"I booked an appointment online so we shouldn't have to wait too long for your stylist," she assures me. I nod in anticipation and open the door, guiding her in first with a hand on the small of her back, and she smiles sheepishly up at me as she passes by.

"How can I help you?" the man behind the counter asks. He has shockingly white hair with a black streak through the front, all pushed up into a messy, disheveled spike.

"Hello," my Dove greets, "I'm Bel and this is Caspian. I made an appointment for him to get a haircut earlier."

"Oh perfect! I'm Rafe, and I get to be your stylist today. Super nice to meet you both!" his enthusiasm is contagious, and Bel is positively beaming at the man, both of them wearing great big smiles.

Bel pushes me toward the man a bit and says, "Caspian is new to... the states and wanted a cut that would be a little more... modern." She sneaks a look at me like we're sharing a joke, and I suppose we are, so I smile back. She pulls her phone out, and with a few swipes, she's showing Rafe something on it and saying, "I do kind of want it to be a surprise, but I was thinking something like this."

"Oh, he'll look so handsome with that kind of volume. Those waves will be perfectly tousled and it'll make his features really pop." She gives his arm an excited squeeze and releases a little squeal, and I have to ignore the sick feeling in my gut telling me to slaughter this man.

He turns to me and does a little summoning wave towards one of the chairs, "Come on, Prince Caspian, let's get you spiffied up." At Bel's giggle, I turn toward her in confusion.

"It's a movie reference. There's a prince and a lion and some not so vague allusions to Christianity," she wiggles her fingers at me in farewell and turns to walk away, "I'll be waiting right over here, 'kay?"

I sit where Rafe directed me, and he drapes a cape over me. He begins running his fingers through my hair and talking about the length, thickness, and *curl pattern.* I then realize that I'm so clueless about it all that it'll be far easier to let Rafe do as he pleases. He starts clipping away at my hair, switching between scissors and a small buzzing machine.

Eventually, he tells me to stand so we can go wash it, but I inform him I cleaned it no more than a few hours beforehand. He explains that the wash gets the small hairs out, so I don't have to take them with me.

After the wash, consisting of several products and a scalp massage so mind-numbing I nearly fell asleep, we head back to my original seat.

"Your English is impeccable. I was thinking maybe you didn't speak much of it. Where are you from?" he asks.

Vankhala. "Italia, originally." *Not a complete lie, I suppose.*

"Oh, that's wonderful," he says, full of genuine excitement, "I've always wanted to visit. What brought you here?"

"Belissenda." *Also not a lie.*

"Wow, moving across the world for someone? So romantic."

"I would travel farther. No distance would be too great." I've known this woman all of two days, and I know intrinsically that it's true.

"That's beautiful. She's lucky to have you," he states.

At that I begin to laugh, "I think she would disagree with you, my friend."

"Are you kidding?" he chortles with me, "That girl looks at you like you hold the answer to the question everyone asks themselves."

"What question is that?" I attempt to keep the growing hope from my voice.

"Why are we all here?" I have nothing to say to that, wondering if it could possibly be true.

Seemingly finished with our existential discussion and my hair, he spins me back toward the mirror, "I am *so* good."

I have to agree. I am a handsome devil if I do say so myself, but he's managed to make me even more appealing. My hair is far shorter on the sides than I've ever worn, but he's left it long on top and styled it, so it's combed back and to the side. The top seems very poofy to me, but I've seen other men with the same style, so I'm assuming it's proper for this time.

As he removes the cape, a high-pitched whistle travels from the entry area. Bel's huge smile tells me we did something right by coming here. "You like it?" I ask.

"So much better." Turning to Rafe, she gushes, "You are a miracle worker. What's the damage?" Then she pays him his fee and some extra as a thank you.

As we exit the salon, I clutch her hand in mine, thanking her for arranging this. It doesn't do much to help me adjust to this world, but it's a start, and she did it expecting nothing in return. Every moment we've spent together has held an undercurrent of fear from this brave warrior and yet, she has offered me displays of kindness I have never been given before.

"It's nothing, really. I couldn't look at that godawful haircut for one more second. It was an entirely self serving act because now you look like a fucking snack." At my perplexed expression, she giggles, "A snack? It's like... slang. Like you look good enough to eat?"

Her teasing tone and raised brows have me pulling her closer by our entwined hands, "Darling Bel, I think we both know that *you're* the one of us who's going to be *eaten*."

Her face burns pink, pupils blown as she tries to create space between us. Seemingly realizing that's not an option, she clears her throat and announces, albeit clumsily, "Now, uhhh, clothes," and pulls me back to her car.

* * *

A few hours later, we are back in the elevator with just a few items in hand. I only allowed Bel to buy me a couple things, not confessing to her that I simply took the vast majority of the items I wanted. She doesn't need to know that I transported all the rest of the clothes I picked home. It would only upset her that I took that much from the mortals. Clothing in this century is very different, but there were so many options I had to have a bit of everything.

When we exit the hoist and walk towards her home, I make what is almost certainly a foolish, reckless decision. I'm going to kiss her. With no expectation of more, just a little kiss to show my appreciation. Friends do that. Right? In this day and age, surely a little affection between friends is acceptable.

As she unlocks her door and steps inside, I slip a hand around her slim waist and spin her in a dance just for us until her back is against the inside of the door. My other hand cups her jaw, and I pause, just for a moment, giving her the time to refuse.

When she doesn't, I let myself have just one small chaste press of my lips to hers, then I pull back. Why? I don't know. To thank her again? To look at her face in hopes that it wears the same desperate expression as mine? But instead, she takes me by surprise, hooking both hands around my neck and pulling me back for more.

I'm holding myself back, knowing if I don't, my need for her is going to startle her, and this will be over before it even begins. She uses her pillowy lips to gently work mine open and lightly lick inside my mouth. *Fuck.* I use my thumb against her chin to open her further, pushing my tongue to slide greedily against hers. Pulling her bottom lip gently with my teeth, I draw a small gasp from her.

A throat-clearing sound fills the air, followed by, "Uhhh, hi Bel. Bel's friend." I push off the door, spinning to face the threat, keeping Bel behind me.

"Isla! What are you doing here?" Oh. No threat, then. She runs toward her friend and gives her a hug, Isla not taking her watchful eyes off me. I follow a few steps behind, trying to come across as a doting paramour, not a demon who was just considering using my claws to rip through Bel's clothing.

"I was in the neighborhood and figured you were working." Raising an eyebrow, she teases, "But you were doing something *far* more interesting."

"Shit. Isla, Caspian. Caspian, Isla." Guilt crosses her face, and before she can say another word, I reach out to shake her friend's hand.

"It's very nice to meet you, Isla. I'll be on my way so you two can talk." I wrap an arm around Bel's shoulder to kiss the side of her head before walking out the front door. I can't go far, but I could probably get away with sitting in the stairwell. I have no *intention* of listening in on their conversation, but I *do* need to know when Isla leaves so I can go back inside. If I overhear something in the meantime, I cannot be held at fault for that.

"Holy shit, where did you find him and where can I get one?! No wonder you weren't answering my texts. I wouldn't have answered either. I'm so sorry I interrupted you guys. I really had no idea. I just know how you get when you work so I wanted to pop in and make sure you stopped to eat." Good. She deserves a friend who will look after her and give her the same love she seems to give everyone else.

"It's a long story, I... met him through work," I laugh at that, even if technically it is true, "and it's still very new. That was the first time we've kissed."

"You haven't fucked him yet?" *They all really use that language so comfortably now.* I decide then that my first order of business will be to read more of her books so I can blend in with the colloquial language here.

"No, not even close."

"Dude, are you crazy? He's so hot. Does he have a brother? A sister? A distant cousin?"

"I'm not totally sure. It's like I said, it's brand new." *That's an understatement.*

"You both looked ready to get down right there against the wall so it must have been good."

"Yeah, it was a good kiss. A *really* good kiss," I can hear the smile in her voice all the way from here.

Isla gives her a happy little squeal and says, "Fuck yeah. That's awesome. You deserve it. Get laid. Have some fun. Keep him around for a while. Or don't." *I'm not going anywhere.* "Just do it for yourself and not him. Promise?"

"Promise."

After a few more minutes of chatting and Isla mentioning that she brought Bel some dinner, they say their goodbyes. Isla walks into the elevator, hits a few buttons, and it whooshes away.

"Caspian?" Bel sticks her head out into the hallway, whisper-shouting, looking around for me.

I exit the stairwell, and her eyes light up when they land on me. She opens her mouth to apologize, as she does so often, but I stop her with my finger tapping once on her nose, "Do not apologize. Unless it's for distracting me to the point I could not even sense another person in your domain. Little minx, you are."

She rolls her eyes and drags me inside, "Isla brought a ton of food so have some of whatever looks good." *You look delicious.* Before I can respond, she sputters, "No. Not me. Food."

While of course, I'd much prefer to finish what we started against the door, the memory her sweet sigh and ravenous mouth sending shivers down my spine, she's in need of sustenance and her needs come first. I'll taste her gorgeous mouth again later.

I grin at her and settle in to have a mortal meal with my Bel. We spend the rest of the evening talking and eating before she excuses herself to bed. We have only a few days here together before we begin our search in earnest. Somehow, I have to show her that even once we find what we're looking for, I'll not be leaving, and show her that it's what she wants too.

12

Vegas, Baby

Bel

Lunch with Isla always goes one of two ways. One of us cries, or we spend way too much fucking money on shit we don't need. Today was one of those *very rare* occasions that we got to do both. We usually make it a point not to get together for lunch because it's a guarantee neither of us will get anything else accomplished for the day. But when her parents get to their meddling bullshit, all bets are off.

After a long lunch and several frilly little mocktails, we find ourselves meandering through town. We float in and out of shops, and I can't help but remember doing pretty much the same things yesterday with Caspian.

Isla keeps looking behind her, peeking around corners, and all around acting super weird. I ignore it the first few times, chalking it up to paranoia because of her asshole parents. But after a little while, I have to ask her what has her so jumpy.

"Oh. I'm not sure. I just keep getting this weird feeling like we're being followed." *Shit.* "You don't feel that?" she asks.

Lying to her feels terrible, but I can't exactly explain that Caspian has to trail us all day to make sure no more hunters show up. He's brought along the compass, keeping an eye on it and coming closer whenever it stops spinning like crazy. Obviously, we don't know if they can find us without it, but it's better to be safe than sorry.

"No, I don't feel anything," It feels like fucking sandpaper in my mouth, but she doesn't need to be dragged into this, "Maybe hearing from your parents is making you a little paranoid? It wouldn't be a huge stretch since they managed to find you even after changing your email address and phone number again."

As soon as I say it, I spot him again. His sly little smirk as he stares at us from the shadow of the closest building. He points at the wristwatch he got... somewhere yesterday as if he's telling me it's getting late. He can't read the thing yet, but he liked it all the same, and who am I to stop him from being the most extra demon he can be?

"Yeah, I guess you're probably right," she pulls my attention back to her. Then she sighs, "It's getting late and I need to work on a few things tonight before I get to bed. I'll order an Uber and *you* can order for your new man to come pick you up for a nightcap."

After a quick wink, she pulls out her phone and gets to work. I pull out my own and pretend to text Caspian, knowing full well he's been listening and that it'll take him no time at all to get over here.

"Speaking of shitty parents," Isla interrupts my secret gawking, "How's *your* mom?"

I scoff, "She's not shitty. She's just..." I can't think of a better descriptor, but fortunately, Isla has several.

"Dismissive. Self-centered. Overbearing. Superficial. Guilt-trippy—that's not a word, but it should be."

A shrug is the best response I have. Nothing she's said is *wrong*, but that's still my mom.

"Don't you ever get tired of it, Bel?" she asks, not unkindly.

"Tired of what?"

"Giving endless love and forgiveness to someone who is incapable of doing the same for you?"

"That's not fair," I argue, "She's done a lot for me."

"And in return, she expects you to live your whole life for her approval. Her love is transactional, and yours isn't. You love her despite her flaws, and she only loves you when you pretend you have none."

Thinking of my mother this way feels like a betrayal, like I'm doing something wrong by daring to think negatively about the person who raised me.

"She is who she is, Isla," I shrug again, "There's no changing her."

She mhmm's, knowing her parents are the exact same. Some people just get too comfortable in who they are and refuse to grow, even for the benefit of those they supposedly love.

A few more minutes of— admittedly, slightly somber— silence pass as we stand waiting, until Isla suddenly breaks it and I'm in the unfortunate position of having to lie to her again, "What does Caspian do, anyway?"

Shit. "Oh, he uhh models. For book covers," I sputter out.

"That totally tracks. Have you asked about a sibling for me yet?" she wags her brows.

"Isla Parker! You horndog, you," I playfully slap her arm before adding, "I get the impression he doesn't have much family. And if he does, they're not in touch." He hasn't said anything about how demons spawn, but I think I'd know if he had one.

Her knowing nod and slightly glossy eyes tell me the conversation is about to take a turn for the worst if we don't shut it down. The topic of NC family is basically off-limits unless we want more tears.

"I'm sure he has lots of friends that model with him though. You know guys like that are always hot people magnets." I suggest.

"Ooh, you're probably right! You'll have to ask him once you guys have been seeing each other a bit longer. It might scare him off if you ask about other hotties too early in the relationship."

Relationship? That's not what this is. It's just... a weird situation where we're stuck together, and he's just so fucking hot, and I'm—

"Hey babe!" There he is, looking so handsome in his new clothes and hair. My god, it's really unfair how fine he is. "Hey Isla, how are you faring today?"

She narrows her eyes at me in suspicion, presumably at Caspian's quick arrival, before responding, "I'm good, and yourself?"

"Wonderful, thank you." He turns his brilliant smile on me, "And you, little warrior? Are you well?"

"I'm great. We just had lunch and walked around town." His arm slips around my shoulder, and I nearly combust on the spot. He should *not* be doing... PDA stuff. I'll never fucking hear the end of it.

We stand awkwardly for just a moment as he toys with my hair, none of us ever being in this kind of situation before. Who talks first? Has being around other people (and demons) always been so hard? Or is it just this big dummy with his arm around me making my brain go haywire?

"Oh! There's my ride!" I get a signature Isla hug, always just barely less than painful, and she turns to Caspian, "Get my girl home safely, Cas. Got it?"

"Yes, I'll ensure her safety. Have a good night."

"Bye-ee!" she shouts, climbing into the back of the car.

Caspian returns his gaze to me, a strange look on his face.

"What's wrong?" I ask him, curious why he seems so confused.

"It's nothing. Probably just me reacclimatizing to the world. Let's get home, we still have to prepare everything for our journey. And you need rest. Can you call one of those car services?" *He hasn't removed his arm from me.*

Unable to breathe so close to his winter wonderland smell, I shrug him off with a hum of affirmation and start ordering a cab. "It'll be here in about ten minutes."

"Perfect. You can spend that time telling me what you and Isla spoke about." He says it as if he doesn't already know exactly what was said.

"Well, I gave you a job," I mutter.

"A very fitting one, I heard. I do bare a resemblance to a few of the subjects in your studio decor." He lets his eyes flash white for emphasis. As if I needed the reminder that he only looks like a human.

Rolling my eyes, I mutter, "Always with the dramatics, Caspian," but even I can tell my jab holds no venom. "It just made the most sense. I narrate romance novels and you pose for them. I don't go out often enough that I could have met someone anywhere *but* work."

He doesn't say anything, just watches me with humor in his eyes.

"It doesn't hurt that you are *very* hot and sorta dumb." His rebuttal is stopped when I laugh, "You don't have any knowledge of this world, Caspian, so you *are* dumb. Plus, looking like *that* guarantees you a job in front of a camera."

"Fine," he admits, "But I'll have you know, I am doing everything in my power to learn of this time. I read an article entitled 37 *Most Influential Moments of 2020.*"

"Oof, that was a rough year," I say, mostly to myself.

"What is reality television?" he asks, and I don't even know where to begin.

"Ummm, it's T.V. shows that are supposed to be real and unscripted. More often than not though, what is shown to viewers is taken out of context. Or the people behind the camera are like telling the stars what to do and say." That's gonna have to be good enough for now. I'll make him binge-watch *The Bachelor* with me later.

"I see." I am nearly begging him not to bring up the reason for that question because I do not have the energy for that shit show.

Before he can ask a follow-up question, a car stops in front of us, and the driver leans toward his open passenger-side window, calling for me. The journey home is peppered with questions about the pandemic, RGB, and how it is that we had so many fires in one year. I wish I had more information for him, but honestly, we all got fucked sans-lube in 2020.

I tell him such, and for the first time, he lets out booming laughter. A laugh that loud and obnoxious has no place on a man so refined and pretty, but I love it. It's so perfectly surprising that I find myself laughing with him. That's probably not great since the source material causing that laughter is incredibly macabre, but dark humor has always been my bread and butter.

When we arrive home, Caspian informs me that he wants to finish off the remnants in the freezer before our trip tomorrow so he can be at full strength. I hand him all the cleaning supplies he'll need to scrub the guts off the freezer walls, then sprint my happy ass away to finish packing. I don't really have any Vegas-worthy clothes, but we're going on a reconnaissance mission, not a vacation.

I pack up my cutest swimsuit just in case. I think the hotel has an indoor pool, and I fully plan to take advantage of the hot tub once we find what we're looking for. I booked us two nights, hoping that'll be enough time to do what needs to be done. I hauled ass through both of my current books, and if I pull a few 12-hour days when we- *when I*- get home, I'll be back on schedule.

I have to stop letting myself think of us as a package deal. Caspian has been around for only a few days, and while obviously we are attracted to each other, it's only being compounded because we are essentially stuck together. If he had all the freedom he desired he wouldn't still be wasting his time with me. And that's- that's fine. It's good. Once this shit is done, I can get back to my real life.

After giving my luggage another once over, I climb into bed and try to clear my head of thoughts about how quiet this apartment will be once he's gone.

* * *

Okay, maybe I shouldn't have gone about it like this.

But he said he wanted to read during the drive.

He can't read and watch the world around him at the same time.

Thirty minutes into our drive to Vegas, I look over to see Caspian staring out the window, seeing the world pass him by. It must be so weird to suddenly be hundreds of years in the future with no knowledge of the time you missed. He's seeing all these things for the first time that I take for granted every day.

Things like the tall glass buildings sparkling in the rising sun or how you can listen to any song in the history of the modern world from inside the car. Or being able to find information on just about anything you want to know with just a few taps. I'd love to see everything with fresh eyes without fully knowing the insidious truths woven into every touch of beauty.

He breaks me from my train of thought by moving one side of the headphones from his ear and asking, "How long did you say this drive would take?"

"Roughly five hours, just depending on traffic." I explain, "We should make it there around lunch time but we can't check into the hotel until a few hours later."

"Alright. And then what?"

"We will get dressed up like two normal Vegas tourists and... I don't know, go exploring I guess. Until you have some kind of idea where to go." I really hope it's easy once we get there. If demons are drawn to places full of sin, Vegas is probably the way to go. Or maybe a Catholic Church. But I can't imagine demons being masochistic enough to subject themselves to that.

He hums noncommittally and puts the headphone back on. I wasn't brave enough to let him listen to any of my work for this journey. There's absolutely no way I could stomach knowing he's listening to me. But he's listening to one of my favorites. And it's really heavy on the MMC's POV, so hopefully, he's picking up a bit more about how we talk.

I love his uptight way of speaking, but it's no secret that it draws way too much attention. Three sentences had Isla looking at me like I had grown a third tit. Fascinated, curious, and only a little bit worried. He certainly looks the part now, and holy fuck, does he look good. But adjusting to this time will take a lot of work.

So his education starts where every hot guy should start. Spicy audiobooks that are written by women for women. Maybe he'll even pick up some dirty talking skill for— *no. Bad Bel. Stop that.* I will not be fucking this man. Demon. Demon-man. Gorgeous, funny, unhinged, sweet demon man. *God damn it.*

Is he snoring?

I turn down my music a bit and look over. Sure enough, this beast of a man has his head tilted back, mouth wide open, snoring. Moving as discreetly as I can, I grab my phone from its home in the center console and snap a quick picture. I know being on the phone while driving is dangerous, but no one would ever believe this happened otherwise. *I* don't even believe it, and I'm looking right at him.

I'll just let him sleep for now. Let him enjoy the wicked dreams he's probably having, courtesy of the background noise he'll have in them. I turn my music back up and try to focus on just driving. But since I am who I am, my mind tends to wander.

Isla is going to absolutely fucking kill me if she finds out I went on vacation without her. Not that it's a vacation, but I can't exactly tell her that. Maybe one day I'll be able to explain all of this to her. Probably not, because how could anyone comprehend this without seeing it?

And why won't Caspian tell me more about these hunters or the compass? He made it seem so simple, but it can't possibly be. The compass not working around me makes sense because we were bound for protection, and the only threat to him is them, I guess. But have these hunters been around forever? Do they only hunt demons, or do they hunt all kinds of monsters? Are there other monsters out there? If there are demons, it makes sense that there would be. Vampires and sirens and werewolves and Fae? It's all impossible. But I've seen it.

"You are thinking very loudly over there, Little Dove," Caspian mutters without so much as cracking an eye. I didn't even realize he had woken up.

"Am not," I argue.

"Your heart is racing, your breath coming in very quick little heaves, and you reek of fear suddenly. What is happening?" Now I have his full attention. Headphones around his neck, eyes trained on me, "Is there a nearby threat?"

"No, Caspian, everything is fine." I try reigning it in, but it's just hitting me how much bigger this is than just him and I. Everything I've ever known is wrong, and the proof is right in front of me. After a quarter century of life, that's a disastrous upheaval to deal with in just a few days. "I just... I think I need to take a breather," I announce.

Since we are on a somewhat deserted road, I decide it's best to just pull over before I crash us into a cactus. As soon as the car is in park, I unbuckle my seat and hop out, walking to a nearby curb to sit and put my head between my knees. He follows behind me and sits a respectable distance away, giving me the space I need to breathe.

"What has put you in such a state, Belissenda?" He's so concerned that it makes me want to retch. *This is humiliating.*

"I just started thinking about what all this means." I throw my hands around as if I can show him what I'm referring to that way.

"What all what means?" He scoots a bit closer and puts a hand on my back, rubbing slow, soothing circles.

"You. Demons being real. I'm just having a hard time wrapping my head around what it means for everything I've been taught my whole life." I bury my face in my hands, the worst of my nausea over. "I don't know what to believe now that my beliefs have been ripped to shreds right in front of me. And if I don't know what to believe, I don't know how to make any decisions going forward.

"If I was *so wrong* my whole life, my judgment is obviously skewed. And I'm just going to keep believing and thinking the wrong things over and over and over again."

"You are being unkind to yourself, Bel." He states. Still comforting me with his warm hand, he adds, "You believe what you do because it's what you've been *allowed* to believe. Those who hold the power control what information you've been given. You made decisions and assumptions without all the pieces necessary. Is your lack of knowledge your own fault? Of course not. You cannot blame yourself for not knowing what you did not know."

He begins to card his fingers gently through my hair, lowering his voice, "You can't go back and fix it. All you can do is choose who to become now that you have more answers. Would you rather go back to having your head in the sand?" I shake my head without looking at him. "No. Because *you* are a warrior who will face this new world head-on. Look, see? We're the same in that. And we shall both rise and make the most of the new world we are fortunate enough to live in."

Without thinking, I throw my arms around his shoulders in this godawful, half hug, half me-sprawled-across-his-lap thing. He wraps his arms around me, holding me to him, and states, "There she is. There's my brave one." He allows me to stay in his arms for as long as I need until I feel steady enough to extract myself from him and stand.

"Thank you." It doesn't seem like a big enough sentiment for the comfort he just gave, but it's all I've got.

"You are most welcome. I... appreciate your willingness to share your feelings with me. I imagine it wasn't easy for you." The sincerity and understanding on his face nearly bring me to tears. *How can this be the same being who tried to kill me?*

I can't let myself think about that right now, or we will never make it to

Vegas. "Let's get back on the road. We're 100% going to hit traffic in the city now."

13

This Place Stinks

Caspian

Getting closer to our destination, I start to feel a bit restless. We've been sitting still in the automobile for hours, and I can feel the energy practically pulsing from the city. From this distance, I can see a skyline full of different shapes and colors of buildings, no two completely alike.

I consider what Bel has been going through. I fear maybe I've pushed her too hard, but what can be done? I could not have avoided her seeing what I am, thus destroying her belief system and giving her countless questions all at once. Being forced to lie to her best friend and essentially being trapped in my proximity, it can't be easy for her.

She knows exactly what and who I am, and she still chose to seek comfort in my arms during her difficult moment. As long as she allows it, I will always stand beside her through her fights. Be it those happening in the world or just in her head. She just has to realize that she wants that as much as I do.

But how do I do that? Seduction is easy enough, I could use her body to show her how much she wants to be mine, but it wouldn't be enough if it's just physical. She needs more, and I'm not sure how to give it to her, but I'll work on it for as long as it takes.

I try not to let my mind wander too far when Bel informs me that since we can't check into our hotel for a little while, we will park somewhere called a strip. A strip of what, I do not know. She tells me that it's slang for the most populated part of the city.

As we turn into the *strip* full of flashing lights, honks, and people walking along every spare stretch of asphalt, I fail to see the magic of this place. It looks like maybe once it was a grand place full of adventure, but it's been allowed to fall into disrepair.

Bel pulls us into an underground parking garage like the one in her home and parks. She turns to me, ready to give me a speech, I'm guessing, "Look, Caspian. This place can be a little overwhelming. Just stay with me, please, okay?" *Oh, is that all? Easy enough.*

"I will not leave your side. It seems a bit dangerous, I wouldn't dream of allowing you to come to harm," I assure her.

"You tried to kill me... three days ago," she phrases this almost like a question.

"That I did. I was under the impression you were responsible for the murder of an innocent in your quest for power," I explain, "Simple mistake."

"Then you killed three cops. Were they not innocent people?" That is a bit more of a gray area.

"Simple answer, no. The more complicated answer? At that moment, yes, they were innocent. They were simply doing their jobs, but the stench they all carried assured me that they deserved the end they were given." She doesn't seem to understand, so I attempt to explain more clearly as we walk back onto the street to join the throngs of people, "Wickedness has a scent; a calling card, if you will. It stinks like poison seeping out of evil peoples' skin. Those who want to cause harm, those who kill and hurt others, they reek of it."

"So you only eat evil people. Not good ones. Why, then, are you considered evil?" she asks as we walk.

"I wish I had an answer on that," I shrug before adding, "However, let's not trick ourselves into thinking I'm some kind of savior. Almost surely, I have killed innocent people. But their blood doesn't *usually* sing to me the way other killers' does." I tell her.

"Usually?" she asks, seemingly terrified to hear what she must already suspect.

"Your blood, my little offering, is the sweetest I have smelled in all my years. It calls for me constantly, begging to be close enough that our hearts beat in time, pressed against each other." Her jaw drops, and I continue, "So it is very different from the way I hunger for their flesh, but I constantly crave you, nonetheless."

She has no response to that, so she walks on. When I can pull my eyes from her stunning figure, I see that every few feet, there are cards covered in lewd photographs of women, piles of trash, cigarette buds, and tiny liquor bottles. The whole place emits the stench of drunken vomit and smoke.

"This is not what I was expecting," I confess.

She laughs without humor before gesturing around, "You said you wanted a city of sin. This is it. Greed, lust, sloth, gluttony, pride, envy, and wrath. You'll find each one in a surplus here. Did you think a place nicknamed Sin City would be beautiful and spotless?" *Well, I had hoped.*

I wrinkle my nose when I'm hit with another layer to the cacophony of smells. "Why on earth does it smell like people are fornicating nearby?" I ask.

"They probably are. There are basically no enforceable rules here. And the idea of public sex gets a lot of people off." Well, I guess that makes sense. The idea of having Bel where everyone can watch as she falls apart for me alone is slightly intoxicating. But there are too many uncontrollable factors around for me to consider such a thing.

We stop and get a late lunch, eating burgers and fries while we watch the city grow busier and busier. I watch a couple throwing coins into the largest fountain I've ever seen. It reminds me of something we might have seen in the old world in Italia. The statues watch over the wishes of mortals, blessing those they find worthy.

Bel catches me staring and grins, full of excitement, "Oh, if you like that fountain, wait until you see the Bellagio. We won't see it now, cuz it's *so* much better at night."

"Is the Bellagio another fountain?" I question.

"Well, the Bellagio is a hotel about a half mile down the road, but it has one of the biggest fountains in the states. And at night they do shows with lights and music. It's gorgeous. And well worth putting off our mission for five minutes." Her eyes glitter with excitement. I want to be excited with her, but the reality of the city around us has me filled with trepidation.

During our meal, I feel... something. It's been so long now that I can't quite recall who it is, but someone familiar. Wherever we are, a demon is nearby, a terribly powerful one, at that. I have my suspicions, but I'd hate to get my hopes up and be disappointed.

"What is the closest large sinning space to where we are right now?" They are nearby. I can feel it.

"Well that fountain you were looking at is part of the Caesars Palace hotel. From what I remember, it has several casino areas, a nightclub, pools, shopping. That's as good a place as any to start."

"Let us go. Someone is here," I announce.

Her face drops, "Already?"

My black heart flutters at that, "Are you not ready for this excursion to be over?"

She clears her throat, "Well, we only just got here. There are a few things I think you'd love to see."

I stand up and reach for her hand to help her up. "Once we have accomplished what we must, we will do anything you desire, yes?"

That beautiful red blooms across her face, and I know *exactly* what she must be thinking. She can have that, too. But not yet, and definitely not here. She puts her hand in mine and gently places some cash on the counter as she stands. I'm going to actually need to find a job because I cannot allow her to keep paying for my existence in her world.

She tries to let go of my hand, but instead, I lace our fingers together and wave a hand in front of us, "Lead the way, my warrior."

She leads me past the fountain towards two huge sliding glass doors, entering a room so large, I wouldn't have believed it possible just two moments ago. Loud clanging and chimes assault us from every angle, people shouting and smacking the machines adding to the overwhelming sound. There is scattered drunken laughter even when patrons lose their tokens.

"We should probably blend in, so security doesn't kick us out," she looks around before pointing, "Oh! There. Let's go buy some chips."

Waiting in line, I tell her, "Bel, we cannot spend any more of your money on this. Just let me... take them. No one would notice. I'll simply pull them through the aether from there to my pocket."

"No, we can't do that. It wo-"

"Oh, darn. It looks like I've already managed it. Oops. Let's go," I wrap an arm around Bel's waist and pull her towards some of the machines. Sitting down and settling her onto my lap, I request, "Okay, Little Dove, teach me."

* * *

A few hours and who knows how many lost tokens later, we've perused the entire casino floor, and I'm about ready to retire so I can clean this city off of me when someone bellows, "Holy shit, look who's topside!"

I turn toward the sound, looking for the familiar voice, when he shouts again, "Caspian, get the hell over here." *Fritz.* Bel looks at me and raises her brows in a silent question before looking at the man— demon calling for me. I nod and pull her towards him with me.

"Hello, Fritz. It's been a long while." I tell him. Nearly 400 years, if memory serves. "This is Belissenda. She's my..."

"Your sacrifice." He supplies. *What the fu—* "I can sense that she's a *hostia* from here, and there's no other way for you to be back."

"Uhh hi," Bel gives him the tiniest wave, pulling herself deeper into my embrace, "Just Bel is fine."

Fritz's grin turns licentious, and he pulls out a chair next to him. "Just Bel, it is. Come sit down, both of you. I would love nothing more than to spend time with an old friend and his new friend." She glances nervously between the two of us before turning to me for direction.

I whisper into her ear, "He's incredibly powerful but utterly harmless. He's just a relentless flirt. Sit."

Strangely enough, she picks the seat that would put her between us rather than putting me closer to him. She looks at me again and then back at Fritz.

He doesn't tear his eyes off her, clearly as captivated by her stunning features as I am. A slimy sensation begins in my stomach, begging me to tear out his eyes so that, for at least a while, they can't consume what is mine.

Another part of me is relishing in his relentless perusal of my girl. I respect Fritz. I would even say we were dear friends when we knew each other. He and I gave in to the temptation of each other more than once over the years and seeing him crave her the way I do has my mind wandering places I would have thought implausible not five minutes ago.

I watch as Bel quickly appraises him right back. His wild hair is much different than how I remember it. The style is similar to mine, but no amount of product could tame those dark curls, one always flopping right into his face, his eyes so dark brown they're black in this light, his build slightly smaller than mine, more angular and agile.

A mischievous grin graces her beautiful face as she looks at me, "So you two know each other." She states.

That sly bastard slings an arm around her, pulling her close, and starts, "We do. But I'm more interested in knowing *you*, Sweetness." And God's damn him, Bel's grin transforms into that shy, coquettish smirk that plays with my heartstrings and my cock in equal measure. Emboldened, he continues, "What has brought you to my table?"

Only then do I notice that he is in the seat generally reserved for staff. It seems Bel realizes it then, too. "You're the dealer?" she asks.

He smiles, still barely giving me a glance. I can't say I blame him, as Bel is a magnetic force, "I am, and you two seem to be the only ones at my table. How fortuitous." The space around us is devoid of life, as if no one dared to enter his circle before he allowed them.

Laughing, I tell him, "I seem to have forgotten just how powerful you are." I scoot myself closer to Bel and lean in, "Fritz is what we call an *Exhaurié*. He feeds off the energy of those around him, so a place like this is perfect for him."

"Wait. You don't all eat people?" She asks in disbelief.

Fritz laughs, and his eyes meet mine, "You were unfortunate enough to see him in action, were you?" At the disgusted look in her eyes, he continues without humor, "No, only demons of Cas's order. *Devoré's.* There are also *Biberé,* but those bloodsuckers are a whole other nightmare, and hopefully, you'll never have to deal with one."

"Oh. How do you... do what you do?" She asks, looking back at him. *They look so good together.* Between his fingers gently toying with her hair and her eyeing him with wicked curiosity, I can't help the depraved turn my thoughts take.

Suddenly, the table is filled with mortals slapping down their chips again, and the change in volume level has me momentarily distracted. When I look back at Bel and Fritz, I see he's whispering something in her ear that I didn't quite catch in time, and she giggles in response.

Before he can get any closer to bedding her, something I'm admittedly *very* interested in seeing, I interrupt, "Actually, Fritz. We are here because of a dire matter. Things we cannot exactly discuss with the present company."

"Ah, yes. Unfortunately, I have to work for the rest of the night. Blah, so boring. But needs must," he shrugs. "Where are you staying?" He's dealing cards and playing with the rest of the mortals while talking to us like he's done this a million times. Then again, he probably has.

Bel looks to me again for guidance, and holy Gods, do I love that she trusts and defers to me. At my encouraging nod, she answers, "We got a little hotel room off the strip."

"Ew," Fritz emits a high-pitched whistle that has me cringing from the sound, and a round, short, red-faced man comes lumbering up to us. "This is Norman. Norman, please show Caspian and Belissenda to my suite. Give them a parking permit, and tickets to whatever show they want to see. Oh! And they're welcome to my VIP pass to the club should they decide to use it. And give them whatever else they ask for. They're my guests."

"Oh, my God. No, absolutely not. We're fine. You don't need to do any of that for us," Bel gushes nervously.

"Bel, Sweets. It costs me nothing and helps us to find each other again easier," he explains while continuing his game without having to give it any attention. "I have a three bedroom suite so you will both have ample private space. I simply work late and cannot imagine you want to be traveling here again in the middle of the night."

She tries to protest again, and his face softens, "I have no ulterior motives here. There are no expectations attached to my offer. You two have traveled here in search of something, and what kind of person would I be if I didn't help?"

"*No* ulterior motives?" I deadpan, knowing him better than he apparently knows himself.

"Well *obviously* I'd love to fuck you both, but that has no bearing on me showing you basic kindness, Cas." He rolls his eyes, "You should know better than that. May I see your phone, Bel?"

She unlocks it and hands it to him. Taking ten seconds from his impatient audience, he taps away before giving it back. "There. I have just texted myself. I can call you when I'm finished here tonight, and you two can let me know where you'd like to meet so we can discuss whatever it is that you need. If staying in my suite makes you uncomfortable, Norman can arrange for your own personal rooms, no problem."

"I don't think that's necessary. It seems as though that would be much more work for your... assistant," I tell him.

"Okay then, that's settled. Go get your stuff, have a fun evening and I'll be in touch. Ta ta," then he redirects all of his attention to his table of clamoring mortals.

As we walk away, I tuck Bel under my arm and ask, "What did he whisper to you, Little Dove?"

She blushes, looking up at me and saying, "Oh, that. Nothing," she waves her hand around as if she could brush away the pink staining her cheeks, "it's like you said. He's just a big flirt."

"You're attracted to him?" I ask, doing my best to hide the excitement it brings me. She tentatively nods, so I tease, "He was *very* interested in you."

She stifles a giggle, and I continue, assuring her, "It's not a bad thing, my Dove. Far from it," I lower my voice to ensure she knows exactly where my thoughts have gone, "I think it could be great fun."

Her jaw drops, and I drag her along, off to waste some time before we meet back up with my oldest friend.

14

Old Friends and New Enemies

Caspian

After Norman escorted us to the suite and showed us the spare rooms, he departed. Bel picked the one with the floor-to-ceiling windows facing the setting sun, leaving me one that will be full of early light due to its eastern windows. That'll work much better for me, seeing as Bel will want to sleep far longer into the day than I will.

Both rooms have unnecessarily large four-poster beds, covered in smooth silk and fur throw blankets, with fluffy pillows piled high in coordinating colors. Each room has a small couch at the foot of the bed, positioned to whether in bed or sitting, you'll have an incredible view of the desert and cityscape.

Having received a set of keys from Norman, along with a permit for Bel's car, we head to the parking structure where we left it. She drives us to our new parking lot, and as she pulls into the spot, she whistles, "How did someone who is just a card dealer pull all these strings?" After a moment, she clarifies, "Someone with that job at a casino is relatively low on the food chain. Why would he have the authority to have an assistant, a full three-bedroom suite, and access to all these extra amenities?"

I think about how best to phrase this without scaring her, "His abilities do not always make sense to me. Feeding on others energy gives him the power

102

to influence them. Not directly, but people will notice they feel better or worse around him, depending on what he wants them to do. If he makes everyone around him feel good, they are likely to give him whatever he wants."

As she grabs her bags from the trunk, she pauses, "Oh. That seems…"

I grab everything she's trying to carry and throw it over my shoulder, "Dishonest? Manipulative? It can be. But he's a good person. I knew him for a long time and never once saw him hurt anyone who didn't deserve it. When he uses his power for his benefit, it's material things. He would never use his abilities to take advantage of people, or harm them." I explain.

"How can you be so sure?" she asks, "He's a demon."

"As am I. And you have seen already that we are not all you've been told we are, yes?" At this, she nods her head, so I proceed, "He will answer our questions, then we can be on our way in the morning if you wish. We do not have to stay the entire planned duration of our trip."

Putting a hand on my arm, she quietly says, "Thank you." Then she uses a little plastic card to let us into the suite once again.

After I set her things on the bed in her chosen room, I wrap both hands around the tops of her arms and face her to me, "Belissenda. I will follow your lead every step and will not let any harm come to you. Nor will I allow a single soul to make you uncomfortable without them facing the most painful death imaginable. I promise."

Instantly, she blesses me with another crushing hug. I don't think anyone has just hugged me before. I want more of these pure, affectionate embraces. I will spend forever earning them from her.

"Can we have a code word?" She pops out suddenly.

"A code word?" I ask in confusion.

"Yeah," she nods, "A word just the two of us know that basically means, *I'm done. Fuck this. I'm out.*"

"So if I'm understanding, the *code word* is your signal that you are feeling uncomfortable or unsafe and I need to stop the situation," I clarify.

"Exactly!" she snaps.

"Is that not just a safe word?" Her eyes get so large I fear they may pop out of her head, "What?"

"I guess it is like a safe word, but contextually, it's not quite the same. A safe word is almost exclusively used in sexual situations."

"I see. But the idea is the same?" She nods noncommittally, but I've come to recognize that as her *good enough* gesture when explaining things to me, "Wonderful. What word would you like to use?" Something terribly vulgar, I imagine. Though the thought of her shouting the word *cunt* to get away from danger has me smiling ear to ear.

"Avocado," she tells me without even a moment of deliberation.

What? "Avocado. Wh-why?" I must be missing something.

"Because it's a word that is rarely used in conversation. So I could say something like *Hey I think those avocados on my sandwich were bad,* and only you would understand what I'm trying to tell you." She explains.

"My little warrior is a genius," I kiss the tip of her nose and spin towards her bags. "Go take a shower and get ready to go out. Do any of the shows tonight pique your interest?"

She shakes her head and wrinkles her nose, "No. Honestly, I'd rather go check out the club. I've heard it's gorgeous, but I really didn't bring any kind of upscale nightlife clothing."

Smiling, I tell her, "You can just leave that to me. Now go get ready and I'll leave the dress right here," I pat the couch at the foot of her bed.

* * *

An hour later, we enter something called a night club, led by Norman. He scans a card with the man at the entrance and explains that we are Fritz's guests, not so subtly threatening that there will be consequences if we are not shown a good time.

The man grabs a little device that looks similar to a cell phone but without a screen. Bel leans over and whispers to me, "That's a walkie-talkie. Like a phone but... for closer distances I guess?" as the man calls for someone named Marie.

Within moments, a young lady in a black get-up and an apron approaches us. She looks at Bel, glances at me, then her attention immediately goes back to her. *As it should, she's a vision.* Bel looks so incredible tonight that I'm surprised I didn't drop dead when I spotted her.

"Hi! I'm Marie! I'm your bottle girl! So, so happy to meet you! Follow me!" I lead Bel in front of me with a hand on her bare back, thinking again that I *definitely* made the right call on the dress. With each step, the short dress lets me almost believe I'm going to get a glimpse of her perfectly lush backside.

"I'm Bel, and this is Caspian," she tells her as we walk.

"Oh, believe me, I know," Marie grins at us and holds her arm out, showing us to a table far too large for just the two of us. "Fritz sent word over earlier that his guests be shown every luxury and that you not be allowed *to spend a fucking penny.*" She holds her hands up and curls her index and middle fingers of both hands at us for emphasis, "Have you guys ever had bottle service before?"

We both shake our heads, so she continues, "So, basically, you tell me what kind of liquor you want and how you like it. I'll bring you a bottle and all the goodies to go with it. If you want a mixed drink, let me know and I can have the bartender make it for you. Same for beer. As long as you guys are here, I am at your beck and call." She hands us both a copy of a cocktail menu from her apron before continuing, "You look like a tequila girly, and I'd bet all the money in my pocket that you're a craft beer kinda guy."

"You are 100% right," Bel laughs as she grabs my arm in humor. "He would be a fancy beer guy. Just bring us whatever's good and will make you the fattest check."

"You got it," she winks at us and spins on her heel to get our beverages. We sit in awed silence, looking around us at the scenery for a minute before Marie comes back with a small team of women in matching outfits behind her, carrying an array of drinks.

"I couldn't decide on just one thing, silly me." She shrugs, "So I had a couple girls pick their favorite shot, cocktail, and beer." I watch as Bel's whole face lights up in excitement.

"Now listen, babes. The goal is *not* to get wasted. I'm here to take care of you, not hospitalize you. So a few ground rules." She starts lifting her fingers to count, "Number one, drink water. You have ten bottles in that little ice bucket so you have no excuses. Two, try a few little sippies of each drink, and then just keep your favorites. Three, get up and dance so you keep the blood flowing, not just the liquor. And four, when you're done partying, let me know so I can send some food up to your suite. Got it?" At Bel's energetic nod, she moves aside so all her colleagues can start placing the drinks on the table.

"I will be right there," she points behind us to where more servers are in similar attire, "Just wave me down if you need me. Enjoy!" She wiggles her fingers and bounces off, smiling and chatting with her teammates.

"I like her," Bel tells me as she starts sampling all the colorful drinks in front of her.

I agree, "She is very friendly and seems to enjoy her job."

Bel picks a favorite, continuing to sip just the one, "And this place is gorgeous. I can't believe we get to be here."

"*You* are gorgeous. Do you like your surprise?" I can't help myself, I want to please her. I need to know she loves the garment as much as I love it on her.

Bel rubs her hands up and down the sleeves, "It's *sooo soft.* It kinda reminds me of–" she stops short.

"Reminds you of...?" I push.

"Your antlers." She looks down, trying to hide her blush, but it practically glows in the dim light dancing across her face. I really do my best not to, but I laugh so hard that she jumps. Now that she mentions it, her dress does bear a striking resemblance to my antlers. Were she to draw a few little white stars and fasten some gems on them, they would look the exact same as her dress.

"That was not on purpose, I assure you. I just saw these," I tell her, running my finger along the little v–shaped slits on each thigh that have spread wider now that she's seated, one and then the other, "and knew I had to see it on you. You are even more stunning than I imagined." I kiss the side of her head and continue sipping on the drinks around us.

Before too long, she stands up and starts dragging me out of the booth towards the dance floor. Immediately, Marie pops up and says, "Go ahead, I'll keep an eye on your things. Have fun!"

"Thank you," I respond, allowing Bel to drag me to whatever she has in store for me. I haven't the faintest idea how one is supposed to dance to music like this, and it appears that no one else does either. I would argue this is closer to fornication than dancing, but perhaps that's the point.

Bel stops me in the middle of the cluster of humans and starts to sway her body to the music. Unsure of what to do, I find myself just standing, entranced by the way she moves. Laughing, she puts her hands on my hips and tries to help me move the way she does.

"Come on, Cas! Just move! Feel the music and move!" I try to follow her lead. Truly, I do. But it's impossible to *feel* anything but the bumping of sweat-slicked bodies every step and the overwhelming stench of alcohol and smoke in the air. She attempts to guide me a few more times before seemingly giving up. "Just watch then," she shouts to be heard over the music. *Gladly.*

I'm happy watching, just being drawn into her orbit, relishing her elated face and sparkling dress catching the light as she spins and sways. That is until some dead man decides he can put his hands on her. Big, meaty hands land on her hips, and she freezes, her sweet scent instantly being doused in fear.

She moves away from him, and I step toward her, but he doesn't relent, following closely behind her. "Come on, gorgeous. He doesn't wanna dance with you, but I do." Her eyes land on mine, and her terror has just signed his death warrant.

I gently pull her hands and maneuver her behind me, telling her over my shoulder, "Go back to the table, little dove."

"Caspian, it's fine. He didn't do anything. He's just being drunk and overly friendly." She sounds brave, but her trembling hands, currently fisted in my shirt, tell another story.

"Hey, Fuckface, we were dancing," he slurs at me, spittle falling from his mouth. I grab him by the throat, my claws barely starting to grow, causing little droplets of blood to start cascading down my fingers. No one even seems to notice the violence happening in their midst, too consumed by drink and each other to see the danger around them.

I repeat to Bel, "Go sit down. I'll be there shortly," while cutting off the grabby man's airway.

She doesn't say anything, but I can feel her releasing me, and her eyes begin to frantically wander around, searching for the exits. I already know where her mind is headed. "Do not run away, Belissenda." I face her, dragging my next meal with me, "I will find you, and I'll be forced to make you suffer."

Despite herself and her fear, the unmistakable fragrance of her arousal hits my nose, causing my cock to stiffen. *Does she want to play again?* Between the promise of violence, followed by the possibility of chasing my sweet little sacrifice, this night is taking the best turn. I need her to run just as much as she craves for me to follow.

I groan, ignoring the man dangling from my grip, "Or is that what you want, Little Dove? You want me to hunt you down, pin you to the floor and make you scream for mercy?" She shakes her head but doesn't use the special word she chose to use when she's uncomfortable, so I press, "Oh, but I think you do."

Truthfully, I think after the little exchange with this stranger that has clearly frightened her, she needs the distraction, but I wouldn't force that on her. I change my tone to drop the game for a moment and ask sincerely, "Tell me, Bel. Honestly. Do you want me to chase you?"

She nods sheepishly, eyes wide and trained on me.

"Then fly away, my sweet. I'll be with you shortly." She takes one last look at the almost-dead man, then takes off into the crowd.

Oh, fuck yes.

15

Run, Run, As Fast As You Can

Bel

I cannot fucking believe I'm doing this.

This is crazy. I should not be running. Caspian's killing someone right now for putting his hands on me, and instead of trying to stop him, I'm letting him chase me while he's probably still covered in that guy's fucking blood. Then what?

What happens when he catches me? He said he would make me suffer. But it left his smiling lips like a promise, not a threat. He can't hurt me anyway, so what meaning could it possibly have other than something sexual?

Even if it is sexual, is that something I want? I haven't let anyone touch me like that in... well, basically ever. But I *want* him, don't I? Every wicked lick of his eyes on my skin had me on fire, and when he traced the edge of my dress, I wanted to straddle him right then and there, damn every pair of eyes who could possibly see it.

And if I don't want this, he already gave me an out. I can tap out with one teeny little word, and the whole game would be over. *Do I want it to be over?*

Absolutely not. I'm more exhilarated than I've ever been in my life. I have no idea what he has in store for me, but I'd let him do any vile thing he asked, strangers blood on his hand or not.

I push my way through the packed bodies, searching for the exit when I see Marie looking strangely at me. *Shit.* Running up to her, I quickly ask her to send my purse up to our room for me. I'm not risking losing that on this little excursion. A knowing smile comes over her face, and she gives me a two-finger salute and a *have fun.*

I spot my escape route just as people behind me start yelling about some asshole pushing them over, and I know I'm already almost caught. *Fucking fuck.*

A strong arm wraps around my waist, and he breathes in heavily with his nose buried in the crook of my neck before moaning and uttering, "Caught you. It's almost as if you wanted to be captured."

"No fair. I expected that to take longer," I pout.

He sets me down and cards his hands through the hair at my nape, grabbing a fistful and turning me towards him, forcing my neck back so I can see his face while pressed flush against his rock-hard body. His eyes are pure white, and I can feel the hunter inside him begging to be freed.

"I'll give you one more chance." He says, licking a stripe from the base of my neck all the way up to my ear, causing me to whimper before biting the lobe with another small groan. "I'll even give you a two-minute head start before I find you, okay?"

I nod, unable to speak, and he leans in until he's speaking against my lips, "Words, baby. I need words." *Baby.* That makes me wanna melt into his big fucking arms, but I wanna play more.

"Okay. Two minutes, then you... hunt me," I force out, swallowing down my fear. His eyes flash even brighter, and I'm in fucking danger, but my panties have never been wetter.

He plants a brief, rough kiss on my lips and pushes me away, mouthing the word *run,* and I'm off. Hauling ass toward the club exit and back onto the casino floor. I veer to the side instantly, deciding to use the shadows of the machines to my advantage. I keep an eye out for security guards, but they're busy enough dealing with all the angry patrons flushing their cash away.

I pick up speed, pumping my arms and trying to get a glimpse behind me. I can't see Caspian, but I can feel him. I sense the change in the air that surrounds him, like a predator lying in wait. I dive between two slot machines, scaring the shit out of an old lady. I mouth the word *Sorry*, then pantomime zipping my lips together. I just needed a second to catch my breath.

Daring a peek around the slot machine, I see him. He's barely keeping his eyes and body in this mortal facade, and I can see tiny wisps of black smoke coming from his shoulders the way they do in his true form. I distantly wonder what it would take to coax the monster inside of him out.

He hasn't spotted me yet, so I take this moment to admire how terrifyingly strong he is. Those massive shoulders and biceps, hands tipped in tiny claws, looking as though they've been dipped in a vat of black tar, and it's trying to climb up his forearms through his veins. I've never had more reason to fear someone, yet I've never felt safer. All that strength and he wants to use it to protect me.

When I've caught my breath and looked my fill, I slink back out of my hiding spot and begin to run again. I hear a growl and try to go faster, sensing my time is almost up. He isn't close enough to catch me so after rounding another corner, I spot a small side door that's opened just a crack.

I slip inside and cover my mouth to quiet my loud breathing. *It's pitch fucking black in here.* I try to feel my way around, hoping for a light switch of some kind, but as I stumble forward, I bump into a soft and firm rounded edge right at hip level. I run my hands over it as my eyes start to adjust, and it's... it's a chair. Next to it is another, followed by another, and even more of them as far as I can see. There are more in front of it and behind it.

The theater. Shit. I get myself out of the maze of seats and push against the wall again, trying to see which way is the exit. I inch against the wall and get hit with deja vu. I ease slightly off the wall, thinking there's a light ahead.

I don't even hear him sneak up on me.

"Got you," he growls into my ear before wrapping one arm around my waist and the other hand around my mouth, taunting me. "Poor lost Little Dove can't see in the dark, can you?" before licking from my jawline up my cheek with another growl rumbling from his chest. He drags me along the pathway, up a small flight of stairs, and across the wooden floor. I fight against him fruitlessly the whole way up, the exhilaration causing me to break out in goosebumps.

He releases me before spinning me and forces me down onto my knees using a firm grip on my hair. *My punishment is going to be a blowjob?* I have to admit, that does sound hot; just thinking about choking on his— no doubt *enormous*— cock has me dripping. It just seems a little... simplistic for someone so calculated.

"Lie down, Bel," he utters quietly. "On your back and lift your arms above your head," *Oh.* I do as he says and find a small ledge behind me. "There's a good girl, hold on to the edge of the stage there." *STAGE?* "Now, hold still." He lowers himself close to me and runs one of his clawed fingers down the front of my neck, leaving a tingly stinging feeling. He drags it lower and lower until ***rip*** he tears the dress completely down the middle.

"Hey! I loved this dress." I protest, though, admittedly, it is a halfhearted one at best.

"Oh, but it's *so* much better now. In fact, it's almost perfect," with another small scratch and tug of Caspian's claw, my bra is in a similar state to the dress. He groans and mumbles, "So fucking pretty." He covers my body with his, pressing every inch of himself to me. He rocks his hard cock against my hip once, forcing a quiet whine out of my throat.

It's so dark the only thing visible is the outline of his shadow and the glow of his unearthly eyes. He lowers his lips to my neck, gently mouthing it, using the tip of his tongue to tease my skin. He nibbles on my ear, and I'm trying so hard to stay still, but it's impossible.

With each wiggle against him, he grows more insistent with his touches, nibbles turn to bites, and his tongue presses longer and firmer against my neck. One hand supports his weight while the other reaches down to grip my leg, lifting it behind the knee to bring it to his waist, opening me up fully to him.

With his first full grind against me, barely anything between us, I moan loudly, and he chuckles against my neck. Trying to play off the sounds I'm making, I pant, "I thought this was supposed to be torture." *Why the* fuck *did I just say that?*

His laughter turns wickedly dark, responding, "How right you are." He bites down where my neck and shoulder meet, hard enough to have me crying out and involuntarily lifting my hips against him. He licks to soothe the spot before suddenly kneeling back and standing. I lift my knees, keeping them together, and plant my feet on the floor, hoping that it might give me some semblance of protection against him witnessing how embarrassingly wet I am.

"Take them off, Bel," he commands.

"Take *what* off, Caspian?" *I must be a glutton for punishment.*

"Take your fucking panties off, spread those pretty thighs, and show me my new plaything. Now," he orders again with a rumbling growl.

I move as slowly as possible without earning more of his wrath, lifting my hips and sliding my panties down past them. When I get the panties to my knees, Caspian gently takes over, forcing both of my legs into the air. Once he has the panties in his hands, he steps back even further until I haven't a clue where he is.

I lower my feet back to the ground, keeping my knees locked together.

"Spread," he demands again, and my body listens without waiting for my lust-addled brain to catch up.

From his spot in the dark, he releases a monstrous, desperate growl before he begins slowly stepping toward me again. The glow of his eyes is gone; I can't see where he is at all. By the sounds of his footsteps, he's circling me, trying to decide where to begin, before rumbling, "Look at my sweet little sacrifice, all splayed out, just for me."

I whimper, so horny I'm beyond the possibility of any sense of shame. I need Caspian to touch me *right now*. But he doesn't, just keeps watching me writhe and try to control myself.

Finally, he stands between my spread legs and lowers himself to his knees. He leans in and runs a single finger through my wetness, the teasing sensation enough to force a small moan from me.

"All this from a game of chase? Poor, needy thing," he mocks. He trails his finger away from where I need it, teasing my entrance, using two fingers to spread me open, "*Christ*, you are *dripping*. You need me to play with this pretty pussy, baby?"

Okay, maybe letting him listen to all those audiobooks was a bad idea. I nod, unable to formulate words, hoping he doesn't ask me for any.

He finally shows me mercy, rubbing my clit in gentle circles, watching for my reaction. His fingers already have me moaning softly, rubbing myself against him, trying to get more friction. He follows my lead, adding more pressure and using his other hand to pin my hips in place.

He increases the speed, keeping his fingers on that little nub. I feel my whole body start to tighten, my breaths coming in little pants, my moans getting louder and more insistent. *Fuck, I'm so close already. I'm gonna—* he stops, removing his hand from me completely.

His bright white teeth shine in the dark, grinning at me and my frustration, "Oh, I'm *sorry*," he says, not sounding sorry at *all*. "Did you need something?"

Realizing the game, I know I'm fucked. I've never been edged before. Why would I when I'm always the one in charge of my own pleasure? Through gritted teeth, I tell him, "No. I'm fine."

"Good." He hovers over me, with one hand beside my head and the other lightly trailing along my bare lower stomach. "You look *so* good like this, Bel. All this beautiful flushed skin on display, chest heaving, nipples rock hard, begging for my touch." He emphasizes his words by barely running his thumb across one of the peaks of them.

He leans down, wrapping his warm mouth around my nipple, using the tip of his tongue to flick it, causing me to whine and bury my hand in his hair. Instantly he grabs my wrist, lets my breast fall from his mouth, and tsks at me, "Oh, Little Dove. You were supposed to keep your hands above your head."

"I'm sorry. I didn't mean to," I beg. Caspian lets go of my hand, and I immediately return it to its spot, white-knuckling the edge. I don't need feeling in my hands anyway. He goes back to working my nipple with his hot, wet mouth, then plants sloppy kisses on his journey to the other one. With the first contact of his tongue, he starts rubbing those circles on my clit, building up the pressure inside me again. He bites down on my nipple and slides two fingers inside me at the same time, and I cry out.

"*Oh*, so wet and warm. You feel fucking perfect." He's curling his fingers inside of me, reaching that elusive spot that has my eyes squeezing shut. "You gonna come, baby?"

"Yes. Yes, Caspian. Please!" I'm going to come harder than I ever have in my life.

"Aw. Too bad," he stops again, and now I'm fucking pissed. Before I can yell at him, he silences me with his lips, prying my mouth open and sliding his tongue against mine.

While I'm distracted, he shoves his fingers inside me again and starts pumping in and out at a relentless pace. The filthy sound of me soaking his fingers is so debauched I'm ready to combust. He's thrusting his hips against me in time with his hand. Every sound I make, he mimics back, almost mocking me, and fuck, if it doesn't make me wetter.

I'm so ready to come that I think I'd do anything he asks. So close, *so close* again, and he stops. Again and again, he does it, until I've lost count of how many times he's forced me to the brink of bliss and then denied me the release.

I've never been so frustrated *and* angry *and* horny in my life. Tears are streaming down my face, and my knuckles and fingers have long gone numb from my grip.

He chuckles darkly, wiping away a tear, "Oh, you poor thing. You need to come *so* bad, don't you?" I nod, letting out another sob.

Once again, he starts fucking me with his hand, each pump grazing his palm against my clit. *Sweet fucking hell, yes.*

He orders softly against my lips, "Beg for it." I hesitate for a second, and he reiterates, slightly louder, "I *said* beg."

"Please, please, please," I'm chanting over and over again, every utterance a plea, whimper, and moan rolled into one.

He groans loudly at my pleading before urging, "Come on, Little Dove. Gush all over my hand." Instantly, I explode. The orgasm sends me straight into orbit, waves and waves of bliss rushing through me, my soaked pussy pulsing and squeezing his fingers. I scream his name, fucking myself on his hand through it, him moaning with me like my orgasm brought him the same relief.

As I come back from my little death, he's brushing my hair from my face, peppering soft kisses against my face and chest, whispering little praises.

"Did so good."

"So perfect, Little Dove."

"You came so beautifully."

I'm practically glowing from all his attention.

"Are you alright, Bel?" he asks a few moments later, and I'm not ready to speak yet, so I just nod. "You were so good for me," he says against my forehead before placing a kiss on it.

"Thank you," I blush.

"Can you stand?" he helps me to my feet, then eases something over my head. "Slide your arm through here. And the other here."

"Clothes?" I ask, dumbfounded. *Where did they come from?*

"It's just one of the soft dresses you brought," he explains. "We should get out of here before security catches us. I'm surprised they haven't yet as I do not think we are supposed to be here."

We stumble our way back through the casino, mostly undetected. A few people give us knowing, judgmental looks, but they're pissing away money like it grows on trees, so I don't really care much for their opinions.

Approaching the door to Fritz's suite, Caspian pulls a keycard from his pocket, not removing his other arm from my shoulder. He's looking at me like I'm the answer to all his prayers. *Do demons pray?*

We walk inside and see Fritz sitting on the couch in the living room of the space. We both freeze, but he just grins, "I tried calling. Imagine my surprise when I hear the phone ringing from my entryway table."

"Sorry," I mumble.

"No apologies necessary. From you, anyway. But *you*, Caspian owe me both an apology and a thank you. A murder in the middle of the dance floor? Have you no decency?" He mock scolds, smirking.

Caspian only shrugs, "He put his unwelcome hands on Belissenda. He *scared* her, so he had to die."

He nods and hums in agreement, stating, "He's in the deep freezer in the basement if you get hungry." He looks at us for a second, then stands, "Go take as long as you need to get cleaned up. I'll make drinks and we can talk business."

"Do we look that bad?" I ask Caspian quietly.

"No," Fritz interjects, "In fact, you both look and smell so delicious I cannot promise to be a gentlemen until you appear slightly less freshly fucked."

"Oh."

"*Oh.*" he repeats with a smile, "Go on, I'll be right here waiting for you."

16

Supernaturally Stupid

Bel

After hopping in a quick shower and throwing on some sweats and a matching hoodie, I go back out to the common area of the suite, somehow having made it out before Caspian got himself cleaned up.

Fritz catches me looking around for him, smiling before he says, "Oh, I'm sure he'll be a few more minutes. Your little game had him all worked up." I go to ask how he knows, but before I can, he asks, "You know this hotel has security cameras covering every inch of it, right?"

"Oh. My God. I didn't even think of that." I cover my face with both hands, utterly humiliated, trying not to panic.

He hurries over to me, gently prying my wrists away, saying, "No, no, no. Shhh, it's fine. I took care of it. No one saw or will see anything, myself included." I look up at him, tears starting to blur my vision when he says, "Hey, it's alright. I jammed all the circuits when I saw him chasing you across the casino floor."

"Really?" I'm almost too nervous to be hopeful.

"Really. You are safe here," Fritz searches my face, "okay?"

"Okay. Thank you."

"I can't have you two getting public indecency charges on my watch, can I?" He teases.

"Or a murder charge?" I ask, somehow finding humor in the situation.

"Oh, that. That's nothing," he pauses, "In fact, let me tell you a secret." He urges me closer, "I would have killed him if Cas had not."

"Why?" I'm truly dumbfounded.

"Because he put his hands on you against your will. He frightened you." He's acting like it's the most natural thing in the world.

"So you would *kill* him? For me?" I ask, dumbfounded. "You don't even know me."

"I'm sure we will be getting to know each other *very well* before too long," his tone has me thinking about just how well he'd like to know me. "And besides that, I don't need to know you to protect you. You are my guest, so you're under my protection. Plus, you are Caspian's lady friend. Anyone who matters to him matters to me," he tells me vehemently.

This brings another question to my mind, one I can hopefully get answered before Caspian interrupts. "What were you and Caspian to each other? Before he... died?"

He grins salaciously before answering, "Well, technically, we can't die. Not exactly." He drops one of my hands but holds onto the other, pulling me toward the couch to sit. Once I do, he hands me a jalapeño margarita, and *holy shit, I'm in heaven.* "To answer your question though, we were friends. Begrudging allies first, then friends."

He drapes one arm behind me on the back of the couch and holds his drink out for a toast. Even through my sweats, I can feel his attention gracing every inch of me, making me hot all over. As I clink my marg against his, a smug voice sounds from behind me, "We were, in fact, very good friends who *occasionally* enjoyed each other over the years. Or did you forget?"

Oh, fuck.

The images filling my head at his admittance are utterly depraved, but I can't help myself. I wonder who— *no. Stop that. Don't think about it.*

"Of course I did not forget," Fritz begins, pausing to take a drink before continuing, "I just wasn't sure what you were willing to *share* with Bel," he finishes with his eyes locked on mine. *Do all demons speak in double entendres, or am I just reading into things that aren't there?*

"I do not keep secrets from her," he explains, sitting down on the couch across from us. I find it odd that earlier, he literally killed a man in cold blood for touching me. Yet Fritz is being far more familiar with me, practically cuddling me, and Caspian doesn't even seem to notice.

He picks up a drink and looks at me, and I love how he finally seems a little more comfortable. Like he's finally found something familiar in this new world. We sit quietly and drink for a moment before Caspian sighs, seemingly not ready to break the comfortable silence but knowing we must.

"As you know, we are here for business, *not* pleasure," he tells Fritz, allowing a bit of mirth to sneak through.

"Pity," Fritz comments, and honestly, I feel the same way. I've already been pleasured beyond what any human should endure in one night. And yet, sitting in the proximity of these two powerful men has me tingling from head to toe with anticipation.

My whole body tightens at the image in my head of them together, of me joining them. Shame coats my tongue as I'm reminded what we're actually here for. I should be focusing on our mission, yet here I am, wondering what it would be like to be sandwiched between them. Caspian holding me in place with his rough hands while Fritz teases me—

I shake my head, dispelling the imagery. It isn't fair to them for me to sexualize them this way while they're trying to have a conversation.

Caspian reaches into his pocket and holds out the compass, which is now pointed directly at Fritz, asking, "What do you know of this?"

Putting down his drink, he leans forward to take it, "*Sanctus Scutulis*. Nasty fuckers. How'd you come across this?" he raises a brow at Caspian.

"They found me," he begins, "however, they stated that for the first little while that I was back on this plane, the compass could not track me. When I am in Bel's proximity, it spins and spins, but never lands on me. She has made me invisible to their technology."

"That makes sense since she's your *hostia*." *There's that word again.*

"What does that mean?" I ask. I have to know, even if the answer won't be pretty.

"You're his sacrifice. The incantation used to retrieve demons from

Vankhala... bonds you two together, kinda. It's essentially a vow of protection. He is a guest on this plane, and you're his host or *hostia* in the original Latin," he explains.

Between the two of them, they go back and forth using a lot of what I think is more Latin phrasing, deciphering exactly what the fake not-so-fake spell said to get Caspian here. I'm just happy sitting here, sipping on my drink. Without breaking his focus, Fritz reaches and pours me a refill, gifting me with a sly smile and a wink.

I shouldn't let him flirt with me so blatantly in front of Cas. It isn't fair to either of them. But I get the feeling that if he minded, he would say something. He even seemed... encouraging about it earlier, but maybe that was because of *his* interest in Fritz, not anything to do with me.

"I don't see how that's possible," Caspian says exasperatedly. I realize now that I haven't been paying attention, "I've never even heard of such a thing. Why have you not told me this?"

Fritz shrugs, "Well it never really came up. The sacrifice can't be harmed by the summoned. It's just not usually an issue because the one whose blood is spilled..." Fritz trails off, waving his hand in the air like it will finish his sentence for him.

"Is always dead before we arrive," Cas looks as dumbfounded as I am.

"Wait, wait. So you're saying that demons who are summoned can't hurt their sacrifice?" That makes no sense. "But that would make them more like... protectors. Why would people kill the one person the demon is called to protect before they even get there?"

"Because then they have an uninhibited monster that they believe they can control. If the sacrifice gives the summoned a sense of humanity, the sacrifice can do all the controlling. But if the sacrifice is dead, that tie to humankind is gone." Caspian fills in, realizing the horrific reality at the same time I do.

"But that still doesn't explain why I could summon him," I blurt. "How can a not-virgin sacrifice call for a demon?"

Fritz shakes his head, "They can't. Period. Back to your earlier question, though, there *are* theories that demons were originally protectors of the innocent. Called upon in times of need to keep children safe from enemies. A few drops of blood, nothing more than a finger prick, and they would be blessed with a terrifying creature who would stop at nothing to protect them.

"But, as always, men who craved power above all else found ways around this caveat. Just kill them before the demon arrives. It worked a few times until we caught on and started killing the killers," he pauses, then adds, "But, as I said, this is all just a theory. There's no way to prove what is true.

"Who am I to say that the original demon hunters were just power-hungry fucks, willing to slaughter anyone and everyone around them in their search for magic? Who am I to say that a handful of warlock families all stood in a circle and slit their eldest daughters' throats to make that there trinket, along with many others, to find our people and send them back to Vankhala?" he finishes, waving around his drink for flourish.

The nonchalance with which he discusses such monstrous acts has goose-bumps popping up along my arms. In every bit of modern religious texts, demons are the evil ones. But what if it was really mankind all along?

Seemingly finished with this rant, he turns to me and narrows his eyes in cautious curiosity, "How many men have you had, Sweets?" His sudden change of subject gives me whiplash.

"One," I answer, clenching my fists to keep my voice from shaking, inhaling the sweet and spicy scent of my drink to keep myself firmly planted in the present. I will not be dragged into the memories of the past. It's a simple question with a simple answer.

"Hmmm. And how many times?" He's watching me so closely now, and the warmth of Caspian's gaze on my face is equally suffocating. At my lack of answer, he prods, "I don't *want* to ask you these questions. They're none of my- *our* business, but I can't help you if I don't have all the information."

God damn it, I'm so sick of crying. "One," I tell him, unable to hide the quiver in my voice. Through my slightly blurred vision, I watch them share a quick glance. The look on their faces is one I've dealt with countless times from therapists, my parents, and even Isla. Understanding and then, horrifically, pity.

I slam my drink down and stand, "Don't do that. Don't look at me like I'm some kind of fucking victim."

Fritz sighs, starting, "Bel... I— whatever happened to you, it wasn't your fault."

"Yes, it was," I tell him through gritted teeth, "I made my choices. I agreed to go somewhere alone with a boy, I chose to have a drink, and I kissed him. if I hadn't wanted to, I could have done more or fought back, could have kept telling him no. But I didn't. I didn't make him stop." The tears are falling in full force now, memories of that terrible night hitting me like a train.

The temperature in the room drops suddenly, and Caspian repeats my words back to me, the sinister tone in his voice freezing me to my spot, "Fought *back?*"

I look up at him as he approaches me, shaking my head, "Don't." I put a hand against his chest to keep him away, as I don't need or deserve his comfort.

Out of the corner of my eye, I see Fritz stand, "I'm going to let you two discuss this privately, but I think you have your answer as to how it all happened." He squeezes my shoulder as he walks past, telling me, "You are stronger than you feel right now. And we," he gestures between himself and Caspian, "will be your strength until you believe it."

Once he's left the room, Caspian drags me to mine, drinks completely forgotten. He slams the door behind him, startling me. As he begins pacing, he demands, "What is his name?" I just shake my head. "Belissenda. Tell me his name, or I will start killing *every* man in *every* place you've *ever* lived until I find the right one."

"Sam. His name is Sam, he's from my home town. We were just kids!" I'm nearly screaming now.

"I do not want to hear you defend that filth one more fucking time, Bel," he scolds, "Do you understand me?"

"Don't fucking yell at me, Caspian! You don't know anything about it! You weren't there. I was," my voice cracks on that final word, and I can't find it in myself to care.

He sits on the side edge of my bed, reaching a hand out to me. "It *wasn't* your fault, Bel," he echoes Fritz's words from earlier. Rather than bring comfort, it just makes my chest hurt.

I put my hand in his anyway, for his benefit obviously, "Of course it was. I–"

"*You* told him to stop. You *told* him. What *he* did was violate you. This is not an argument, nor a gray area. He took what was not his to have." His voice is softer now, and I think I preferred the yelling. At least then, I could yell back.

"He took away the safety of *choice*. The moment saying no wasn't safe, any agreement you made wasn't real," I keep shaking my head, not willing to remember it the way he's painting it out to be. "Your virginity, sexuality, purity, or whatever else you mortals call it is intrinsically yours. It cannot be taken, whether by force or coercion. Did you *want* to have sex with that man?"

"No."

"And he knew that." Not a question. A statement.

I nod and sniffle.

"So you had no choice, and yet here you stand, all these years later, with the weight of *his* wickedness on your shoulders," he reaches up and wipes a tear with his thumb. I shake my head, readying another argument.

"Darling Dove, if you need more proof of what I say, I could not be here if it weren't true. You heard Fritz, and he's one of the oldest of our kind. I am here because you have not made the *choice* to give yourself to anyone," he finishes.

Words fail me. *How can I argue with that?*

"You don't deserve any of this pain he's left you with." he urges me, and I just glare at him. "Say it. Say it back to me."

"I don't deserve this," it's barely a mumble, but I say it.

"Hey, there's my brave warrior," he gently squeezes my hand. "I'll have you repeat it every day until you believe it and can free yourself from the albatross around your neck."

I can't help myself, wrapping my arms around him. I need the physical comfort his huge body promises. He returns the hug, and I whisper, "You can't kill him. He's married. He has kids. He has a whole life."

He freezes, "His *life* was forfeit just for touching you against your will. Him allowing you to feel blame for it all this time has earned him the slowest, most painful death imaginable." He pauses, "but you needn't worry about that. Fritzy and I will take care of it."

I can't shake the sick feeling of knowing I've just condemned a man. But why should I worry about his life? He took more than my life from me. Seven years I've spent harboring shame over this. It won't go away overnight, but I feel freer than I did an hour ago. This is the first time I've ever been able to recount that night without falling into a panic attack and spewing bile all over myself.

I don't want to think about it anymore. I need something else to do, or else I'm going to spiral into that place again. As he draws soothing circles against my lower spine, I settle myself into his lap, straddling him. I slowly release his neck from the death grip I've had on it and pull back enough to look at his beautiful face, the rage still barely trapped under the surface.

His features look slightly sharper, his eyes foggy with the white trying to bleed through, and I can feel the tips of claws where he moves them against me. I lean in to kiss him, and he lets one hand wrap around the back of my head, cradling me gently.

As I rock my hips against him, he gives me a frustrated groan and pulls away, "Little Dove, do not tease me right now. I am barely restraining the monster as it is."

I yank his mouth back to mine, biting his lower lip and pulling. There is nothing I want more than to ride my monster until we're both sated and sleepy. "Please, Cas. I need you."

He makes that noise again, enhanced by a growl in his chest. He all but moans my name, "*Bel.* Not tonight, baby."

What the fuck? The first time I want to go there with someone, and he's rejecting me? I try to climb off his lap, but he doesn't allow me to move.

"Listen here, my brave little warrior. There is *nothing* I'd like more than to lay here and let you have your way with me." I nod, thinking *Yeah, let's do that,* "But you've had too much emotional turmoil tonight, as well as too much to drink. You don't want *me,*" *the fuck I don't—* "you want a distraction.

If in a few days, you want to bless me with the gift of your body, I will cherish it and you for all of my eternities. But you're not in a place to make that decision right now."

Somewhere in my half-drunk lust-and-sorrow-addled brain, I know he's right, but my traitorous body doesn't want to listen. She just wants to replace the shitty memories with new ones of his perfect body beneath me, letting me take what I need.

He stands, holding me against him with one hand and pulling down the soft comforter and sheets with the other. Once the bed is ready, I disentangle myself from him and clamber in. Instead of leaving, as I expected, he slides in next to me and pats his chest with a soft smile.

I curl myself into him, listening as he tries to slow his breathing and shake off the righteous fury still fighting against his hold. Even though both of us are furious and restless, laying in his arms is utter bliss. I've never been held this way by a man. Never wanted to. Now I fear I'm going to be addicted. If it were up to me, we'd never leave this little heaven we've found with Fritz. Going back to the real world will be a bitch after knowing what life here could be like.

Surrounded by his snowy scent, while feeling his heartbeat slowing against my cheek and his fingers tracing patterns on my arm, I fall asleep almost instantly.

17

The Greatest of Gifts

Caspian

After I'm certain Bel is sound asleep, snoring away, I go in search of Fritz. There's no way he's sleeping, probably pacing to burn off the rage the same way I am. Thankfully, he's already waiting for me, sitting on the couch he shared with Bel earlier.

I know I should find their familiarity concerning, but having someone else to look after her brings me comfort. He knows this world far better than I do, and he's fantastic in bed. If I was going to trust anyone with her, it'd be him. She certainly doesn't seem opposed to the idea, so who am I to keep her from her desires?

He hands me an amber-colored drink before commenting, "She's a firecracker, that one. Yelling at you even while you're more monster than man?" He whistles, "Brave girl."

I sit and take a sip. "Indeed, she is. She shot me when we met," I recall with a smile. Fritz's laughter fills the room, and I'm granted a small semblance of peace, finally having something familiar around me. "She even yelled at me, *in my true form*, because I killed a few cops."

"That does not surprise me in the slightest," he remarks with a smile before turning serious. "So when do we kill this fucker?" I knew he'd want a piece of the filth who dared harm my girl.

"She does not want us to." At that, he rolls his eyes, mirroring how I feel about that sentiment. "And as you know, I cannot leave her without being tracked by the hunters."

"How? You have their little compass," he crosses one leg over the opposite knee, relaxing into the couch.

I sigh, "I do not know. The two I killed made it sound as if they have an array of sensors for our kind. How have hunters not found you yet?"

"I'm sure they know exactly where I am, I am simply not enough of a threat for them to hunt me, plus I am constantly in a sea of mortal witnesses."

"Not a threat?" I laugh, "You are one of the most powerful of our kind."

With a shrug, he explains, "And yet I use it to deal blackjack and live quietly in a hotel room. Why should they come after me? I'm harmless unless crossed, and if they provoke me, they won't live long enough to gain anything from it."

I have to admit, he makes a point. "Well, once I get Belissenda back home, we can sneak away and take care of him." The promise of releasing my fury has every inch of me begging to let the monster out.

He nods, then asks, "What will you do now that you have your answers? Apparently you are in no hurry to relieve her of her virginity," he snickers.

"I am not worthy of the gift she wants to give, and she was not in a position to be doing that tonight anyway." She needed rest after our game and the revelations about her past. "I suppose now we will go home in the morning. She needs to get back to work, and I need to find my way in the world, somehow."

At the mention of us leaving, all the humor leaves his face. He tries to cover it up with more questions, asking, "What does she do?" Part of me is becoming irked by his curiosity, but I cannot fault him for that, can I? She's a fascinating creature.

"She's an audiobook narrator, specifically books with *smut*," I explain, hoping I used the proper phrasing.

He looks at me strangely, "That seems... odd, given her history with sex."

"I get the feeling she uses her career as a way to explore her sensuality without having to trust anyone else with it," I respond, adding, "She's built an entire career within the walls she erected."

"Can't say I blame her," he comments, and I nod. "But she's definitely... *curious* about things," he says in that mischievous way of his.

"In what way?" I'm sure I know the answer, but I crave hearing it anyway. It seems wrong to discuss this without her present, but I'm too enthralled to stop.

"You may not have been close enough to sense it, but her reaction when you confessed to our dalliances was *so sweet*," he finishes with his eyes closed in elation. "Her entire body froze in place, her pupils fixed on me as they widened, and the scent of her wetness was so powerful I had to bury my face in my drink to stop myself from getting a taste straight from the source."

Christ, I'm getting hard again. If Bel *is* into that idea, I don't know how long I could stop myself from acting on it. Fritz would obviously be ecstatic, but I don't want to push her into anything too soon. "We shouldn't seduce her, Fritz," voicing the protest I've been trying to tell myself all night. "She hasn't even had one man, let alone two at once. Had I known about her past, I never would have dragged her into my rough desires."

After an overtly dramatic sigh, he responds, "I suppose you're right. We *should* just step aside and let some mortal man have the honors." The growl building inside me at that thought has him looking at me skeptically, "You and I both know that you won't let anyone else have her. You care too deeply for her. And her, you."

"Do I only care for her this way because of the summons?" I ask the question I haven't dared even ask myself. "I mean... I did try to kill her when she summoned me."

"Try?" he laughs.

"I tried. I had my hand around her throat, using all of my strength to crush her," I recall, "I was so confused as to why I couldn't squeeze the life out of her."

He raises his brows in question, "And did she yell at you before or after that?"

"After. She shot me before," the memory has me smiling.

More laughter before he answers me. "The only thing the *hostia* bond promises is just that. Protection. Whatever else you may be feeling is all on you," he explains.

"She is magnetic," I confess, "I'm unsure how to deal with these feelings I'm having. I'm not ready for our journey here to be over. I fear she still wishes herself rid of me, but I'll never be ready to leave her side. As I can see from your face, you feel the same pull I do," I consider throttling him for it, but I can't bring myself to harm someone who would only ensure her safety and happiness.

He nods in thought, saying nothing to refute my statement about their connection, "You two should stay another day or two. I'll schedule Bel a day at the spa. She needs a little TLC."

"I don't understand anything you just said," I hate the modern world.

"TLC is tender, loving care. It's like colloquial for relaxing. Kinda. A spa is a place where they'll let her lay back, take care of her skin, maybe a massage, style her hair. I don't know, Cas. It's just fun. All three of us can go if you want."

"It will be relaxing for her?" He nods, "Then let her do it by herself. She has not been allowed to leave my proximity for days. Let her have some semblance of privacy for a moment."

"I'll have them schedule a full day for her, then we can get a table to drink and dance tomorrow night. No playing chase or murder this time, okay?" He's barely containing his laughter.

"Yes, yes, very funny. I'm going to bed. Be quiet in the morning, Bel prefers to sleep well into the day." I begin to make my way to my room when he yells goodnight to me, so I respond, "Goodnight, Fritzy. See you tomorrow."

As I crawl back into the warm embrace of Bel, I wonder if we could somehow make this work. If we could stay here indefinitely in the safety of Fritz's home. Right now, she lives alone, paying for her home all by herself without the income necessary to do so. Nowhere could be safer for her than right here.

I can't stop my mind from wandering to indecent places. Images of Fritz cradling her the way I am, images of them in far less innocent embraces. The jealousy I feel is greatly overshadowed by the need to see it come to life. She'd be so beautiful falling apart wrapped around him, so stunning lost in the rapture of us both worshipping at her altar.

I've never felt anything like this craving for the three of us together. Like something is pulling is all here, against all odds. As if this is where we were always made to be. I fall asleep wondering if fate could be kind enough to me to bless me with such a gift.

* * *

Walking into the common area in the morning, I find a scribbled note with drops of last night's liquor from Fritz. Instructions on summoning Norman so he can show me where the body is being kept. He leads me down to the lower level of the hotel, allowing me privacy to have a little bit of the dead drunk man for breakfast. I don't want to take too long, but I *do* want to be at full power before the day begins.

When I return to the kitchen, I realize it's nearly time for Bel to get out of bed, and I search for breakfast and coffee. Thankfully, Fritz has a machine similar to the one in Bel's apartment, so I place a premeasured cup into the brewer and find a mug. While they're nowhere near as humorous as the ones she has at home, they'll do for now.

"Good morning, Caspian. No Sleeping Beauty yet?" Fritz asks, snatching the freshly brewed coffee from my hand.

"That's for Bel." I tell him.

"Yes, I know," he winks at me, "Does she use creamer?" I nod at him, and he prepares it for her, not unlike how I would.

Just then, she toddles out of her room, rubbing the sleep from her eyes. She spots me, and her whole face lights up before she becomes more solemn and states, "You weren't in bed when I woke up."

"I wanted to start your coffee," I explain, pointing at the cup in Fritz's hand. He gives it to her, and she glances at him before expressing her gratitude with a little kiss on the corner of my mouth.

"Thank you," she tells me, "and you," she points her mug at him, a smirk playing on her lips.

"You're welcome," we say in unison, and Bel's sleepy, flirtatious smile as she looks between us has me grabbing behind her neck to give her a *real* kiss. When I try to slide my tongue into her mouth, she releases a peal of laughter and pushes me away.

"Come now, Caspian," Fritz begins, slinging an arm around Bel's shoulder, pulling her close, "you two have all night to do that. For now, we have plans."

"We do?" Bel asks, practically bouncing in excitement. She returns his affection with an arm around his waist. Whatever he plans, I'll go along with, so long as she keeps smiling at us that way. She turns to me, "I thought we were going home?"

"It is your choice, Bel. If you'd like to go home, we can pack up and go right now. I know you wanted to finish your current read and there's no *need* to stay." I tell her.

But by her curious nature, I already know what her next question will be. Looking up at him, she asks, "What do you have planned?"

He runs the tip of his index finger down her nose before answering quietly, "So much." I should want to gut him for the way he speaks to her, but I love every second. I love watching her react, anticipation written all over her soft features. "But first, how do you feel about a spa day?"

"Oh, my God, yes please," she looks at me, "Is that okay?"

"Of course it's alright. We can do whatever you want." I don't need to tell her that I mean that in more ways than one. I've never felt the desire to bed someone with Fritz, but my attraction to both of them, coupled with my overwhelming need to please Bel, has my cock begging for the chance.

"Perfect," Fritz chirps. "So you, Sweetness, will spend the day at the spa, and I will spend the day catching Cas up on everything he's missed in the last couple of centuries."

She raises a brow, "Just the two of you?" There's no malice or venom in her voice, only a playful lilt. She can't hide her excitement from either of us, and she knows it.

"Do not fret, Little Dove. We won't have any fun without you." She tries to hide her face in her coffee mug, and *by the Gods, she wants this so bad.* Fritz must have the same thought if the hunger in his eyes is any indication.

I toy with a couple strands of her hair while she stays in the comfort of his embrace, stealing just another moment of joy before the source of it is whisked away for some *TLC* as Fritz called it. "I truly need to be informed of the advancements the warlocks made while I was gone. And someone who can tell me what's different and what is the same between now and before."

"I totally understand. I was only joking," she assures me, "When do I need to be ready to go?"

Fritz explains, "Finish up your coffee, then we'll escort you. They'll have a robe, but you need to bring a swimsuit in case you decide to use the sauna or jacuzzi. We'll have clothing delivered before the end of your treatments."

"Treatments?" She beams, and her happiness is so warm I want to bask in her light for eternity.

"Anything you like," he tells her, "I haven't been myself but I know they do all the facial and massage stuff, hair, make up, the works."

"You're full of shit. You 100% have had spa days here," she laughs at him.

"Fuck, okay, you caught me," he snickers, pulling her closer until they're nose to nose before he whispers conspiratorially, "Michele is a miracle worker. Look at my pores. There are none. She'll take great care of you." He spins her out of his hold, gently pushing her toward her room.

A few moments later, she emerges again, little purse in hand, looking like a child about to enter the world's largest candy shop. *She deserves this.* She's done nothing but adapt to all the horrible things she's seen. After being forced to reevaluate everything she thought she knew about the world *and* herself in only a matter of days, she's taken up arms to fight still. She needs to relax and have nothing to think about except her own wants for a little while.

As we walk her down, Fritz explains a little more about each part of the hotel. There are so many towers, restaurants, and shops that I haven't the faintest idea how he remembers it all.

He walks into the spa area before us, talking to the receptionist as I turn Bel to me. "You've got your phone, so if you need anything, just call, okay? We will not be far."

She gently slaps my arm, "Yes, Caspian, I will call if I need you. You don't need to worry about me. In fact, I'm more worried about you." At the confused look on my face, she explains, "Well, you *were* being hunted, if you remember. No one is looking to hurt me."

"Well if *you* remember, I killed everyone who was hunting me," I grin, and she slaps a hand over my mouth.

"Shhhh. You can't say shit like that. Someone will hear you," she looks around in a panic. The only thing holding my laugh in is her hand. Grabbing her wrist, I mime taking a bite from her palm before releasing her.

Before I can say anything else, Fritz waltzes over and hands her a robe, telling her that Michele will give her a tour and be in charge of her pampering. She nods as he walks her over, then she shakes hands with the older woman, instantly making a new friend. With her robe draped over one arm, she gives us a little wave and disappears down the hall.

Walking back to me with a wide grin on his face, Fritz says, "So, you got a hankering for some grabby hands, or did I hear you sneak off to the basement already this morning?"

"I did, in fact. I appreciate you taking care of that, by the way," I tell him.

"Of course. As I told your girl, I would have done the same." He begins walking, and I follow, lest I lose my way.

"Why?" I press casually. He wasn't willing to share much about his obvious affection for her last night, but hopefully, now he will be.

"Why what? Why would I have done the same?" He seems baffled by my question.

"Yes. Why would you have defended someone you don't know?" I clarify.

"Well, my reasoning is twofold. First of all, I don't like bullies, and that guy was a big, drunk, ugly fucking bully. And second, you are my oldest friend. What's important to you is important to me."

I narrow my eyes, "And?" I prompt.

"*And* I... like her," he admits, "I may not have had the time to bond with her that you have, but I *like* her already. I want to protect her, too."

I have nothing to say to that except to maybe tell him I wouldn't keep either of them from the happiness we could all have. It would be strange and take a lot of adjusting and working at it, but I care for them both. Why would I try to keep them apart?

Before I get the chance to tell him any of that, he goes on dejectedly, "I thought you were as good as dead, Cas."

"I was." *I was.*

"Then you show up, centuries later, with a gorgeous girl on your arm, smiling like a loon," he grins. "I would do anything to make sure that happiness is not taken from you. You may just have to... share some of your joy with me," he smirks.

I breathe a sigh of relief. Having Fritz here has lifted much of the invisible weight off my chest. "I have missed you, friend," I tell him earnestly.

"Likewise, Cas. Now let's go educate you on the 18th, 19th, 20th, and 21st century. Only the important stuff. Indoor plumbing, modern politics, the MCU," he pauses to think, "Oh! The invention of the dildo."

I huff out a laugh before telling him I know plenty about that last one, thanks to Bel.

"Jesus *Christ,* Cas. You shouldn't tell me that. Fuck, I already wanna do vile things to her. Now the thoughts of her fucking herself on a fake dick are never gonna go away," he groans.

Trying to keep my tone light despite the rising heat in my body I ask, craving the answer, "What kind of vile things?"

"Do not toy with me. That's your girl and you said no. It's true that I can't help but flirt, but I would *not* go so blatantly against your wishes," he points a finger at me.

As he unlocks the key to his home and I enter, I murmur, "She seems very intrigued by the idea," with a shrug. I pretend the thought is only occurring to me. As if I haven't been considering it nonstop since last night.

He groans even louder, "Bro, you're killing me."

"Answer the question," I demand gently, sitting on the couch. Ordering Fritz around comes naturally to me, and his obeying is the sweetest surrender.

"Fine," he starts pacing, waving around his hands as he confesses, "Last night when you guys got back, and you had her panties in your pocket, both of you looked and smelled like sex on legs. Even after she changed into sweats, the scent of that sweet pussy kept creeping up on me.

"All I could think about is bending her over the couch and pounding into her while she choked on your cock. I wondered what kind of sounds she'd make, if she'd cry from overstimulation." I smile at the memory of her doing just that. Her tears *were* gorgeous. "You fucker, I see that face."

I grin wider, just to spite him, "She's beautiful when she cries, but she is *ethereal* when she comes." I have to spread my legs to relieve the pressure at the thought, and it doesn't go unnoticed. I probably shouldn't entertain this alone with Fritz, but I get the feeling that he doesn't really want to play without her either.

"I wanna lick her little cunt while you pin her legs wide open for me," he blurts, eyes fixed on the very obvious reaction his imagery is causing, "I want to tie her to the bed and let her watch us." His eyes dart back up to mine, "Fuck, she wants to watch us together so bad, Cas."

"She does," I agree. Her face always gives her away, "but it has to be about her. She needs to have control and freedom to feel safe. We can... suggest it, but we follow her lead no matter what."

"Obviously," he tsks. "I only want to give her what she wants. And what I want. And I guess you can have what you want, too. Win, win, win."

"We will bring up the idea *delicately*," I reiterate, and he nods. "Okay, great. Now can we talk about something else? I can't think about this any longer or I'll storm down there and grab her right now."

"Absolutely," he tries to shake the growing tension from his body, "I'm assuming you have another dress for her to wear tonight, yeah?"

"Of course, I do."

"Okay, then as long as it's dropped off within the next six hours, she's good to go." He walks toward the kitchen, and I pop up off the couch.

"*Six hours?*" He must be joking.

"She's getting pampered from head to toe, with half an hour or so where she can just lounge in a private heated tub with music and dim lighting. That gives you six hours to study up on what you've missed. Let's start with the fucking demon hunters."

He drones on and on for what feels like an eternity. He tells me about the hunters growing exponentially over the last couple of centuries due to some magic they discovered. Then something about a demon he knows that started an organization to counteract their reach. Ammon? Aimon? I don't fucking remember.

At some point during the day, he escapes for a while, explaining he needs to check in on how one of his proteges is doing for their first shift on the floor. While he's gone, Norman arrives to deliver the dress and shoes to Bel for us.

The only part of the *homework* Fritz left me I find even a little bit appealing is the movies. If I remember right, Bel had a couple of these on her shelves. Although I hardly understand how two friends having a little tiff constitutes being called a *Civil War.*

When Fritz returns and *finally* informs me it's time to go, I nearly run to grab my best clothing and ready myself for seeing ou— my girl. Walking down, I notice that he dressed similarly extravagant, and I can't wait to see how she feels about all the attention she's about to receive.

18

TLC

Bel

As I close my eyes and let the scalding water soak my feet, I hear a mock surprised voice, "Oh. My goodness. What a coincidence. Fancy meeting you here."

I crack an eye, peering at Fritz, looking adorable and silly in a robe that matches mine. He plants himself on the chair next to me, assuming the position for a pedicure and greeting the salon staff like old friends.

"What are you doing here?" I laugh in disbelief.

"Teaching Cas about the modern world was such a drag, I needed a break. I was due for a little pampering anyway and I thought I'd just join you so we can get to know each other outside of Caspian's constant growling and wandering hands," he raises his brows in mock suggestion, and I laugh again.

Getting comfy, he reaches over and grabs my hand closest to him, admiring the manicure I just got. He gives Michele a thumbs-up before releasing me.

"Michele, darling, will you pretty please grab me and my girl here a bottle of champagne?" She stands to do so, and he turns back to me, "So, Sweetness, Caspian tells me you have a *very* interesting job. What's that like?"

I fight against the heat rising in my cheeks, "It has its moments. Most of the time it's just reading. The spicy stuff is only usually like 15% of the book."

"I see. How does one stumble into that kind of job?" He seems genuinely interested in my work, unlike most people who ask about it just to get their rocks off or pass judgment, so I indulge him.

"It kind of found me, I guess." I shrug, "I have always loved reading, ever since I was a kid. I can read really fast, too, so that helps. My best friend, Isla, actually gave me the idea." As I talk, Michele returns with an opened bottle and two glasses full of the pink bubbly liquid, and I mouth *Thank you* to her. She smiles and nods before starting my pedicure.

Fritz nods intently as I keep talking, "She said my voice is really soothing and interesting and I should try animation voiceovers. But that industry is really hard to get into unless you have connections, and I like being my own boss. I make my own deadlines and expectations. I choose my clients. It's a dream, honestly."

He hums before commenting, "I've found that people who work for themselves often work the most," and I have to agree.

"Oh, 100% I overwork. But I've got bills to pay, ya know?"

"Mmhmm. And when you're not working? Do you have fun? You're not having sex, so you must be doing something." I nearly choke on my drink, causing a self-satisfied smirk to light up his gorgeous face.

"I read for fun, too. I go out with Isla, I visit my parents, see movies, and travel a bit. All the usual stuff," I tell him as I try to sneakily admire him.

He really is so unbelievably hot. Smaller than Cas and softer, somehow, but equally terrifying and thrilling. His always calm and laughing demeanor tells me he's never worried about someone more dangerous being around the corner. His eyes are so dark they're like black pools, always swirling with wicked playfulness when he looks at me.

His body is equally enticing. Before recently, I thought all men were essentially built the same. They've all looked basically the same to me, anyway. But these two men are undeniably different. While Caspian's muscular frame is large and nearly overwhelming, Fritz seems more lithe, almost serpentine, while still being utterly fucking ripped.

He peers at me, "Little Songbird, if you keep looking at me like that, this spa day is going to end with a very unhappy Caspian and a very, *very* happy me." His sultry voice promises endless pleasure that I'm almost willing to take him up on.

Instead, I simply mumble a quiet, "Sorry."

"No, no, no. No sorry's here. You are admiring, as am I," he says with a slow, thorough perusal of my frame. "There's no shame to be had here. I only tease because I adore the soft pink that spreads across your cheeks."

I say nothing, too embarrassed that I got caught checking him out so blatantly.

"Bel," he draws my attention back. "Honestly, you've done nothing wrong. I sought you out. Obviously, I'm *very* attracted to you, much to our mutual friend's chagrin. If the feeling is mutual... all the better for me," he beams.

We don't talk much for the remainder of our pedicures. He just occasionally looks at me with a small smile, allowing me to relax and sink into the massage chair beneath me. After a while, he reaches over and grabs my hand again, entwining our fingers together. He starts drawing slow circles with his thumb on my hand.

Every stroke of his thumb sends pulses between my legs, and I wonder again how I could possibly be this horny after my... adventure with Caspian. His grip slowly tightens, his thumb becoming slightly more aggressive, like the small point of contact affects him the same way it does me.

"Have you had a chance to soak in the pool yet?" he asks me suddenly, pulling me from the errant thoughts of that thumb rubbing circles elsewhere.

"Uhhh, no. And I hadn't planned on it, seeing how I just got my nails done," I wiggle said fingers.

"It's gel polish, perfectly safe for the water," Michele reminds me. *Oh.*

"Come, we'll go now," he practically yanks me out of the chair now that my toes have finished *curing.*

"Thank you, Michele, Connor. You two are a fucking dream," he calls behind us on our way out. He leads me down a corridor before opening up a door that leads to a small room with dim lighting and a hot tub large enough for six or seven people.

"Strip, Sweets." He says as he takes his robe off and practically leaps into the water. I expect him to linger and watch me as I disrobe, but he doesn't, just closes his eyes and sinks into the water until it reaches his neck.

I drape the robe over a nearby chair, down to just the swimsuit I had on under it. As I sink into the hot water, I sigh, causing Fritz to tense up momentarily, still giving me the space to get comfortable without his eyes on me. I make myself comfortable, letting the scalding water relax my limbs.

Done with the silence, I ask him, "How did you become a blackjack dealer? That's not a job you hear about every day."

He grins, keeping his eyes closed, leaning his head back on the tub wall behind him, "I've been doing it for nearly 20 years now. I came to Vegas looking for adventure, as one does. I played a few rounds and found I could beat the house fairly easily." He laughs as he remembers, "I ran through every single casino, outplaying their best until one stopped me and accused me of cheating.

"When I explained how I played and showed that I most definitely did not cheat, they offered me a job on the spot. I've bounced around to a few of the local casinos since then, but this one felt like home immediately. I make these greedy fucks so much money they'll give me anything I ask for to keep working."

I laugh with him, enjoying the easiness of his company. I'm half naked, yet he hasn't even looked at me. These demons are downright tame compared to what I was expecting. The longer I'm in their presence, the safer I feel. Physically, of course, but even mentally. Emotionally. I feel like they're willing to give me whatever I need to feel comfortable.

With that thought in mind, I'm feeling a little daring. Maybe Caspian wouldn't like being left out of this moment, but he definitely seemed to enjoy the idea of us together, so if I dip my toes in the water, so to speak, I think he'd be encouraging.

I slowly make my way towards Fritz, and he peeks one eye at me, "What are you doing, little temptress? You're going to get me in trouble. Caspian might have half a mind to punish me if I take liberties with you."

Thoughts of Caspian *punishing* Fritz fill my mind, only urging me forward more until I'm left standing right in front of him, knee to knee. He opens his eyes and trains them on mine, "You are looking for trouble, aren't you? Do you *like* the idea of Caspian hurting me?" I nod sheepishly, and he slightly widens his legs, making room for me to stand between them.

He leans forward and hooks his hands behind my knees, urging me closer and staring up at me. "Little deviant, you are," he whispers with his signature playful mirth. "Kiss me, troublemaker. I dare you."

Using a gentle grip on his hair, I lean down and place one soft kiss against his lips.

"Again," he tells me, and I smile against his lips before placing another teasing peck and pulling away.

"Again, *Christ*, please." He keeps his hands on my legs, gifting me complete control. Having such a powerful being submit to me in this way, beg me for kisses– it's intoxicating. I lean in again and pull his bottom lip between mine, sucking it into my mouth, and he groans quietly, fighting to keep still.

The sound spurs me on, so I climb onto his lap, keeping myself upright on my knees rather than sitting fully on him. His hands climb slightly, wrapping around my thighs in a barely there hold. I tighten my grip on his hair and deepen the kiss, fully pressing our lips together.

He gently opens his mouth against mine, tentatively licking against me, seeking permission, and I meet his tongue with my own, sliding them together. His fingers flex, digging into my thighs, and I moan into the kiss. His movements are slow and teasing, allowing me to lead the kiss only as far as I want it to go. *Fuck, he's good at this.*

I never thought I'd be the type to crave control in bed, but I guess I also never thought the day would come when I'd be thinking about enjoying anyone that way. He pulls away from my mouth and kisses my shoulder, full of affection.

"Bel, Sweets, I'd like to take this moment to remind you that Caspian probably would not appreciate this going any further without him." Despite his words, he continues his assault on my shoulder and collarbone.

I nod in agreement but don't stop him. If anything, I think I've pulled him against me harder, loving the attention he's laving over my wet body.

"Gods above, I want you so fucking bad," he mutters, using one hand to finger the strap of my bikini bottom, "I wanna see if this little pussy tastes as good as it smells."

His words send a flood of warmth to the apex of my thighs, and I fight the urge to start rocking them against him. I look down at him again, ready to say something else, but when he kisses between my breasts and then licks the same spot, I can't.

An unintelligible word escapes me as I try to express how good it felt, but he just chuckles against my skin before leaning his head back with a sigh. He closes his eyes for a few moments, then opens them again, looking slightly less hazy than a moment ago.

"You have 20 more minutes to soak, then you have your next treatment," he begins to lift me by the waist to remove me from his lap, "I suggest you use that time to actually relax while you can."

"You're leaving?" I ask, feeling the sting of rejection for the second time in as many days.

"I must, my Songbird. I hadn't planned on staying this long, to begin with, but I wanted to spend time with you," he confesses with an almost timid look on his face, if he's capable of such a thing.

He places another kiss against my shoulder and exits the tub, wrapping himself in the robe, "Enjoy this time you have to yourself, Bel. Once Cas and I get you back in our arms, you won't have any time to rest at all." My jaw drops, and he winks before walking out of the room, presumably back to his suite.

19

Swim

Bel

I've never felt more relaxed. My toes and fingers are painted, though that'll last a week. My skin is fucking glowing, and my hair has never been fluffier. But mostly, I'm just happy I got to sit and relax for a few hours. The hot tub was heavenly, both with and without company; whatever oils they had in there had me floating my way to nirvana.

As I emerge, feeling like a new woman, the sight of them in the lobby stops me short. *They look so good.* Obviously, they're both gorgeous men, but standing side by side, they're so beautiful it's almost an uncanny valley situation. There's no way anyone could see them and not know something supernatural is afoot.

They smile at me, surely sensing my thoughts. *Can demons read minds? I meant to ask.* That would be fucking awkward. Caspian approaches me first, wrapping me in a hug, enveloping me in that unmistakable smell, before turning us toward Fritz, keeping an arm around my shoulder, "Shall we?"

"I was thinking we should grab something to eat, I'm sure after your *relaxing* day, you are famished," he smirks at me knowingly, and I absolutely am, what with the few glasses of champagne he and the spa staff supplied me with. While I love fruits and cheese, there's only so much of them I can eat.

I don't say any of that though, just nod my assent.

"What are you hungry for?" Caspian urges as we begin to walk toward the casino area.

"I could go for something spicy, I think."

"I know just the place. Follow me." Fritz walks just ahead of us, continuing, "After we have dinner, we shall head over to the club again? Dance, drink, all that jazz. Cas already promised me no more murders so it'll be a little less fun than last night, but I'm sure we can keep it interesting." He turns and winks in our direction.

Caspian squeezes me a little tighter for a second, and I suddenly get the feeling I'm being cornered by two apex predators. Once again, I think to myself that I should probably be scared shitless, but I'm just excited.

As we eat dinner, which is, in fact, the best, spiciest phở I've ever had, I realize Caspian was 100% right last night. I'm definitely not ready to have sex, but it would be fun to dance and drink and flirt with them both. Maybe I could even get a little glimpse of what they're like *together*, but I'm not expecting that. They both seem more interested in me than each other, and all the attention is making my head spin.

They both keep finding small, innocent ways to touch me, and it's causing rampant thoughts that are anything *but* innocent. Fritz will brush the inside of my wrist with his fingers as we walk, or Caspian will brush my hair behind my shoulder while talking to me.

At one point, Fritz wraps an arm around me and takes a selfie as he's pretending to kiss my face, and I push him away, laughing my ass off the whole time. I finally relent and allow him one little peck on the cheek before I shove Bánh gối in his mouth to make him relent.

By the time we make it to the table inside the club, I'm in dire need of a drink, and I need to go dance, just to expel some of this energy building inside me.

Marie is an absolute and utter joy again, of course, gushing about my hair and my makeup and *that fucking dress!* as she brings us a couple different drinks again. We all give her approximately 23762 thank you's, and she heads off with a wave.

After a few minutes of talking and sampling everything, Fritz stands up first. "I'll be on the floor, I fucking love this song," he announces, not waiting for a response before he's gone.

I turn to Caspian, asking, "Are you going to attempt to dance tonight?" while I sip on my sweet, blue something or other. I'm trying not to laugh at how wooden he seemed the night before, but it's funny. He's always graceful and smooth, so his complete lack of rhythm shocked me.

He looks at me, deadpanning, "Fuck no." I take another sip to hide my laughter, and he adds lowly, "I'll just watch." *Okay, wait.* I set down my drink and narrow my eyes at him. I'm reading too much into it. He doesn't mean what it sounds like he means.

I turn my head to find where Fritz is already spinning someone in circles, ignoring the patrons around them, grinning, and meeting my eye. "He *is* entertaining to watch." I concede, "Though his rhythm is about as good as yours." As I look at Caspian, the look in his eyes is nearly feral.

"There is no way to dance to this music that is not thinly veiled foreplay. Would you prefer he stand there and rub himself against her for your entertainment?" he smirks at me, knowing my answer would be a resounding *yes.*

"You could go dance with him, I'm sure he would be happy to teach you." I bat my lashes at him.

He makes a sound like he's considering it but says, "Actually, Little Dove, I think *you* should go dance with him. I would enjoy the lesson infinitely more that way."

I freeze with my mouth open in shock, "But- but you just said-"

"I know what I said, and I know what I want. I also happen to know what he wants." I swallow, considering his words. I've been wondering if Fritz mentioned our time together, or if I should. Based on how hungrily he's looked at us both all night, he's well aware of what's taken place.

He slides closer to me, draping his arm onto the backrest behind me, using his free hand to trace little circles on my bare thigh, "But the question, Bel, is what do *you* want?"

"I don't know," I say too quickly.

"Yes, you do. You're just afraid that you shouldn't have it," Caspian gently cups my jaw with the arm draped around me and presses his lips to mine, surprising me with his softness. Opening my mouth wider, he slowly and thoroughly glides his tongue against mine, and I moan into the kiss. In answer, his fingers still their movement and grip my whole thigh in his big hand. He whispers against my mouth, "Look, baby," before using his grip on my jaw to turn my head towards the dance floor.

There I instantly find Fritz, still moving to his own rhythm, eyes glued to us, looking starving and slightly dazed. Caspian lips find my neck, and I let out a sigh, not allowing my eyes to drop from Fritz's smoldering gaze. Between Caspian's slightly too-hard grip on my thigh and his urgent nibbles on my neck, I'm a mess already.

"Go dance," he begs, "please. Put us all out of our misery." *How can I say no when he asks so sweetly.* I pull back and give him one more kiss on the lips before making my way over to what is probably the most dangerous being in the room.

"Oh, hello Sweetness," he greets, "having fun?"

"So much. But unfortunately, Caspian refused to come dance with you, so you'll have to make do with me," I tease.

With one brow raised, he holds a hand out to me, "I'm sure you're a far better dancer than he is. He's always had two left feet." His eyes sparkle with humor and excitement, and I'm sure my face mirrors his. He pulls me into his arms, spinning me how he was his partner before.

I admit I was expecting him to instantly make this an obscene display of lust, but instead, he spins me, holding my hand and waist in a downright respectful manner. Before I know it, I'm giggling like mad and twirling again and again without a single thought in my head.

I'm sure we've danced for several songs, just laughing and playing, and I can imagine this is how they used to enjoy themselves at balls in their world before. I make eye contact with Caspian a few times, and he's always smiling, either giving me a wave or lifting his drink in salute.

After I've been spun in countless circles and dipped nearly the floor several times, the beat slows into something sultry, heady, and drugging. Fritz spins me out again, this time catching me when I return to him, spinning me until my back is against his front.

He grabs my hands and slowly raises them up to wrap around his neck, trailing his fingers down the backs of my arms. As his hands trail lower, his fingers lightly graze the outside of my breasts. The back of his fingernails leaves a tingling sensation over my chest and ribs as he continues the slow drag downwards. I lean my head back against him, closing my eyes.

Once his hands finally reach their destination on my hips, he pulls me against him, lightly rolling his hips while we sway. He's rock hard against me, and I'm practically panting, letting him control the pace and movement, his hands getting more forceful. After one particularly rough drag against my ass, he moans in my ear, "You feel *so* good, Bel."

My fingers dig into his neck, trying to somehow pull him closer. He moves one hand to the front of my stomach, salaciously low, fully possessing me, while the other drags back up my body, grazing along my chest before he grips my neck, forcing me to look up at him. "Fritz, I-" I blink, trying to clear my head enough to make words form.

"You what, baby?" he drags his nose down mine.

"I ummm, I- I need more," I plead, not really sure what I'm asking for.

"More? More what?" he teases. "Tell me what you want and I'll fucking give it to you, I swear." He's grinding against me harder, breathing heavily, the sweet smell of liquor and cinnamon wafting from his mouth. "So good of you to join us, Caspian. I was beginning to wonder if you were going to stay up there all night."

I try to snap my head to see where he is, but Fritz keeps me locked in place, a challenging smirk lighting up his face. "Bel here was just about to tell me what she wants. You go ahead, Songbird." He eases up his grip on me, changing his movements to be slightly less lewd so I can think almost clearly for a second.

When I do look at Caspian, I almost wish I hadn't. He looks at us like he's not sure if he wants to hurt or fuck us. From being so viscerally turned on, he almost looks angry. *Christ, I'm soaked.* If this man wanted to hurt me, I think I'd beg him to do so.

He tries his hardest to rein in the monster, stepping forward and claiming my face in his hands, sandwiching me between them, "What do you want, love?"

"I want... I want both of you." *There. I said something, at least.*

Fritz chuckles, "Oh, we know," before sucking on a spot beneath my ear that has me whimpering.

"Be more specific," Caspian urges, and I shake my head, unable to voice a single thought. He chuckles darkly and yanks Fritz's head away by his hair to stop his torment, "Stop for a second so she can think. What are your *no's?*" he asks.

"I don't want to have sex. I just- I don't think I'm ready, but I want other stuff," Caspian nods encouragingly, asking me what else, so I keep thinking. "I don't want to be tied up or anything," I finally say.

"Keep going," Fritz pushes. I think about what I really want, and even though I probably shouldn't ask it of them, I do.

"I wanna watch you two. Together." They groan in unison, causing a new flood of warmth between my legs. *I need to hear that again.*

Caspian leans in and places a chaste kiss on my mouth, telling me, "Good job, baby," while Fritz restarts mouthing my neck, moaning at the taste of me. "Would you like to go now, or dance for a bit longer?"

"Dance with her, Cas. I'll guide you," Fritz spins me to face him, pushing me against Caspian's hard chest. He copies how Fritz was gripping me earlier, one hand holding my body against his, his other hand collaring my throat.

"Oh, fuck, that's gorgeous," Fritz mutters to himself, eyes locked on my neck, palming his cock through his pants. He crowds in closer, instructing Caspian, "Now just pretend you're *gently* fucking her to the beat of the song. Show her how bad you want it."

I honestly think I might come from this, the feeling of being claimed so wholly by Caspian; Fritz being so taken by the sight that he seems to have forgotten we're still in public. Once we find a rhythm, Fritz steps forward again, slotting a thigh between mine, placing a hand on my hip to push and pull me against it. I can't stop the moan that rips from my throat.

He watches my face for a few seconds, no doubt feeling me soaking his fucking pant leg. Without breaking eye contact, he reaches a hand up, wrapping it around the back of Caspian's neck. He drags him in and slams their mouths together. Caspian tightens his grip on me, forcing my head back, so I have no choice but to watch their tongues tangle against each other. Honestly, nothing could make me look away.

Caspian bites and pulls Fritz's lower lip hard enough that he whimpers at the pain, his hips jolting against mine uncontrollably. *He likes the pain. Fuck, this is so hot.*

They've never stopped their movements against me, and I can feel the tension building in my body. If they don't stop right now, I won't be able to control it. It's too much, too intense. Caspian moves his hand from my stomach, grabbing the back of Fritz's head and forcing our mouths together. I instantly open, craving the taste of them in his mouth.

I distantly register that I'm moaning, riding his thigh like a wanton whore, but it all feels *so good.* So much better than I ever could have imagined. I'm so close, I'm gonna come in public twice in as many days, and I'm completely powerless to stop myself.

"Let go, baby. Come all over his thigh." At Caspian's gruff command, my whole body tenses, and I practically scream into Fritz's mouth. He moans with me, rocking his hips, working me through my orgasm, only stopping when I'm fully spent. As soon as my breathing returns to normal, Caspian extracts himself, grabs my forearm, and starts storming out, barking at us both, "It's time to go."

Fritz and I share a private, playful smile at Caspian's reaction, and he follows closely behind, linking the fingers of my other hand with his.

20

Showtime

Bel

I knew Caspian would be the dominant type, but even I'm surprised at how bossy he is. I almost want to fight back, just to push him. But I think after the dance, he's probably barely holding himself in one form, so I'll save that for another day.

As soon as we enter the suite, he barks at Fritz, "Take her to your bedroom and strip her down. Do what you like while you wait for me. I need to get something."

I want to ask what he's getting, but I don't get the chance before Fritz has his mouth on mine, trapping me against the wall, grinding his cock between my legs. Both his hands are buried in my hair, holding me still for his assault on my mouth.

He suddenly wraps both hands around my thighs and grunts a single word, "Up," so I jump and wrap my legs around him. He pulls me away from it and carries me into the primary bedroom, slamming me against the wall again once we're inside. The jarring motion of hitting it draws a soft cry from me, and he pulls us slightly away to do it again, giving me every bit of the rough treatment I didn't know I was craving.

Grabbing both of my hands in one of his, he holds them above my head, using his other hand to grip my ass. He starts rocking against me, every grind against my clit making me moan. I lean my head back and close my eyes, rubbing myself down on him, his grunts and groans music to my ears. He leans in, tongue running from between my tits all the way up my neck before plunging it into my mouth.

"You were *supposed* to be getting her naked." Caspian's amused voice interrupts us, and Fritz gently puts my feet on the ground, muttering a little *oops* with a shrug. "Take off her dress. Now."

Before I can say anything, he's almost tearing the dress in his haste to unzip it. This dress didn't require a bra, which is fortunate since my good one was ruined last night. As it pools on the floor, they both stare slack-jawed at my tits before Fritz cups them both, whispering, "They're so fucking pretty. Let me-"

"No. *You* didn't listen so *you* don't get to touch them," Caspian orders, walking closer, "Take off her panties, but do not touch her pussy as you do. Leave the shoes. They'll leave such pretty scratches all over your back if I let you taste her later." Just thinking about him licking me between my thighs has me rubbing them together to soothe the ache.

Caspian looks to me with that amused look in his eyes, "Aw. You need to come again already, my dove?" I refuse to give him the satisfaction of an answer, so I do nothing. He watches hungrily as Fritz lowers to his knees and slowly works my panties down my legs. "I'll take those."

Fritz pouts, "Hey, you got to keep the ones from yesterday. I earned the orgasm soaking these, they're mine." And he sticks them in his pocket.

He gets an eye-roll from Cas, but he concedes, "Fine. Go strip to your underwear while I get our little voyeur ready." *What does that mean?* At the scared look on my face, Caspian holds both hands up to show me what he's brought. In one hand he has a bottle of lube, while the other holds a small box that looks vaguely familiar.

"Did you take that from my house?" I ask, knowing he did, but not sure what exactly it is.

He nods, "Go lay on the bed, propped up against the pillows." I start walking, trying not to let my nudity unnerve me. Once I get positioned as he instructed, he climbs onto the bed and kneels at my feet, handing me something from the box.

Oh. "I haven't used this one yet," I confess.

"I had hoped not," he answers with a smirk.

Fritz sits on the bed, waiting very impatiently. He looks at the objects in question and starts palming himself again. I get the sentiment. I wish I had a way to relieve this growing ache inside me.

I twist the vibrator this way and that. It's a relatively small, red toy shaped kind of like a U or a C. Both ends of the toy are bulbous and vibrate. It's designed for G spot and clit vibration, and Caspian holds up and wiggles the remote with a wicked grin on his face. "I will be in charge of this," he tells us, "Do you want to put in the toy, or would you like one of us to?"

My eyes widen; I've used toys countless times before, but obviously, no one has ever done it for me. Before I can answer, Fritz interjects, "Oh, shit. Lemme do it. Please, Cas. Please let me."

He narrows his eyes, "After you stole the panties? Why would I let you do anything?" A whimper escapes Fritz, and either Caspian takes pity on him or wants to torture him further because he sighs, "Fine. You may do it."

Fritz frantically reaches for the lube and Cas pulls it back momentarily, "Make sure it's perfect, but you don't get to taste her or play with her breasts." Then he takes the toy from me and gently places it in Fritz's open palm.

"You got it," he climbs up and lays beside me, pouring a bit of lube onto his fingers, warming it up before putting it on one end of the toy. "Open up for me, Bel." I let my legs fall open, feeling two sets of eyes on my very wet, *very* exposed center.

He groans before saying, "Hold her legs out, Cas. Spread her wide open." I feel Caspian's hands prying my thighs apart as far as they'll comfortably go. Fritz plants kisses all over my neck and collarbones, still respecting Caspian's order to not touch my tits. I feel him dragging the toy down my stomach, and I try to rock my hips in anticipation, but I'm stopped by Caspian's bruising grip.

As the toy slides through my wetness, the vibrations start super low, but I'm so sensitive already it makes my legs twitch. Fritz inches it inside me slowly, his kisses getting longer and more greedy. Once it's placed, he looks at my face, silently asking for confirmation that it's in the right spot. *Holy fuck yeah, it is.* I give him a desperate nod, keeping in the whine begging to escape. Showing me a small amount of mercy, Caspian stops the vibrations.

"Good job, Fritz. Look how pretty it looks in her little pussy," he comments, and we both soak in the praise. He tears his eyes away from my center and looks me in the eyes, "Okay, baby, you're going to have full reign to move, but I'm trusting that you won't do anything naughty." He winks, "Remind me what your safe word is if you need to stop."

"Avocado," I pant.

"Avocado. Good job." He climbs off the bed and starts undressing, causing both me and Fritz to ogle and practically drool. "Get over here, Fritz. Let's put that loud mouth to use and give our girl a show," I can't help the whine that escapes me at his words.

Fritz plants one last peck on my cheek and joins Cas on the floor. They're positioned at the foot of the bed, so I can watch them without having to move at all. As he drops to his knees, Caspian frees his cock, giving it a few lazy tugs, causing all three of us to moan. The beading at the tip of him has me licking my lips. I never thought I'd be into sucking cock, but I think I'd make an exception. Two, now.

He slaps Fritz's cheek with it, ordering, "Open." The second he does, Cas shoves himself roughly into Fritz's mouth, and the buzzing in my pussy starts again. The stimulation against my clit and that sweet spot inside has me fighting the urge to roll my eyes back into my head. *Fuck, it's so good. It's too intense. I'm not gonna last long like this.* He's slowly fucking the other man's mouth, one hand gripping his dark waves, directing the pace. His other arm is hanging at his side, with the little red remote in hand.

As I watch him get rougher and rougher with Fritz's mouth, they're both moaning and grunting, Fritz's muffled and gargled and *so fucking hot.* He's clutching Caspian's thighs, and the vibrations are getting more intense as he continues choking on it. My moans are getting higher and louder, closer to frantic cries than anything else. He eases up on the intensity, not letting me fall over the edge, and if he edges me like last night, I'll kill him. I can't fucking take that again. I'm already gripping the sheets next to me, twisting my fingers into them to hold myself on solid ground.

He moans loudly as he buries himself all the way to the hilt, holding Fritz still against him, "Oh, look how fucking good she looks right now. She's dripping on the bed." He pulls out, slapping Fritz's cheek again before plunging right back into his throat, "You love this, don't you baby?" he asks me.

I nod, but that's not good enough for him because he turns the toy all the way up and barks, "Tell me. Tell me you love it."

I'm practically sobbing when I finally force out the words, "I love it. Fuck, I love it. Looks so fucking good." Fritz trying to watch me out of the corner of his eye while he swallows Caspian's cock nearly brings me to the edge. I'm so close, whimpering and moving my hips, desperately seeking release.

Caspian pulls himself out of Fritz's mouth and turns the man to face me, still on his knees, with tears running down his face. They wear matching expressions, chests heaving as they watch my cunt with undisguised hunger.

I can't hold back anymore, and I scream as I come. The orgasm feels like it goes on for hours, and I throw my head back, squeezing my eyes closed as I cry out with each wave of pleasure. It's so intense it almost hurts as I clench around the toy again and again, turning from pleasure to the pain of overstimulation.

As I start to wiggle to stop the onslaught, Caspian finally stops the vibrations. When I can eventually register anything happening around me, the first thing I notice is them laying on each side of me, watching as I come down.

"You're so fucking beautiful when you fall apart, Songbird," Fritz tells me, looking awestruck.

"You alright, Bel?" Caspian asks, and I nod, "Can you take more?"

"More what? More vibrator? No."

He grins before gently removing it, and I hiss as it slides against my clit. "Good girl, telling me what you need. You're doing great, baby." He grabs the lube from next to me before looking back at Fritz, "If you want a taste, now's your chance. You'll want to be distracted for this next part." He raises his brows once in suggestion, and Fritz strips his underwear off faster than I thought possible.

I let out a small giggle that's cut off when Fritz plants his lips on mine. When his tongue brushes against mine, I moan at the taste of him. I've never tasted cock, but I know the delicious, slightly salty taste has to be Caspian.

With my eyes closed, I sink into the kiss, letting Fritz lead me into a dance of tongues and teeth before sucking my tongue into his mouth. He climbs until he's hovering over me, straddling one of my legs. I wrap my arms around his neck, then he suddenly whimpers into the kiss. I open my eyes to see Caspian kneeling behind him. I can't see a damn thing from this angle, but with the way his forearm is flexing, there's only one thing he could be doing.

I pull Fritz away from me enough to watch his face. The pleasure-pain combination of his furrowed brows and panting breaths is intoxicating to watch. I keep switching my eyes back and forth between his face, an expression between pain and pleasure twisting his features, and where Caspian is getting him ready.

He moves one of his hands down between my legs where I'm still so sensitive I whine at the sensation. "Shhh," he urges gently, "It'll feel better in a second, just breathe." As he works my clit in gentle circles, I start moaning and rocking my hips in time with his hand. He sinks two fingers in before whispering in my ear, "Next time, I'm gonna fuck this hot, wet little cunt while Caspian enjoys your mouth." The imagery and his wicked fingers force another cry from my throat, and I'm sure I'm soaking Fritz's hand already.

"Stop stalling, Fritz. Come lick her sweet pussy while I take your tight little fuckhole." *Jesus Christ, where did that come from?* Looking at me with wild eyes, he says, "Neither of us gets to come until you do, baby. So direct our boy exactly where he needs to go."

Fritz moves down my body, planting wet kisses all the way down. At the first swipe of his tongue against my clit, I bury my hands in his hair. "Oh shit, that feels so good."

"You lucky fuck, you get to be the first person to ever taste her." Caspian tells him, "Make that pussy squirt and you can have a treat." Suddenly, Fritz cries out against my pussy, and I know before I open my eyes the sight that will greet me. But knowing it and seeing it are two very different things.

Caspian has Fritz bent over, one hand on his hip, the other holding him by the back of the neck against my drenched core. He throws his head back in bliss, groaning out, "Oh that's so *good.*" He punctuates each word with a slow thrust. His eyes meet mine, and he asks, "You like this, baby girl? Me using Fritz to bring us both pleasure?" he pauses and adds, "Yeah, you fucking do." I quickly nod, moaning at each swipe of the tongue that's working me over. "Should we keep him, baby? Do this all the time?" I nod again, not in a space to think about the implications of that, but I don't fucking care.

Fritz moans again before sucking my clit into his mouth, forcing me to scream his name. Caspian lifts him up by the throat, still fucking up into him, and asks, "How does she taste, Fritzy boy?"

"So good, Cas. So fucking good," he whines out, and my jaw falls slack at the image in front of me. Caspian licks across Fritz's already shiny and wet chin before shoving his tongue into his mouth, giving him painfully rough thrusts as he does.

Caspian growls out his pleasure at the taste before muttering against his ear, "Make that pussy gush or you don't get to come," then shoving him back down against me. Fritz loops both hands under my hips to hold me still while he restarts his onslaught. He buries his tongue as far inside me as he can reach, way further than he should be able to, and I feel the overwhelming tension building inside me.

"It's too much," I start babbling, "I ca-*fuck,* I can't come again."

"Yes, you can, and you will." Caspian orders, "Fritz, don't you dare fucking stop until you hear a safe word or she floods your face."

Fritz sucks my clit back into his mouth, using the tip of his tongue to draw little circles against it, and I detonate. My body tries to close my legs around his head to ease the pressure, but he holds me still, forcing me to take more and more of this sweet torture. Even as I'm clenching and my hips roll of their own volition, he doesn't stop. He keeps hitting that bud with his tongue and sucking on it over and over while I'm crying out, "Please, please, please."

I can't stop coming, and I feel the pressure building in me, and- *Oh fuck.* I drench Fritz's face and the bed beneath him, more than I ever thought would be possible. Every clench of my cunt gushes more liquid, and he drinks down every drop like it's the finest wine.

When I'm utterly and completely spent, barely able to keep my eyes on them, he finally stops. Caspian drags him up by his neck again, moving his other hand from his hip to wrap it around his cock, working it up and down in time with his quickening thrusts.

"Oh, *good boy*, Fritz, making our girl squirt so hard," he praises before looking at me, "What do you think, does he deserve his reward?" I give him a nod, unable to tear my eyes away from where Fritz is leaking precum all over his hand. Fritz seems about as lust-drunk as I feel, unable to do anything except fuck into Caspian's hand and take every ounce of pleasure he's being given.

"Where do you want it, baby?" Caspian asks me, and I don't understand what he's saying until he continues, "There's a little towel right there if you don't want it on you." *Oh! No, I definitely want it on me.*

I do my best to spread my legs a little more, even though they're shaky and heavy, trying to make it clear what I want. I may not be ready for sex, but there's nothing I want more than to be covered in the evidence of Fritz's immense pleasure.

"You want me to paint those pretty pink pussy lips with his cum?" At Caspian's filthy fucking mouth, Fritz moans so loud I know he's seconds away from coming. "Ask nicely." So I do. With the small amount of voice I still have left, I ask *please* very, very nicely. "Come on, Fritzy, she's begging for it. Give her what she wants. Make a mess all over that perfect, sopping cunt so I can fill you up with my spend."

Within seconds, Fritz is shouting out his release, coating my pussy, thighs, and stomach with his cum, followed by a long, rumbling groan as Caspian follows him off the edge. They keep moving together through the final waves of their pleasure, and Caspian mumbles, "You both did so fucking good for me," before kissing Fritz's cheek and gently pushing him to lay beside me and catch his breath.

I look over at the blissed-out smile on his face and suddenly feel Caspian's hot mouth give one long, wet swipe along my slit while watching my face. He sits up and gives me a salacious grin, "You two taste incredible together."

At my slack-jawed expression, he leans in and gives me sweet kisses all over my face and neck, "Good job, baby," he pauses, adding, "you too," before ruffling Fritz's hair and grabbing the towel from the bedside table.

He walks to the ensuite and gets the towel wet before coming back and cleaning up the atrocious mess all over me, then giving Fritz the same gentle care. He hands me his shirt and throws his briefs back on before laying down beside me, playing with my hair. Fritz barely manages to throw his underwear back on before he, too, is snuggled up, drawing patterns along the bare skin of my leg that he draped over himself.

In my half-asleep state, I hear Fritz mumble a thank you, which I don't understand at all. *Who is he thanking?* Then he gently pinches my leg, and I reply with a very dignified, "Huh?"

He sleepily laughs, "I said: Thank you for trusting me with your body in this way."

"Mhmm. Thank you both," Caspian adds. "You did so wonderfully, Bel, setting boundaries and communicating your needs. I am so proud of your bravery."

"Here, here." Fritz agrees.

"You guys are amazing," I tell them honestly. But I can't be too vulnerable, so I add, "Now shut the fuck up and go to sleep."

And after a few moments of chuckles, we all do, snuggled in the warmest sleep pile imaginable.

21

Breakfast of Champions

Caspian

Waking up the next morning with Bel wedged between Fritz and me is not something I would have expected to bring me such joy. It feels like this is where the three of us were meant to end up, but I haven't the faintest idea how we could make this work.

My feelings for Fritz have always been affectionate but never romantic, and as far as I know, he feels the same way. He has never looked at me the way he already does my Little Dove. He looks at her the way I'm sure I do. Like life didn't truly begin until she entered it. I know that I need her, but does he feel that same compulsion?

Who am I kidding? Of course, he does. It doesn't matter that they've only just met. He's willing to travel across state lines and commit cold-blooded murder for her. *We will need to discuss the details of that this morning before leaving.*

I try to extricate myself from Bel's grip without waking either of them, but based on the way he's caressing her sleeping form, Fritz is already awake. I reach across her and flick him gently on the hand. His eyes burst open, ready to defend against whatever threat dare interrupt him. When his gaze becomes clearer, he looks up at me and raises his eyebrows in silent question.

I nod my head towards the bedroom door, so we can go discuss all the events that have transpired while Bel continues her rest. Gods know she needs it. Last night Bel was utterly and thoroughly sated, just the way she always should be. The way she always *could* be if we stayed. I can't just ask her to pick up her life and bring it here on a whim, though, can I?

He looks back down at our sweet girl, still deep in her dreams. The distraught look on his face tells me he knows once we leave this bed there's a chance the fantasy world we've created is over. He grabs a strand of her hair that's fallen over her face and brushes it back, chastely worshipping her with his fingertips across her cheekbones and slightly parted lips.

I feel as though I'm intruding on an incredibly intimate moment. One just for them. The reverence with which he watches her now is wholly at odds with the depraved animal he was last night. She deserves this version of him, too; the soft vulnerability, bare from the jokes he always wears as armor. He breathes out a sigh and gives her a goodbye kiss on the forehead before sliding away from her and out of the cocoon of a bed we've made.

I quietly follow behind him, settling the blankets around her to mimic bodies, ensuring she does not wake too quickly. It's barely sunrise, so she should still rest for a few hours. Long enough for him and I to talk.

In the kitchen, I take a seat at a table and watch him as he prepares us both a large mug of coffee, generously pouring some kind of sweet and creamy liquor into each cup. He hands one to me and drops into the seat next to me.

"So," he begins.

"So, where do we go from here?" I finish his unasked question.

"Mhmm. Where indeed?" I think for a moment, ready to answer, but he proceeds, "You shouldn't have asked if you can keep me last night. It wasn't fair to her. Or to me."

That's not at all what I was expecting him to say. At my confused face, he looks at me as if I'm the most dense man he's ever met. Perhaps I am.

"Something like that can't just be said in the heat of the moment. Because now you either have to actually consider letting the three of us see where this goes long-term, or you have to take it back. All this time, I have been under the impression I get only a couple days with you and your girl," he tells me. *Oh.*

"I have no intention of taking back what I said. I never did. I had considered it already. I've never seen you look at anyone the way you do her. With the flirting and your *visit* yesterday, I thought it went without saying," I explain, hoping that excuses my slip of the tongue.

He's so shocked it takes him a moment to respond, "Does she know that? Or is she going to come out here ready to leave with you, never to return?" he asks, then holds both palms up to stop me, "No. Even if she did want to *explore* this with us both, there's no fucking way you could do it. Sharing for a weekend is one thing but you're too possessive for anything else and I am *not* going to become an enemy of yours over a girl."

"You've known her nearly as long as I have. I don't have any kind of claim on her," those words grate on my tongue coming out, but they are true.

"Do you have any intention of... *claiming* her?" he prods.

The thought of that makes me gag, "To be frank, I'd rather you do that. I'm not sure that I could. It's too risky, the margin of error too great."

"It's far more dangerous if I do it. Yours might be more... grotesque, but there's less risk involved." He's right, of course, but I don't think I could ask that of Bel. There's also the chance that it won't work. I've heard of a few people over the years whose bodies rejected the claiming, leaving them sick or mad for the rest of their lives.

"She's not ready for that discussion any time soon. She's taken everything very well thus far, but I think the idea of eternity with one of our kind would have her running for the hills before we could explain what it means or what it entails." Demons rarely claim mortals, or anyone for that matter, just due to the horrific acts it requires. Except for the *Biberé*, but those guys are sick fucks.

"Oh? You are not in the mood for another game of chase, then?" he chuckles under his breath, adding, "Could be fun. I have lots of ideas for what we can do next time."

I'm sure he does. I roll my eyes, "We have to go *slow* with her. W-"

"*Slow?* Were you there last night? What part of that could be considered slow?" He looks at me incredulously.

"Okay, yes, she is incredibly adventurous. But thus far, all of her adventures have been solo. I do not want to overwhelm her and quite honestly, she does not even know us yet." I want her to pick us– *both of us, apparently.* But I don't want to scare her with our intensity.

"And if she did want me too, you would be willing to give me equal time with her? No competitiveness, no possessiveness?" I understand his trepidation. I did not expect this to be something I would want so fiercely, but I feel it down to my black heart that she needs us.

"Yes. I can do that. I could not, were it anyone but you," I confess, "You are the only person I would entrust with her body and heart. Anyone else would be dead before they get the chance."

"*So* romantic, Cas," he says, hiding his laughter.

"I am serious, Fritz. What if you two spent more time together today before we leave?" I ask," You may... state your intentions and ask what she wants."

"You aren't supposed to be apart from her, remember? Am I supposed to believe you'll just stay here while I take your girl on a date?" I nearly growl in jealousy, realizing this will be a bit more difficult than I originally planned. I want to be there with them for every moment.

But it's not about my desires, it's about theirs. "I will be perfectly safe here. I shall take a trip down to the basement freezer, and then I will find a store to get myself one of those little screens everyone is so addicted to now."

"A phone? You want a phone?" he asks, surprised again.

"Well, from what I've gathered, it is nearly impossible to live without one. Where do I acquire one?" I answer with a shrug.

"You can't just grab one like you can clothes and stuff. You have to talk to a person who sets up the service under your name and stuff. Honestly you should just wait for Bel to take you," he tells me.

"But how will the two of you alert me if you need me?" I do not *want* to be one of the mindless drones I see attached to their tiny computers like it's their drug of choice, but the advantage of instant communication cannot be overlooked.

"We can leave Bel's phone with you and I'll have mine. And I'll text Norman right now to get you your own. It'll be here before you leave this afternoon." He picks up his device and taps away on the screen, "See? Now that's done."

"Thank you," I swallow down the rest of my drink before choking out, "If you are going to take Bel for breakfast, you'll need to go wake her now."

"Can I have Bel for breakfast? That would be a great way to wake her up." *Actually...*

"No. You got to taste her last night." I slide my empty mug in front of him and stand, saying, "I will go wake her. You may watch."

"Fuck, *yes*," he jumps up to stay with me as I sneak back into the room, seeing our girl sound asleep. She'll probably be mad that I woke her up later, but for now, she's going to be a *very* happy little dove. I silently point to the foot of the bed, right where he sucked my cock while Bel watched in rapture, showing him where he can stand to watch.

I slowly climb over her, pushing her fully onto her back, trailing wet kisses along her collarbone. I'm whispering for her to wake up, telling her it's time to get out of bed, practically begging her to open her eyes so I can make her come on my face.

Finally, her eyes flutter open and land on me, "Good morning, baby," I growl, lowering my mouth to her neck again, fingering open the buttons on my shirt she's wearing. "Fritz wants to take you to breakfast without me, so I need to eat before you go."

The sleepy confusion on her face takes a few moments to clear before she's blushing, looking around me to where Fritz wiggles his fingers at her, "Morning, Songbird. You look ravishing. Let Cas have his breakfast real quick then we'll go spend some time together, yeah?" She hesitates only for a second before nodding and breathing out a gorgeous little noise of assent.

I move further and further down, tonguing and biting every inch of skin I can reach, pausing to give each of her perfect breasts the attention they deserve. Once they're both pebbled and she's panting, I continue my journey to the sweet heaven between her thighs.

I pause to dip my tongue into her belly button, and she jerks at the tickling sensation before Fritz whines, "*Ca-as*, I can't see from back here. Your big fucking body is blocking the whole show."

I chuckle against Bel's lower stomach, biting it gently before teasing, "So I have two voyeurs to deal with, do I?" *Mine. My little voyeurs.* Bel giggles between her heaving breaths, and I'm sure Fritz is standing there pouting.

"Get over here," I tell him, adding, "Bel, baby, tell him what to do. I'm going to be a little too busy to do so." Fritz's jump onto the bed makes the whole thing shake, and Bel giggles again. He instantly leans down to start teasing her mouth with little almost kisses that she keeps trying to chase.

I gently slap her inner thigh, reminding her, "Don't let him be a brat, Bel. You're in charge," before I fully spread her legs and take in the sight of her wet pussy begging for me. I groan at how fucking gorgeous she looks right now, soaking wet, skin reddened from her blushing and my marking bites.

Finally listening, she grabs Fritz's hair with both hands and forces their mouths together, taking what she wants. *She's so good at following directions.* As I lean in and swipe my tongue through her wetness, I wonder what else I could direct her to do to Fritz. He can be dominant when he's in the mood, but he likes it best when he's taking orders.

I start fucking her sweet cunt with my tongue, letting it grow closer to its monstrous size to give my girl the best fucking oral she'll ever have. I know Fritz did the same last night, and fuck, did it work. Her frantic little screams left her mouth in perfect rhythm with her gushing, clenching pussy, and I almost came right then and there, watching her soak his face.

Her moans are getting louder, and I'm not ready for her to come quite yet, so I ease off the pressure, switching to slower, teasing licks. She whimpers her frustration and tries to push her hips harder against me, chasing her orgasm. I pin her down by her stomach, fully easing my tongue out.

"What's wrong, baby?" I ask, but her mouth is too busy keeping up with Fritz's relentless kisses. He's absolutely devouring her, sucking on her tongue, biting her bottom lip, and moaning at every sound she makes. I rest my head on her thigh, angling up so I can watch her core and her face at the same time.

I slide a single finger inside her, and she disconnects from their kiss, a surprised moan ripping from her throat. I curl my finger to hit that spot inside her to make her eyes flutter, and we both watch her, entranced. I gently rub that spot again and again before adding a second finger. At the intrusion, she cries out, reaching for my hand to hold my wrist against her.

Fritz starts fucking her mouth with his tongue again, using one hand to play with her breasts, pinching her peaked nipples. Every thrust and curl of my fingers inside her matches a stroke of his tongue. I lean in and gently suck on her clit, turning her moans into cries.

I pause to ask, "Can you take one more, love?" I won't be happy until her body is stuffed full, but three fingers will sate me for now.

Fritz mutters, "Please say yes," mostly to himself, echoing my thoughts.

"Yes, yes, yes," she pleads. I pull back, almost completely removing my fingers before sliding back in, my middle three stretching her so beautifully.

"*Christ*, that's so fucking hot," he rumbles. Once she adjusts, I start moving my hand in earnest, filling her cunt again and again. Her short, staccato screams echo off the walls around us, and *she's so close, just a little lick right there–*

Yes. Oh fuck, yes.

Her wet warmth squeezes my fingers, trying to suck them in deeper as I work her through it, her cries slowly turning into near sobs at the overwhelming pleasure. I keep licking and fingering her until she hisses and attempts to shove me away.

I raise myself into a kneeling position, looking at her blissful expression, eyes closed and lips open. She takes a few breaths and calms down a bit, then looks at us both, squeaking out, "Good morning."

All Fritz says in return is, "Pussy. Breakfast of champions."

I grab the nearest pillow and throw it at his head, causing Bel to burst into laughter. I'm hard as a rock, and they're laughing and making jokes. Once they leave for breakfast, I'll need to find release immediately.

I playfully shove Fritz out of the way so I can give my girl a kiss before telling her to get dressed quickly so they may go. She hops out of bed and runs to the other room, my shirt hanging halfway off her body. I look at Fritz and grin. I've never felt this good before.

They depart 10 minutes later, and I decide to do a little research on a topic that's been plaguing me as of late.

After I make myself come in the shower, of course.

22

You Didn't Hear It From Me

Bel

Fritz whistles and swings our interlaced hands back and forth the entire walk to breakfast. I have to admit, I'm just as excited to hang out with him. I have no fucking clue how we got from strangers to *this* in less than a few days, but it's been such a whirlwind. I've never felt seen by *anyone* the way I am by both of them.

They fulfilled my most wicked fantasies without even fucking me. They gave me everything I never knew I wanted while respecting and even *encouraging* my boundaries the whole way. Is this what sex is supposed to be like? I'll never be able to go back to just toys now. Nor will I ever be willing to settle for anyone else, which is the real problem.

As the host leads us to a table towards the back of the restaurant, Fritz releases my hand, instead guiding me with a hand on my lower back, sending tingles all the way up my spine. We sit across from each other and silently start looking over the menus, but I can't even focus on the words in front of me, too consumed by my spiraling thoughts.

I don't even know how something like this is supposed to work with humans, much less demons. Will they want to do this again? It seems like they're both very into the idea, but maybe this little trip is a one-off? And even if it's not, they're both immortal, and I'm decidedly not. I'll age, and they'll stay the same. It's not like I can expect them still be attracted to me in ten years, much less 30 or 40.

He says something to me, but I don't quite catch it. Looking up at him, I utter an undignified, "Huh?" before amending, "I'm sorry, what did you say?"

His gorgeous face is pulled into a humorous smirk, and he repeats, "Penny for your thoughts? They seem to be very intriguing. Unless there's just an item on the menu that has you enthralled enough to cease blinking." *Shit.*

As I'm about to answer, our waitress arrives, asking about drinks. I order the largest, sweetest coffee they offer, and he does the same.

When she walks off, he waves his hand, wordlessly asking me to proceed.

"Well, I umm, I just- I don't know- I don't know how- or where-" I don't even know how to explain what I don't know.

"Look, Bel. Having a plan for your whole life, filling in the neat little bubbles, meeting deadlines, all of that is important and worthwhile. Truly. But there are some things you just can't plan for." I begrudgingly nod, and he continues, "None of us knew where this chance encounter would take us. But would you go back and change it?"

"No, absolutely not. But the logistics of it all are just so... complicated." That's an understatement.

"It doesn't have to be so complex, Sweets. We'll just take it one step at a time. Keep it simple," he shrugs with nonchalance, "Did you have a good time last night? And this morning? Let's start there."

"Obviously, I did," I laugh.

"See? Easy. All three of us had an incredible night. Are you interested in more nights like that? Or were you only willing to experiment like that for a short time?" Before I can answer, he grabs my hand and adds, "There is no wrong answer, here. If your interest in me ends when your trip does, I will remember this time fondly. If you want to explore more, but only with Caspian present, I'll treasure every moment of that, too. Even if you only want my friendship and alliance going forward, I shall give it to you, no strings attached."

Now I'm confused, "Wait, wait, wait," I hold my free palm up, "Are you telling me that you would want to *spend time* with me, even without Caspian involved?"

He blinks, "I thought that was obvious." *Oh.*

Throwing my hands up in defeat, I explain, "I have no idea what I'm doing here, Fritz. I've never dated one man, much less two."

He gives me a sympathetic smile and grabs both my hands in his, "You're overthinking it. Cas and I are hundreds of years old, so we have exorbitant amounts of patience. There's no need to rush into anything with labels. We want you, you want us. Right?"

I nod again, and he lifts a hand to kiss my palm right as the waitress arrives and places our ridiculous, gorgeous drinks before us. We place our breakfast orders, French Toast piled high with strawberries and bananas for me and some kind of potato and bacon skillet for him.

"I think maybe you're having a hard time because you're thinking of this as an all or nothing situation, yeah? But we aren't a package deal. There's your growing relationship with Caspian, and then our... whatever we are. Two completely separate things that sometimes coincide. Okay?"

It's definitely not as simple as he's making it out to be, but maybe it can be. I'll just... go with the flow. Just thinking that phrase has my stomach dropping. *Going with the flow* has never been my strong suit. But, for them, I'll do my best.

Once the food arrives, we eat quietly for a few minutes, enjoying the comfortable silence. Until one question forces its way out of my mouth, "Would you come visit me? Back home?"

"Of course I'll come visit you," he says around a mouthful, "Although, I think eventually you'll want to move here."

"Move? Here?" I'm dumbfounded. He wants us to move in after two days? "We haven't even fucked and you wanna move me in?"

He chokes on his food, surprised by my abrupt wording. After clearing his throat he answers, "Bel, as I said, we've been around a while. I instinctively know that you are supposed to be here with me- with us," he amends. "In all my years, I've never felt this pull, the... rightness. I don't need more time to learn what my soul already knows."

Dejectedly, I utter my fears, "But I'll... get old. I'll die," his face drops, losing all color, "And what happens then?"

He shakes off the imagery of my death, seemingly debating something in his head before correcting me, "Actually, you don't *have* to die. There are ways around it."

"*What?*" I can't fucking believe it, "How?"

He groans, "It's a really gross and dangerous ritual. And honestly, that's a conversation for you to have with Caspian because *I* will not be doing it."

"Why not?" I prod.

"Because in all likelihood, I'll kill you," he says casually, like we're talking about the weather.

"Kill me?" I repeat, hoping for clarification.

"Yeah," he keeps talking while eating, and I want to reach over and close his fucking maw for him, "Ya know how Cas and I are different types of demons? Well, each classification of demon has their own way of giving immortality to humans, depending on how we gain power."

I narrow my eyes, still not following what he means.

He makes a face like he's disgusted that he even has to bring it up, swallowing down the bite he's been working on before clarifying. "I feed on the life force, the energy. So in order to bind a mortal's life to mine, there has to be an equal exchange, given freely by both parties. I have to drain almost all of their life force, before then filling their body with enough life force to sustain them for presumably forever."

I think about the implications of that, then ask, "But finding the right balance without draining all their life or overdosing them would be too difficult?"

"Exactly! The *Biberé* do a simple exchange of blood," he waves his hand around in emphasis as he speaks, practically weaving the story into the air. "They drink of their chosen human and then the chosen drinks of them. Nasty, but arguably the least dangerous."

"And those like Caspian? The... *Devoré?*" *He can't possibly mean... no, we would have to,* "Absolutely fucking not."

He nods in concession, "Yeah, it's not pretty. But it's far less risky than the other option," I go to argue, but he continues, "Look, Sweets. We don't need to be discussing this now. It's too early. There's no pressure on you to even be thinking about next month, much less eternity."

"Couldn't we just find one of the vampy ones to like help me with the immortality thing?"

He laughs like I just told the funniest joke, "No, Caspian would find a way to killl the unkillable before he allowed it. The exchange creates a bond of sorts. You can feel the others emotions, and find them like a homing beacon. I've heard the sex is mind-blowing." He wags his brows at me, "Not that we have any need for improvement there."

I feel warmth spread across my cheeks and have to shut that shit down, so I ignore the comment and take another bite. Fritz's scorching gaze warms my face further, so I look back up at him, and he smiles, "Hurry up, Songbird. I have more plans for us before you two go back home."

"Really? What are we going to do?" Now I'm so excited I push my plate away immediately. Fritz's enthusiasm is contagious and I want to see whatever he has in store for me right now.

"I'm going to teach you how to play blackjack," he grins and throws a couple $20s on the table before standing and holding out a hand to me. I gladly take it, lacing our fingers together to go on to the next adventure.

* * *

An hour or so later, we are sitting in a private room with a huge poker table. In the middle of a hand, Fritz's phone begins to ring. "Oh, look at that. It's you," he places the phone against his ear, "Why, hello there, Caspian."

I can't hear the other end of the conversation, but I'm assuming it's something about needing to hit the road.

He gasps, dramatizing his revulsion at whatever the other demon said, "I am offended that you would even think such a thing. We are on our best behavior."

He pauses, listening while his eyes traverse my frame for the 100th time before responding, "I am teaching her to play poker. We are fully clothed, unfortunately."

Another pause, "Ugh, okay, fine. You can talk to her," he hands the phone to me.

"Hi" *Why did I say it like that?*

"Hello, my Dove. Are you having a good time?" he almost seems... nervous.

"Yes, we are having a great time. I think I'm getting better," I chirp. Fritz mouths at me, *You're not* before falling into a fit of silent laughter. "Okay, I'm not. But I *am* having fun."

"That's so wonderful to hear. I'm sorry to call and interrupt but if you want to make it home on time, we need to be leaving within the hour," he informs me.

"When can we come back?" I ask without thinking, and Fritz's reaction is to launch at me and grab my face to plant a big kiss on my mouth while Caspian answers.

"We can visit as frequently as you like," I can nearly feel him smiling through the phone, "We can even find the gear you need to record your books so you may work while we're here as well."

Fritz nods with his mouth still locked to mine, then says, "I'll get you whatever you need, just need a list," he puts the phone on speaker, "One of you just send me a photo of her set up and I'll recreate it her room." *My room.* "I'm hanging up now, Cas. I'll return her in ten minutes," he hangs up before letting Caspian say anything else.

"Get up on the table, baby," he murmurs against my lips. *Holy shit, I don't think I can take anymore.*

But his sweet command has wetness flooding my center, so I oblige anyway. I stand from my chair and clamor into a sitting position on the table, legs dangling off the edge. I would know what to expect from Caspian right now, but Fritz is still a mystery to me.

Instead of the treatment and demands I would expect from his rougher counterpart, Fritz stands and gently parts my legs with his knee so he can stand between them. He looks down at me and uses both hands to cradle my face, running his thumbs along my cheekbones. He gazes at me, and I at him, slightly terrified at how vulnerable this closeness makes me feel.

He leans down and plants his lips against mine, using his hold on my jaw to angle my face so he can slide his tongue into my mouth just how he wants. The slow, sensual pace he sets has my head spinning. *He's so good with his mouth.*

I wrap one of my ankles around his calf, trying to pull him closer to me. He smiles into the kiss before upping the intensity, using a stronger hold and firmer strokes of his tongue. I yank on the belt loops of his pants, needing him pressed fully against me. Once I feel the evidence of how affected he is, I rock myself against it.

I must be the most wanton virgin to ever exist. Once one of them fucks me, I'm going to be insatiable.

He moans at the contact before pulling away and placing his forehead against mine, "My Sweet, we don't have time for anything but a few kisses." He runs his nose up and down against mine, "You'll be back soon. Or I'll come to you."

He steps back and helps me hop off the table, wrapping an arm around my shoulder to lead me out the door and back to Caspian.

As we walk, I realize this might be my last chance for a while to ask what I've been wondering for days now, "How did Caspian... die?"

He freezes for a second, then tries to play it off with a shrug, "Hunters sent him to Vankhala."

"Yes, but how? What happened? You guys seem so... invincible," I urge.

"You should be asking him these questions. I was not there," he tells me.

"But you know what happened." His reaction to my question told me as much.

"I do," he sighs. "Long story short. He trusted the wrong woman and she betrayed him, turned him over to the warlocks. They used one of their fancy warded objects to separate his body from its tie to this plane and send it back to the prison realm."

Jesus. "Is that painful?"

"Immensely," he answers tensely. I want to ask more about the woman, but I think that would be an invasion of Caspian's privacy. If he wants me to know more about her, he'll be the one to tell me. "When we are ripped from this plane, we are broken apart to the molecular level, shoved through time and space, and left a formless, thoughtless mist on the other side."

"Has it happened to you?" I ask.

"Thankfully, no. But I've seen it enough times for it to haunt my nightmares."

I wonder if it hurts to come back. I would imagine so. Forcing an entire being together like that has to be torture.

Like he read my mind, he states, "I've heard coming back is worse than going down," with a shudder.

"It is," Caspian's voice utters from behind us, "It is the absolute worst agony you can imagine."

I spin around to face him, his gaunt face proving the truth of his words. Before I can stop myself, I wrap my arms around him.

He laughs without any real humor, "It is alright, Little Dove. I am here now, with you. And those who sent me there are long since dead, nothing but rotten earth." I look up at him, "So who *really* won in the long run?"

His words are so at odds with his expression, but I won't press him. Instead, I just hug him closer before he tells me, "I'm sorry to rush you again, my warrior, but we have to begin our journey home."

After a few hugs and kisses goodbye, along with about a thousand fucking promises to call and FaceTime, we leave Fritz and the glittering city of Vegas behind us. As I begin driving, Caspian doesn't speak much, and I worry he's thinking about the same thing I am.

How could someone betray him like that? I mean, yes, he's a flesh-eating demon. But he's also kind and funny and obviously cares so much for the people lucky enough to know him. If this bitch wasn't already buried, I'd make it my life mission to put her six feet under.

As it is, I have half a mind to find her grave and cuss her the fuck out. I'm too superstitious to really fuck with someone's grave, but I think spitting on hers would make me feel better.

It must be horrible to have those memories brought up. I shouldn't have asked about it. It's really none of my business, and now Caspian is probably reliving the worst day of his life because of me. This is going to be the longest drive ever.

23

Blast From the Past

Caspian

Our drive home has been nothing short of hilarious.

Bel has hardly spoken, but she's fuming so hard she nearly has steam emerging from her ears. Her face has been beet red, and it's as though she's been having a silent argument with someone for nearly an hour and a half.

I would not like to be the one on the other end of her imaginary fight, but watching her have it might be the most entertaining thing I've ever witnessed. Her ire, presumably on my behalf, brings so much warmth to my chest. If Fritz was telling her what it seemed like he was, she's probably cursing Tasha as much as I did when I first learned of her betrayal.

After so long, I cannot help my curiosity, "Darling warrior, won't you tell me what has you so ready to take up arms?"

She snaps her head at me as if she'd forgotten my presence altogether, "What?"

I chuckle and ask again, "Why do you look as if you want to commit murder?"

"Oh. I thought I was being subtle." *She was not.* At my raised brow she gives me an exasperated sigh, "Okay. I was just, like, thinking about this mystery girl who set you up with the hunters. That's fucked up, dude."

She *is* angry for me. For an act hundreds of years ago, this wonderful, brave woman wants to go to war for me. I do not deserve such devotion, but I'm a selfish fuck, so I'm going to soak up every ounce of it.

"As I said, my would-be killers are long dead, Bel. There is no need to curse them," I twirl a finger through her hair and tug, "They are nothing now. Probably being tortured in the mortal version of Hell, possibly even in Vankhala itself."

"Mortals can go there?" she asks, always so curious.

"Only the worst of the worst." I explain, "A soul sent to Heaven or Hell can be... retrieved, in a sense. Not often but it happens. So the worst souls, those who cannot under any circumstance be allowed rebirth, belong to Vankhala. Trapped. Always on the cusp of consciousness, but never able to reach it.

"It's a constant ache of something almost like thought, without the clarity of it." There truly is no worse torture in all existence. "Some of us believe that they fuel the creation of my kind. That their souls are split into three pieces, creating one of each kind of demon. The theory is supported by our growing presence over the millennia, but obviously there is no way to prove it."

She's nodding, soaking in the overwhelming amount of information, without taking her eyes off the road, "And the woman?" she asks, voice full of malice.

"Are you jealous, Belissenda? You did not mind the idea of sharing my affections last night," I joke with her, reminding her of the debauchery she loved so much.

She ignores it, answering, "I- I'm not *jealous.*" *A lie.* "I'm just fucking mad. Why would someone do that to you? What a bitch."

I run a hand through my hair, considering how to explain this to her. I understand her fury, as I felt it too. But she doesn't know any world besides this one, doesn't understand that for Tasha, it was a matter of life and death.

"She had no choice, Bel." I shrug.

"No *choice?*" she repeats, incredulous.

"Things were not... the way they are now. Tasha was a young woman, one I cared for," not anything close to my growing feelings for Bel, but I digress, "I was not her first, but we were intimate several times."

Bel scoffs, "And then she found out what you are and turned you in?"

"I am not in the habit of hiding my true form from those I'm intimate with. A lie about my existence would make any consent given null, don't you think?" I explain, and her jaw drops.

"So she knew? She knew the whole time?" Her voice is growing in volume with each response, and her righteous fury is so beautiful I want to kiss her. All over. I want to turn her cheeks red for entirely less holy reasons.

"She did. She even spoke on one occasion about the claiming," I had no intention of doing that with her, but that is beside the point. "But then her family discovered that she was no longer *pure*." *I hate that fucking word.*

She's lost, so I explain, "In those times, in many communities, it was common to kill an impure woman. They deemed it a matter of morality. An impure woman was considered a disgrace to her family. Usually they knelt around them, prayed for God's *forgiveness*, then hung her in front of the entire town."

"Jesus," she mutters.

"That's the guy," I wink, trying to downplay the horrors I witnessed. She doesn't need to know just how many young women and girls were subject to this heinous practice. "When Tasha was found to not be a *maiden*, her choices were to accept that fate or to place blame on the demon who *tricked* and *seduced* her."

"You," her voice shakes, a tear running down her face.

"Me." I confirm, "Of course I was furious, and I could have confessed about her other dalliances, had I been a crueler being. But it wouldn't have mattered. My life was forfeit either way, being what I am."

"So she turned you over to save herself."

"Can you blame her?" I ask, "I do not." Bel releases countless tears and silent sobs, all for me and my suffering.

I grab the hand she has clenching the center divider, "Bel. She did not deserve the end they would have given her, and my time in Vankhala allowed her to *live*, possibly even have children and grow old. I suffered immensely, but truly I would not take back my choice to remain silent."

Suddenly pulling over, she buries her face in her hands, stating, "I don't care. She made you suffer. She's horrible and I hope she's in Hell."

I awkwardly pull her closer to me, "She did what she had to do to survive. Anyone else would do the same."

She pushes me away, "I wouldn't. I would *never* do that to you."

"You absolutely fucking better," I argue.

"No. I'll die before I let myself be the reason you do."

I grab her behind her jaw, cupping her neck and pulling her to me, I order, "If it ever came down to it, and you had to choose between saving me or yourself, you pick yourself. I do not care what happens, you do not suffer for me. Ever."

She wants to argue further, but I don't let her. I plant a firm kiss on her lips before I pull back and urge her, "Please. Promise me." with a broken voice that sounds wholly unfamiliar to me.

Her tears slow, and she whispers, "Okay, I promise."

"Thank you," I breathe a sigh of relief, then proceed to lick every tear from her face like the depraved animal I am.

The idea of anyone or anything thinking they can take my Bel away from me has me feeling murderous. I'm going to need to go take care of those urges once she's safely tucked in bed. Although Fritz still has the compass, so I'm unsure how far my circle of protection ranges. I sigh internally, surmising I'll have to hold off on any more violence until him and I can go in search of the dead-man who hurt Bel.

Getting to see Fritz again was a pleasant surprise. Bel wanting to watch us fuck was an even better surprise, and she was ethereal in her pleasure. I have never needed to fuck someone as badly as I do her. I need to have every bit of her; I'll have to claim her eventually.

I shouldn't. It's morally reprehensible, and Bel doesn't deserve the torture of being tied to me in such a way. But knowing that she would live through anything and everything, even if I'm not here to witness it, gives me peace.

It should be Fritz. He thinks he would kill her but I know he wouldn't. He feels her as intrinsically as I do, somehow. He would stop before he harms her, of that, I'm sure.

But would she even want that kind of bond with one of us? She would be constantly influenced by our emotions, drawn to us like a magnet, no matter how far we are, or if she one day changed her mind.

It's eternal, and she's not ready for words like eternity.

In an effort to entertain myself on the drive, I play around with the phone Norman retrieved for me. I have no need for most of the features on it, but being able to call Bel when we are apart will be wonderful. Fritz also added a contact number for himself, and someone called Eamon. *That must be his friend who runs the counteraction against the hunters.* Hopefully, I never have need to call him, but better to be cautious.

Bel begins humming along to the songs again, and I know I could live in just this moment forever. When she sings something about a hideaway, she lulls me straight to sleep.

* * *

We arrived home a few days ago, and other than when she has to work, we've spent most of our time together. I've tried my best to refrain from touching her, but I know I've failed. I've finger fucked her to climax countless times since we've been here, and she stroked me until I coated her stomach in my spend earlier. Only a few soft touches from her hand, and I came harder than I thought possible.

She's been working nonstop again today, only pausing long enough to inhale the food and coffee I bring her. I heard her phone tell her it was time to use the restroom earlier, and she *ignored it,* forcing me to drag her out of the studio long enough to take care of herself.

Once she's done for the day and we have dinner, she tells me that she needs to get cleaned up, so I allow her a few moments to herself, settling into the couch. Looking around, I think again about how much happier she could be back in Fritz's home. This apartment feels like a corpse, like there was once life in it, but it's all gone now. If she doesn't want to move, maybe we can get her some artwork to adorn the walls. Fritz had paintings on every available surface, so I'm quite sure he could find her something.

I text him, albeit very slowly, to give him the idea, and within seconds he responds,

Fritz: Why? She's going to move here before long anyway.

I tell him, **You don't know for certain that's what she wants.**

Fritz: She does. It may take her some time, but she knows as well as we do that she's ours.

I'm unsure of what to say to that, but I cannot negate what he's saying. Her tears the other day over my pain stem from more than just her deep sense of empathy. Instead of taking the next hour to tell all of that to him, I simply reply, **Have patience. She may never be ready for that.**

He sends me a picture of a little yellow man who appears to be rolling his eyes. *Ugh, another thing Bel will have to explain to me.*

Distantly, I register her starting the shower. Generally, she takes long, leisurely showers, so I decide to spend some time catching up on more current events. I use the television remote to turn on a documentary that I understand is about the king of tigers, although I don't see how a tiger can be important enough to have sparked millions of people talking about it.

After watching for a few minutes, I understand that it's not about the tigers at all but about the self-proclaimed king of them. Human beings are so fascinating. I feel Bel sneaking up on me much faster than I expected her to be finished cleaning herself.

"Tiger King, huh? This show came out when we were all in quarantine. It was all anyone talked about for weeks," the smile in her voice has me turning to face her.

Instantly I see my mistake. I should not have looked. She's wearing the *smallest* clothing that could possibly be considered pajamas. Teeny blue shorts and a lacy matching tank, hair piled on top of her head haphazardly.

"He is uhhh..." I barely manage to push words out of my mouth, "He seems quite eccentric." I should stop staring, but she's a fucking siren, calling me to sin.

"It starts off funny, but it gets really dark. You might wanna watch something else?" She walks closer, that sweet almond and vanilla scent wafting over me. As she sits beside me and leans forward to grab the remote, I gaze at the soft curve of her breasts, nearly toppling out of her shirt.

She's feigning nonchalance, but her smirk gives her away. She wants to be a tease, and while Fritz might be a little upset he's missing out on so much, he understands the arrangement, and we will make it up to him later. Probably several times if she continues to be as insatiable as she seems.

Cuddling up against me, she releases a content sigh, kicking her feet up onto the coffee table in front of her. All that soft skin, only inches away from me, begging for my touch.

"What are you thinking about, Caspian?" she taunts, having caught my leering at her legs.

"What are *you* thinking about, Belissenda? You smell exquisite, like a sweet dessert and sex all rolled into one, barely clothed in your tiny little sleeping garments." She blushes but doesn't answer, just snuggles further into my side. I wrap an arm around her shoulders, whispering in her ear, "You are playing a dangerous game. Do not forget that *I* am an apex predator and *you* are the pretty little prey I've trapped." I snap my teeth at her in reminder, and her whole body shivers, but she ignores it and pretends she did not come down here to taunt me.

If she wants to be a tease, I'll let her take this game as far as she wants. I run my fingers along her bare shoulder as she selects something else to watch. I do not even pay attention to what it is.

She watches a show about... something, but all I can do is stare at her. She must feel my eyes because she says, "You're supposed to be paying attention."

"I am paying attention," I counter.

"To the *show*."

"But it is not nearly as entertaining as you," I grab hold of her and pull her onto my lap, positioning her so she can still watch her show. I can feel every inch of her body as she attempts to flee. She turns to face me, presumably to express her discontent, even though we both know it would be a farce. "Keep watching, Bel. Pretend I'm not here."

I continue to run my fingers across every inch of skin I can find. I'm not rushing, because for once we have nowhere to go, nothing we need to accomplish tonight. I can just explore my sweet sacrifice and all the sounds she makes for me.

When my thumbs slide against the underneath of her breasts, she sighs quietly, attempting to press herself into my hands. Rather than give her the direct touch she's craving, I slide my hands down across her legs and waist, gently caressing her skin, lightly scratching up her thighs, leaving trails of goosebumps.

Fresh waves of her arousal hit my nose with every touch, intoxicating me. I reach one hand up to wrap around her neck, and she whines. "Did you think you could tease me without consequences, Belissenda?" My hand on her thigh spreads her legs open just a few inches before I scratch up the inside again, getting closer to the heaven waiting for me.

"Caspian," she begs.

"Yes?"

"I want- I think I want-" *By the Gods, please say what I think you are going to say.*

"You want what, baby?" I'll start begging soon if she doesn't say it.

"I want you to fuck me." My whole body reacts to her vulgar words. I groan and roll my hardness against her, fingers on both of my hands flexing against her soft flesh. She releases another whimper, and I can deny her nothing, but I'll try one last time.

"I am not a gentle man. I don't think I'll be able to hold back with you," I try to explain through my lust-addled brain.

"Well, see, that's the thing. You're not a man at all." She stands, and I instantly want her back on her perch in my lap. She begins pacing, and I'm starting to get nervous. She wants me, and I crave her, so what else could she have to say? If she's unsure, we should not do it. Once I have her, there will be no going back for us.

She bites the skin on her thumb before shaking her hands out, then kind of rubbing one over the other as if to soothe her nerves.

"Belissenda," I start, "There is no need to do this. You are free to do as much or as little as you want with me. We can continue watching your show and I'll keep my claws to myself."

She looks at me like I've just uttered the most ridiculous words she's ever heard, "Of course, I want this. That's not a question. I just think... I just was thinking about what you said the other day. About how, like, your existence not being disclosed would make consent not real or whatever?"

"I'm not quite following. You are perfectly aware of what I am," I search for clarity.

"Yeah. Right. Exactly. So like this person in front of me is not you. Not really." *She can't possibly want-* "So it wouldn't actually be fair to you if we fuck with you like-" she gestures at my body, "this, right?"

"Well, that's not *exactly* true. They are both me. The other one is just *more* me," I explain, and she begins to respond, but I keep going, "But you *want* my true form?" I raise a brow at her.

Covering her face with her hands, she nods yes. I bark out a laugh in disbelief, "Oh, Little Dove, I should have known. You truly *do* prefer monsters to men." Allowing a growl to escape me, I stand and grab her face in my hands, tilting her up towards me, "If that's what you want, I'll gladly give it to you."

"Really?" her whole face lights up with that familiar sordid anticipation I've grown to adore.

"Bel, there's nothing I'd love more than to watch your pretty face morph with agonizing pleasure from trying to take all of me inside that little body," I tell her, excitement growing in every breath. "You'll squirm. And scream. You'll cry so beautifully, and I'll wring every ounce of ecstasy from you before you beg me to do it over and over again."

With her face still cradled in my hands, I allow my body to grow to its true form, watching her expression drop into one of apprehension and wonder. The clothing I'm wearing rips against my skin until it's barely hanging on by its last threads. Bel gazes up at me, and she looks so tiny right now that part of me wonders if she's going to shrink away in fear and change her mind.

Instead of doing anything I expect, she pulls my hands off her face and uses them for stability as she steps onto the couch, bringing herself to my height. Then she slowly reaches out and runs a fingertip along one of my antlers, sending shivers down my spine and all the blood in my body rushing between my legs.

"Like velvet," she mutters in awe.

"Explore later." I grunt out, grabbing her by the back of her knees and slinging both legs around my waist, "I need you. Right now. Hold on tight." She does as she's told and grips my antlers with both hands, yelping in surprise. I nearly run us up the stairs toward her room, ready to lay claim to my sweet sacrifice and make her scream my name.

24

You Can Take It

Caspian

I move as quickly as possible, kicking open her bedroom door and throwing her onto the bed. She giggles and tries to roll off the other side of the bed to run, but I catch her by the ankle and drag her to me. Her deep red tresses create a waterfall of color as she's brought closer to me.

Laughing, she kicks my hand and tries to crawl away again. She wants to play but I am in no mood. With a growl, I claw off the tiny bits of clothing hiding her from me, forcing a gasp from her lips. I crawl over her, pinning her legs down with mine, grinding against her. The only thing separating her from me is the threadbare remains of my *joggers,* as she called them.

She moans at the feeling of me pressing against her, and the scent of her arousal fills my nostrils. Were I feeling less frantic, I'd take my time and explore every inch of her perfect skin, but I'm aching to have her wet warmth wrapped around me. We have all the time in the world to play and learn each other. Next time we have our third playmate, I'll have him pin her arms and legs while I lick her all over.

She seems to be on the same page as me, pleading, "Please, Cas. I've been teased for days, I need you."

"It's not being *teased* if you're getting all the orgasms you could ever want, My Dove." I get up to my knees, straddling her legs, "Teasing is what *you* were up to in those frilly little pajamas, rubbing yourself against me like a wanton whore." She whimpers, looking up at me from her trapped position. I rip the last bits of my pants off and give myself a few slow tugs, watching for her reaction.

Her jaw drops as she eyes my cock, and I swear to the Gods her mouth is watering. "There's no way that's going to fit inside me," she says quietly to herself.

With a laugh, I remind her, "Do not forget, I have seen your collection of toys, Bel. You can take it," she nods, still unsure, "but first, I'm going to eat this little cunt until it's soaked and ready for me."

I drag the point of my tongue between her breasts, all the way up her neck, over her jaw, and shove it into her too-small mouth, nearly gagging her with it. At the intrusion, she moans and subconsciously pushes her hips up, seeking the friction she needs. As I thoroughly ravage her mouth with mine, I run a hand back down the trail I left with my tongue and roughly grab one of her tits. Using the claw on my thumb to rub little circles, I force more delicious, muffled moans to escape her.

After giving the other one the same attention, I start moving down her body, leaving sloppy kisses and gentle bites in my wake, careful not to scrape her with my antlers. Finally reaching my destination, I lift her legs up over my shoulders, baring her completely to me. I bury my face in her, inhaling her sweet honey and growling out my pleasure.

She releases a harsh sigh at the brief contact, already so wet and needy. I start with one long, teasing lick against her, beginning at her beautiful opening and ending with a small circle around her clit. Her little cry urges me on, so I repeat the motion. She's fisting the sheets, trying to remain composed, but I need her as messy and feral as I feel.

I flip us until she's suspended above my face, hovering. She's looking down at me, shock written all over her features. From my position, I slide my massive tongue out again and use the pointed tip to flick her clit before ordering, "Sit."

"Uhhh, I'm gonna crush you," she pants.

With a laugh, I tell her, "You won't hurt me," I lick her again, and my eyes roll into the back of my head at her taste, "Grab the antlers and go for a ride, baby."

She grips me- *finally*- and tentatively sits her soaked pussy on my face. I moan into her flesh, and she begins to rock against me.

Good girl.

I slide my hands underneath her ass and wrap them around where her hips meet her thighs, locking her against me. Each movement of her hips against my face wrings more sweet sounds from her. I use my tongue against her clit with each motion, groaning and growling against her, the vibrations bringing her higher and higher. She's gripping me, using my antlers to propel herself as she rocks again and again. It feels so gods damned exquisite, sending sparks of pleasure down my spine with each surge of her hips.

She's riding me so hard, so fucking good.

I can't wait to feel her doing this on my cock. The thought has me burying my tongue as deep inside her as I can reach, and she screams. I keep it inside her, writhing against her walls as they start to tighten. She's seconds away from coming, babbling half sentences about how good it is and chanting my name in prayer.

I long to tell her she's doing so perfectly, to beg her to come for me, but with my tongue very occupied, I just groan against her and pull her harder to me.

Her whole body tenses for a second, her mouth open in a silent scream before she finally shouts out her release. Her soft, warm walls pulse around my tongue, trying to pull me further inside her sweet body. *Fuck, if I could get deeper I would.* Her sweetness floods my mouth as she whines out my name. While she's still slowly rocking herself through her peak, I gentle my movements, prolonging her pleasure.

When it becomes too much, she uses her grip on me to push herself off my face and rolls onto the bed beside me. The blissful, open-mouthed smile on her face has pride bubbling up in my chest. Leaning over her, I plant my lips to hers gently, using my lips to tug on her lower one. She sighs and wraps her arms around my neck, pulling me in for a deeper kiss. I allow her to pry my mouth open so she can taste herself on me, and she moans when she does.

I pull her on top of me, straddling my thighs. She has the perfect view of my very impatiently waiting erection, though she seems nervous about touching me in this form, so I reach down and fist a hand around it, watching the hunger light up her face.

"Give me your hand, love." She reaches out, and I wrap her hand around my shaft with my hand covering it. I move our hands up and down a few times, pumping myself into them. Moaning, I mutter, "Just like that."

I remove my hand and lace my fingers behind my head to watch her work me over. She doesn't realize it, but with each pump of her hand, she's moving her hips, mimicking the act we're both begging for.

"Caspian, I-" she mumbles.

"You want it?" she nods fervently, "Take it. It's yours." I can't be the one to make this final step for her. She has to be the one to take it for herself, to take her power back.

She's still pumping, letting my precum leak down her hand. If she doesn't sit on it soon, I'm gonna come all over us both, "Just pretend I'm one of your toys and use me for your pleasure," I assure her, trying to remain calm enough for the both of us.

Oh, finally. Finally.

She moves herself to hover above me and wraps her hand around the base, her pale skin contrasting against the shiny blue-black of mine. Her slightly terrified eyes meet mine, and I'm sure I look as wild as she does. I give her a slight nod, not daring to move an inch lest I scare her off. She begins to lower herself onto it, and as she sinks onto the tip of my cock, I have to clench my teeth to stop from lifting my hips and sheathing myself inside her.

She releases a sound that is a whimper and a sigh all at once, sliding down a bit more. Her brows are furrowed from the stretch, and *sweet gods above* she is glorious. She moves back up a bit, and the friction has me digging my claws into the bedding I'll have to replace tomorrow. With a deep breath, she sinks all the way down until we are completely joined at the hips. I groan out in relief as she gasps from the intrusion, eyebrows pinched from the stretch.

I let her have a moment to adjust even though every instinct is telling me to thrust upwards and make her cry out. At the first motion of her hips, my eyes flutter shut and my head lands forcefully on the pillow beneath me. This is the closest I'll ever get to heaven; being inside my gorgeous girl's perfect body. Nothing has ever felt so *good* and *right.*

Another rock on me accompanied by the sweetest moan to ever grace the earth. She's fucking herself on me just like I instructed, taking her pleasure from my body. She gasps when my cock hits the perfect spot, and I grip her hips to steady myself.

"Baby," I sigh, unable to keep quiet any longer, "You feel so good, fuck, make yourself come on my cock." I have to have it. I *have to.*

She rolls faster, moving back and forth, making me hit that sweet spot inside her over and over, drawing a keening sound from her each time. Once she finds the rhythm she needs, I surge up with each roll of her hips, grinding against her clit. Her cries turn frantic, as do her movements.

She uses both hands on my chest for balance, riding me so hard the bed springs add to the symphony of her cries and my panting breaths.

"Cas, I- I'm gonna-" her brows furrow, and her jaw goes slack, eyes locked on mine as she's tumbling toward the edge of ecstasy.

"Let go for me, Little Dove," I pray to the goddess riding me before reaching down with one hand to rub a thumb against her clit, giving her the last push she needs.

Yes, yes, yes, yes. With her next movement, Bel falls apart, strangling my cock with her perfect cunt. Using my grip on her, I keep her moving through it, forcing her to stay in rapture until she's fully spent and her legs are twitching from the aftershocks.

"Bel?" I ask to make sure she's still with me.

"Mhmm?" she answers, unfocused eyes on me.

"You a little cock-drunk, baby?" I chuckle at her dazed expression.

"Mhmm."

"Yeah? Poor thing," I gently taunt as I slowly roll her onto her back, nudging her nose with mine, "You still owe me one more."

"I can't," she whines.

"Awe, that's really too bad for you, isn't it?" I ask her, shallowly thrusting into her. "You wanted to play with the monster, now the monster wants to play with you.”

She moans at that. So loud and primal, showing me how much she craves the depraved. There's a wild beast beneath her perfect flesh, just inches from the surface, never before allowed to show herself. “Wrap your fucking legs around me,” I bark, collaring her throat with a clawed hand, wrapping it all the way around her neck. She does as she's told, and I reach my other hand up to the headboard and grip it so I can pound inside her.

With a growl rumbling in my chest, I bury myself fully inside that hot, wet pussy. *Hard.* I'm using way more force with her than I should, but she loves every second. Her breaths are coming out in frantic shrieks, the sounds of her body meeting mine being drowned out by her cries and the bed smacking the wall.

Her little hands turn into vicious claws, raking across my shoulder, my forearm, anywhere she can reach. *There's my feral animal.* I look down to where I'm splitting her open, watching my cock leave her pussy, practically dripping, before I force it back in. I move my hand from her throat to behind her head to make her watch, too.

“You see that, Little Dove? See that pretty pink pussy taking me so well?” She tries to nod, sobbing from the sight and overstimulation. “My cock was made to fill your little body. And your pussy was made to come wrapped around me. Now *give me what's mine.*”

She screams, the flutters of her cunt pulling me over the edge with her. I don't bother holding back the growling moan it forces from my throat. She keeps screaming while I pump every drop of cum inside her sweet body, prolonging our pleasures.

As I come down, I lean down and kiss every bare inch of her skin within reach; her face, across her chest, and her shoulders, before gently removing myself from her wetness.

“You did so well, love.” I whisper, “So fucking beautiful right now.” I can't stop praising her, she's so perfect. She's always beautiful, but sated, full of bliss and my cum? She's never been more gorgeous. “I'll be right back,” I kiss her nose, easing off her and heading to grab a towel.

By the time I return, she's nearly out cold. I huff out a laugh, telling her,

"Bel, you can't sleep yet. I need to take care of you."

"Nuh uh. 'm fine," she mutters.

Relenting, I do the best I can to wipe up the mess between her thighs before I climb in behind her, wrapping us both in the blanket, cocooning us in its warmth.

"Thank you," she whispers.

"For what?" I play with her hair, loving the new scent covering her. *Mine.*

"For the sex, duh."

"No, Little Dove. Thank *you.* It was entirely my pleasure." I kiss the back of her head, caressing her cooling skin and running my fingers through her hair until her breathing evens out.

Within moments, I follow my Bel into the realm of dreams. *I will follow you wherever you go*, I promise her silently as I doze off.

25

Digital, Digital Get Down

Bel

I think it goes without saying that the next few days are filled with endless sex. We fuck on every inch of my apartment, both in his human and demon form. Okay, except for the kitchen. Not because I don't like the idea of kitchen sex but because I can't walk in there without wondering about the possible contents of my freezer.

I don't think there are any more human parts in there, but I can't be sure without asking, and I'd rather not.

We've also been talking with Fritz a lot. He FaceTimes me or us almost every day, so I feel like we are kind of getting to know each other. I mean, he knows my body very well, so I guess at some point we need to catch up conversationally to *that.*

I think they're planning a trip without me, which is fantastic. I need a fucking break from Caspian's insatiable appetite. Maybe he can fuck Fritz's brains out for a few days instead of mine so I can get some fucking rest.

Last night when he was balls deep inside me, seconds away from making me come, Fritz called. He made me answer it and try to keep my cool while he slowed down and didn't let me come until I successfully got off the fucking phone. It was *misery,* and I loved every second.

There's no way he was fooled; Fritz was cackling during our entire conversation. Plus he texted me not even 30 seconds later, asking when we would all get to have naked time together again.

We're having so much sex I'm basically screening Isla's calls. *Okay, maybe that's not the only reason.*

Isla is too fucking smart. She sees everything. The second she talks to Caspian and asks him about his past for more than two seconds everything will unravel. Plus, it's not like I can just say, "Oh, yeah, this is one of my boyfriends. They're both demons, but, like, nice ones." *Boyfriends? Is that what I have?* I mean, we haven't really discussed it, but if I had to give this situationship a name, I guess they are.

I haven't asked them about exclusivity because how do you ask about that kind of thing in this situation? Do I expect them to abstain from everyone but me? I won't be able to keep up with Caspian's needs forever, plus there are *two* of them. There's no possible way I could do that. Obviously, they have each other, too. But would they want other women?

The idea of that makes my blood boil, but obviously, one woman who has just barely entered into the sex-having portion of her life won't be able to satisfy the needs of two ancient, powerful beings. It doesn't make any sense to expect that of them. But if they did fuck another girl, I don't think I'd like that very much.

"Hello?" Caspian prods, breaking me out of my trance.

"What?" I ask.

"Why do you look the same way you did when I told you about Tasha?" *Oh fuck, busted.*

"I do not."

"You absolutely do. Down to the silent conversation you seem to be having," he chuckles.

"Oh. It's nothing. Just thinking." I change the subject, "Did I hear you and Fritz talking about taking a trip together?"

He freezes as if he's been caught doing something horrible, so I assure him, "I think that's great! It'll be awesome for the two of you to like catch up some more without me around to distract you."

He slowly nods his head, chewing on the pasta he made for dinner before carefully responding, "Yes, we have been discussing spending some time together. He wants to introduce me to his friend that runs the *Arcana Militum*, see what I should be doing to hide my presence from the hunters."

"Oh, that's a wonderful idea. And you two can spend some *quality* time together so you can give my body a break and go to town on his instead." Am I a little jealous that I won't get to see it? Of course. But they deserve time to enjoy just each other too.

He looks at me like I've said something utterly ridiculous, before clearing the expression from his face and asking in a mocking tone, "Have I been going too hard on you, Little Dove? I seem to recall you literally begging for *more Cas* and *harder Cas* and *please, Daddy-*"

I slap a palm over his mouth, muttering, "Okay, I get it." He licks my palm, and I release him. Wrapping a hand around my wrist, he mimicks taking a bite out of my hand before placing it back down in front of me. He grins at me before chomping down on another piece of food, and I just stare at his stupid gorgeous face.

He's right about the begging, I guess. But it's not my fault. Even before he went under, he had over a century to master his technique, and I'm only fucking human.

"You're thinking about it again," he says, voice full of mirth.

"Shut up," I throw a breadstick at him.

He dodges it and lets out his booming laugh that always startles me before standing and holding out his hand for me, "Come. I had an idea I wanted to try, and it seems like you are perfectly ready now."

"Again?" I groan, even though we both know there's nothing I would like more. He just grins, waving his hands upwards to signal to *get my ass up.*

* * *

Twenty minutes later, he's in full demon form, face between my thighs. His hands are behind my knees holding them up and wide fucking open. I've already come once, but he hasn't stopped. He still hasn't told me which part of this is his big idea, and I've only got about ten seconds before the rubber band snaps again, and I lose all sense of time and space.

Suddenly his phone is hovering in front of my face, dialing a video call to Fritz.

Caspian lifts his face from me just enough to tell me, "Do not hang up that phone." I nod and grab it from the air. "Point the camera right here, Bel. Show him what he's missing."

I'm trying so hard to keep the phone still, but my hands and legs are twitching with every pass of his tongue against me. The phone keeps ringing until I assume he's not going to pick up. All the while, Cas has been switching between fucking me with his tongue and working my clit, never letting me get to the peak I so desperately need.

"Hey Cas, what's goin- *oh, fuck yeah.* Christ, you couldn't warn a guy? What if I was working- *oh, that's so hot.* You sound so fucking good, Bel." My eyes are squeezed shut, but I hear a frantic rustling from the other side of the call, so I'm assuming he had to quickly drop trou, "Don't make her come yet, Cas. I wanna come with her."

Caspian pulls his mouth from me again, licking his lips before saying, "This is just the appetizer, Fritzy. You don't wanna come too fast and miss the main course, do you?" *Appetizer?* At my mildly horrified look, Cas winks at me before restarting his ministrations.

"Bel, Sweets, you look so good. Fuck, that pussy's pretty. Get the phone up higher, I need to see all of her when she comes," he pleads, desperation coloring his tone. Caspian takes the phone out of my hand with his powers and hovers it high enough to put every inch of me on display for this lewd call.

Then he *finally* sets a steady pace, working me with his tongue while I try to rock myself against his soaked face. In the background, I hear Fritz moaning and groaning about how good I look, how hard I'm fucking Caspian's face, and how much he wants to be tasting me, making me writhe like this.

It's too much. Too much sound and stimulation, and I'm screaming my release, pulsing around Caspian's far too large tongue as he slowly brings me back down. Once I return to Earth's atmosphere, Caspian orders me, "Flip over. On your stomach. Ass in the air."

Fritz practically chokes through the phone, watching as I lazily roll over, arch my back and maneuver my knees underneath me. Without warning, I'm hit with the sharp pain of Caspian's teeth biting into my ass cheek, nearly hard enough to break skin. I cry out from the magnificent pain, and both of them growl at the sound.

"Oh, shit, lemme get a close-up of that mark, Cas." I overhear the wet sound of Fritz working himself over as Caspian licks the sore spot, soothing the ache. "Christ, that's gorgeous. Looks *so* perfect, baby."

Before I can respond, Caspian gently fists my hair, asking me if I'm ready to take him again. I nod the best I can with my face buried in the pillows, and he kisses my spine before rising back up and slamming to the hilt inside. I shriek at the sudden intrusion before he pulls out almost to the tip and does it again.

The sounds of their moans and my cries, along with the slap of his body hitting mine, fill the air, creating the most erotic song known to man. Caspian's harsh thrusts border on painful, each one causing me to shriek.

It feels so fucking good, so brutal, and my legs are about to give out. They're shaking from the tension, having already endured so much fucking sex over the last few days. Out of the corner of my eye, I see the phone land on the bedside table before Caspian lifts my head, forcing me to look at it. The screen is filled with the image of Fritz tugging on his cock, along with a miniature showing of my face as I'm being filled to the brim and shoved into the bed.

"Oh," Fritz whimpers, "Sounds so incredible. You two-" he moans again, "are fucking perfect." Another loud moan, "Make her come again- *please- fuck*, make her come." His pleading is intermingled with the sounds of him fucking up into his fist.

My legs are pulled out from under me, and I land on my stomach. Caspian sinks his weight down on top of me until he's pressing his giant body against every inch of me, pushing his cock even further inside me. He's pressed right against my g-spot, and I groan, then yelp when he starts to move again.

He loops a hand under me, locking it around my neck while leaning his weight on his other elbow next to me. Leaning down, he licks me from my jawline up the side of my face before telling me, "Every inch of you tastes delicious, my dove."

Each roll of his hips in this position has me seeing stars. I'm utterly boneless, a panting, sweating, mess. I grip the sheets as Caspian thrusts into me in a torturously slow grind. His cheek is pressed to mine, both facing the camera, watching Fritz as he watches us.

"Oh, *baby*, you see how hard he is for you?" Caspian groans, "Look at him fucking his fist wishing it could be you." With a dark laugh, he adds, "You want this pretty little pussy, don't you Fritzy?"

Fritz nods, but Caspian just tsks and condescends, "Tell her. Tell her how bad you wish it was her." He ups his pace, fucking into me and hitting that spot over and over.

"So bad- *fuck.* So bad. I wanna fuck you so long and hard you can't walk for days," Fritz's filthy mouth mixed with the grunts and growls escaping Caspian have me panting out little cries with every breath. "I wanna watch my fucking cum drip from your swollen, pink pussy. Watch Cas lick it up again- *fuck, I'm gonna come.*"

"Come on, Fritz. Let her watch you spill all over yourself in your need for her." Caspian's words are getting louder, his thrusts sloppier, and his grip on my neck is making me lightheaded. *Shit, shit, shit, I'm so close.* Fritz whimpers again and groans, his face looking almost agonized as he lets his release coat his chest and stomach.

Him falling apart while watching us catapults me straight into my own orgasm. I'm instantly hit with waves of pleasure, my whole body shaking while I'm fluttering around Caspian's cock. I'm sobbing as Caspian fucks me harder and rougher through it, cursing in my ear, "Yes, baby, strangle my cock. Just like that, *oh, fuck yeah.*" Then he bites down— *hard*— on my shoulder, muffling the sounds of his orgasm as he gives me a few more pumps, burying his spend inside me.

"Holy shit, I've never come that hard that fast." I barely register Fritz saying in a dazed voice, "So like... when are you guys coming back again?"

I laugh— well, sort of. I still have a giant demon resting on me, so I can barely breathe enough to laugh. Caspian kisses all over my cheeks, leaving the same little pecks he always does after sex.

Through his slowing breaths, he answers, "You are supposed to come here, if you've forgotten."

"Right, right, can we move that up? I can be on the first flight out. In like an hour," he claims.

Easing off of me, Caspian rolls me over, checking my neck first, then the rest of me for bruising. He asks me, "You alright, love?" and I nod, telling him I'm great. "Good girl," he whispers before kissing my nose and responding to Fritz, "No. We have plans. We leave in three days time for our-" he looks at me strangely, "*alone time* trip."

"Our- oh, right, right. Yeah, I'll be flying in on Wednesday to pick you up in a rental." He seems unsure of what to do next, "I uhhh, I gotta get this cleaned up, so I'll talk to you guys later. You did *great*, Bel. So beautiful. Thanks for, uhhh this," he gestures to his body, still covered in drying cum. "Bye!" He blows me a kiss and hangs up the call.

Caspian nudges my cheek with his nose, "Did you like my idea?" he asks in the most innocent voice I've ever heard from him. As if he didn't just rail my brains out in his massive demon form- *that he's still wearing*- with an audience.

"It was definitely inventive. You seem to be adjusting to the modern world very well," I answer honestly, "I never would have come up with something that devious."

He grins, wide and beaming, and I reach up to touch his stunning, terrifying face. He nuzzles into my hand, and it occurs to me that he must not have had this kind of affection in this form before. It makes no sense to me. He's so arrestingly beautiful like this, so inhuman and otherworldly.

I should have known I would be a monster fudger if monsters were real. Though his treatment of me has been anything but monstrous. If anything, he shows me more respect and kindness than any man I've ever known.

"What are you thinking, my Bel?" he asks, searching my face.

"I just... I'm happy to know you. To have you," I admit against my better judgment.

"Truly?"

I nod, biting back the damning words trying to escape. Revealing what

I already have feels like a gamble. Like caring for him means I'm doing something stupid. I probably am, but hey, it's too late now. I really tried to get rid of him, but I know now I'll never be able to. I'd never want to. Either of them, really. Even armed with that knowledge, I'm not ready to surrender the small protection I have left.

Without any more words, he transforms into his human body and kisses me again. Rather than the hungry kisses I've quickly become accustomed to, this one is more like the one against the door last week.

He's slowly, tenderly exploring me, learning my mouth intimately. I feel him hardening against my leg again and I pull away to look at him. His smile is almost sheepish if he were capable of such a thing. But the dastardly man just kisses me more, speaking against my lips, "I need to have you again, Bel. Please tell me I can."

What am I supposed to do? Turn down more orgasms? Absolutely not. So *obviously* I tell him yes again.

And again, and again, and *again*.

26

Teamwork Makes the Dream Work

Caspian

Mid-afternoon on Wednesday, there's a knock at the door. "Are you expecting someone?" I ask Bel.

"Oh, shit. She's early. She wasn't supposed to be here until you guys left." She comes running down the stairs and answers the door. Isla stands on the other side with a big grin on her face until she sees me.

I wave awkwardly, and she returns the gesture. As she enters the apartment and shuts the door behind her, she whispers to Bel, "You said it was just us tonight. I don't care if you bring your boy but you gotta warn me at least. Communicate, ya know, so I can bring a date, too."

"Oh. No, he's not coming. He's about to leave." *Shit. Fritz is here.* Another knock and Bel's eyes go wide as she looks at me.

"Little Dove, Little Dove, let me come in!" Fritz sings from the other side of the door.

"Who the fuck is that?" Isla's confusion and humor are written all over her face, and I'm not entirely sure how much we are supposed to tell her.

Bel answers the door and lets Fritz in, giving him a wide-eyed look and a shake of her head, hoping to signal for him to be quiet. He sees our unexpected visitor and narrows his eyes at her, tilting his head as if confused by her standing there.

When he remembers himself, he reaches out to shake her hand, "Hello, lovely. I'm Fritz. I'm-"

"He's here for Caspian. That's why he's here." Bel hastily explains, "Fritz is Caspian's best friend," to which Fritz puts a hand on his chest as if it's a huge honor and mouths *best friend?* to me. "They're leaving. Going out of town. Guys vacay."

Isla looks at the three of us cautiously before drawling out, "Oooookay. I'm Isla. Nice to meet you." I get the feeling she doesn't believe a single word, but unfortunately, that's an issue for Bel to manage once we've left.

"And you," he gives her a quick nod before turning expectantly to Bel.

"Okay, bye guys. Good to see you, Fritz," Bel practically shoves him back towards the door. He looks a bit wounded, I'm sure he wanted to be allowed some affection, but he understands her need for... *discrepancy.*

I, however, am too desperate to be denied her touch. I grab my measly bag of items and walk towards her, wrapping a single arm around her and snatching a quick kiss. I look at Fritz and give him my cruelest smile, taunting that I got one more taste of her lips, and he's been without them for over a week.

Isla sees everything, as she always seems to, and I truly feel for Bel. Her best friend is far more perceptive than the average human, and having to explain our nontraditional relationship is going to be uncomfortable. Surely, Isla wouldn't care about something so trivial, but I get the feeling discussing her private life at all makes Bel nervous.

I tell Bel that I'll text her as soon as we get to our destination, but she assures me it's entirely unnecessary. Keeping the truth from her causes a pinching pain in my throat, but it's for her own good. As much as she hates the man who harmed her, she doesn't deserve the weight of his death on her shoulders. I'll gladly take that weight for myself, though. I'll relish in the spilling of his blood and ripping of his flesh.

My last kill was lackluster at best, a quick snap on a dance floor, completely bloodless. This one will no doubt be my favorite murder.

As we walk down the hall, Fritz finally asks, "Does she not know where we're going? You've totally avoid-"

"No, she thinks we are going away for some *alone time,*" I use what I've learned are called air quotes, "I do not want her knowing we are killing that man."

"Why not? It's romantic as fuck. Lots of guys *say* they'd kill for their girl, but we're actually *doing* it," he gushes, giddy at the prospect of our perverted form of justice.

Fritz is not usually a vicious man by nature. Because of his classification, he doesn't need to kill or even harm to survive. He just soaks in a little life force from all those around him. The energy he feeds from also gives him an overwhelming empathic ability. As he's explained it to me in the past, emotions are basically pure energy, so he has to feel those of the people he's feeding from.

I do not envy him that. My craving for flesh and the violence that comes with it is far less daunting than the idea of being influenced by those around me. With this sense of empathy, I have found myself wondering occasionally if it's also skewed his view of justice and vengeance. There isn't much gray area for him. If someone has been wronged, he feels the need to extract payment swiftly and with equal pain as the grievance caused.

"By the way, what's up with that other girl? She looked ready to stab me in the fucking eye if I came too close," he continues, unfazed by my being lost in thought.

I laugh, "Isla is Bel's best friend in the entire world. She does not miss a thing so you'll need to watch yourself around her."

"Oh, she totally knows we're both head over heels for Bel." *An understatement.* "But if she's friends with our girl, she's friends with us. We'll win her over. Eventually."

"We shall see."

"So Bel thinks we are going away to just, what? Have fancy dinners and fuck? Without her?" he asks.

"She does. She seemed rather excited by the idea, so I didn't feel the need to correct her." I explain. Her eyes always light up when she remembers the night the three of us had our dalliance, and I'll have to give her a repeat performance soon. I had half a mind to call her while denying Fritz an orgasm so she can see how good *he* looks when he's a needy, desperate thing, but without her near enough to touch and taste, the appeal is gone.

"But, no offense, why would she think we would want to do anything that doesn't involve her?" he asks.

I shrug, throwing my bag into the car he points out to me in the lot, "She seems to think that because we've had each other before, we see each other in a romantic sense."

"Huh," he laughs, "I mean that makes sense, and the sex is *fire* but without Bel? Meh. You're not as hot without her underneath you."

"I wholeheartedly agree, but this was the only way we could do this without gaining her suspicion," I tell him.

He slowly nods his head around in thought before answering in a grave tone, "We'll have to tell her eventually. I won't keep this from her, nor will I let her be under the impression I care for anyone but her."

He's right, of course. I don't want to deceive Bel either. But my bloodthirst is blurring my vision, and I can make it up to her later. I'll spend eternity doing so if I must.

This car ride is exponentially more boring than the ones I've had with Belissenda. Fritz wants to listen to an audiobook, and not one of the good ones like Bel narrates. He tells me that keeping up on current events is a full-time job, but that sounds terribly dull.

I allow myself to doze in and out of consciousness, but I'm suspicious that Fritz is doing something to me in my sleep. At one point, I wake up with a tiny piece of paper in my mouth that could not have gotten there on its own. And Fritz can never hide his amusement, no matter how he tries.

I flick him on the ear, and he just chuckles, waving me off. "So what's the plan when we get there?" he asks, "We didn't discuss much, but since you told her we'd be gone a few days I'm guessing this is not just an in-and-out kind of situation."

I sigh, "It is not." If I'm being honest, I want to watch long enough to prove that he deserves this. I already know that he does, but Bel will not see it that way. People like him do not change; they only get craftier and crueler. She will need to know for herself that relieving him of his body is the proper treatment. "I think we will need some reconnaissance for a day or so, ensure he is not the type of man to have a full team of guards."

"And with the other days?" I grin and snap my teeth at him, making my intentions clear, "Got it," he smiles. It will not be our first kill together. Not by a long shot. But never have we been so on the same page. Anyone who hurts our girl dies painfully and slowly.

We make a quick stop by the hotel to grab the keys to our room and drop off our things. I take the bed closer to the window so I can be awoken by the sun, and Fritz indelicately tosses his bag onto the other before stalking back to the open door, asking, "Shall we?"

Ten minutes later, his phone alerts us that we have almost reached the destination. Not a moment too soon, as the sun has just fully disappeared behind the mountains, fog descending across the ground.

Fritz turns his lights off and pulls his car to the side of the road before pointing, "That's the one."

I give the house a once over. A large home nestled between other large homes. No sign of personality, just two matching SUVs. Every inch of the home is covered in status symbols. They have warning signs for a security company, yet no cameras of any kind. I roll my eyes, *Humans think their money makes them invincible.*

We silently exit the vehicle, both dressed in all black to hide in the dark. As we creep around to the back of the house, I can sense five people inside. Three kids, two adults. *Bel did mention he has kids.*

It irks me that she's spent time worrying about him and where his life has gone while not allowing hers to move forward. This filth deserves every ounce of pain coming to him for taking these years from her.

We watch silently as they put their three children to bed, two girls and a boy, spitting images of their mom. She seems kind enough, though a little timid. In fact, the entire household seems to be treading lightly, like they're moments from disaster.

The pit in my stomach grows, knowing the man in their house is likely to blame for their frightened demeanor. As I thought, he's only gotten better at hiding his monstrosity from the outside world. The background check Fritz ran brought everything back completely normal, nothing more dangerous than a speeding ticket.

"He seems like a fucking asshole," Fritz comments, and I hum in agreement, watching him yell at his wife for not making the dinner he *specifically requested*, though I'm sure he didn't.

"Hundreds of years in Vankhala, and people are still just the same," I mutter, turning to walk slightly away from the window we're watching through. I can't look at that fucker for another second.

"Many of them are, yeah. Some are worse than ever before. And the good ones? They get trampled before they ever get a chance." Fritz sounds as dejected as I feel.

With his unique perspective on humans, I often found myself worrying about how jaded he had become, even before going under.

Seeing not only the worst of humans but the emotions driving their atrocities has turned my friend into someone I nearly don't recognize over the years. His liveliness and joy have faded, leaving behind a man who constantly makes jokes rather than facing the world around him. He tries to keep the farce up, especially for Bel, but I've known him long enough to see right through it.

"Shit," he says suddenly. "Once a fuckhead, always a fuckhead."

With the *no*'s and the *stop*'s I'm hearing, I'm not sure I even want to look. But I have to. The sight makes me nauseous, and I have to put a stop to it right now before this piece of filth truly harms his wife. I warn Fritz seconds before transforming into my larger form.

Fuck reconnaissance. I'm putting an end to this right now.

He grabs my arm, and I look down at his human body, "Just wait," he tells me, trying to quickly formulate a plan before I go insane and kill the man right now, "I'll go knock on the front door. He'll send her to answer it and you snatch him from here. I do not want to frighten that poor woman any more than necessary."

I nod. His wife and kids have nothing to do with this and don't need this kind of terror from us. They'll be much better off without him, but seeing it happen might break all of their psyche's beyond repair.

As Fritz stalks around the side of the house, I see more of his disgustingly rough treatment of her. It sickens me so much that I'm hit with a dizzy spell, a lightheadedness that I have to shake off. Clearing my head, I know I can't take one more second of this, so I tap on the window, slinking into the shadows to ensure I'm not spotted.

"What the fuck was that?" my victim asks his wife as if she has the answer. *Just a little longer. I can almost grab him and begin the fun.*

The door knocker clangs three times, and the man shoves her toward it, "Go see who's at the fucking door," he tells her, marching to the fridge.

As soon as his despondent wife rounds the corner away from him, I silently let myself in the back door leading into the dining area. He has his whole upper body bent into the fridge, seemingly searching for something. As he grabs his prize and slams the door shut, his eyes finally land on me.

I wiggle my giant clawed fingers in a wave, letting the smoke rise from my hands and arms. Sam drops the beer in his hand, and before it even hits the floor, I have my hand wrapped around his face, palm covering his mouth, and the tips of my claws digging into his head for grip. I don't want to kill him yet, but I want him to know exactly what manner of treatment he's going to receive from me.

I overhear Fritz explaining to the woman that he's part of the neighborhood watch and thought he saw an animal of some kind in the backyard. *You should probably call animal control,* he tells her, *It looked to be some kind of deer.* I laugh at that, and he proceeds with *It's probably harmless, but better safe than sorry.*

She thanks Fritz and promises to make the call right now. She's probably relieved to know what is in her yard and have an excuse to escape her husband's disgusting *affections.* As she begins the journey through the house back toward us, I pull him towards me as I waltz backward out the back door. I'm dragging him by the tiny holes I've created in his head, his blood dripping down my arm and onto the floor. *Oops.*

I gently close the door behind him so as to not startle his wife or wake their children, and I'm positively thrumming with energy at the prospect of what to do with him when the smell of urine hits my nose.

Fritz whistles a tune as he walks around the corner and stops dead, looking at us, "Holy shit, dude, you made him piss his pants already?" he laughs.

I shake the asshole's head like a rag doll, answering, "I haven't even done anything yet. He's just a fucking coward," I look down at the trembling man, making a decision, "I will give you one chance to run. Just one," I hold up a finger of my free hand.

I release his face, watching the rivulets run down the sides of his head, one on his right side, four down the right from my claws. He seems discombobulated, but that's no concern of mine. He nods, blinking rapidly to clear his head, and I explain further, "I will give you a ten-second head start to run into those woods there," I point behind him. These assholes, with their little personal forests, so unaware of the trouble it invites. "If I catch you, I'll... well, don't let me catch you," I grin, showing my teeth.

He doesn't even hesitate, just tumbles himself into a sprint toward the woods. I look at Fritz, "Ready?" I ask, anticipation building with every beat of my heart.

He scrunches his nose in distaste and shakes his head slightly, "The hunt is your kink, not mine. You catch him, then drag him around the corner there," he points with his chin, "It looks like there's a foreclosure. That's where I'll be." With a quick glance at his watch, he adds, "Three, two, one. Go fetch."

* * *

After chasing my prey for a few minutes, I realize the only exercise he's done in years has been in the form of tormenting others. I'm sauntering slowly toward him, and he's barely moving any faster than me. This is not a chase; it's the saddest Gods damned thing I've ever done.

Rolling my eyes, I give up on the whole charade. Fritz mentioned this *foreclosure* a few houses down, which I guess is just a home no one is living in. That seems silly, having an empty home when there are clearly so many in need of one, but I digress.

I stalk up, muttering to myself about how fucking pathetic this sad excuse of a man is before I grab him by the back of the neck and start dragging him toward our destination. He tries to shake me off, pleading for mercy already, and it's so pitiful it almost makes me feel bad for him. *Almost.*

Fritz is waiting on the back porch, sitting on a large swing, singing softly to himself, "*She held Wanda's hand and they worked out a plan-*" Then, upon seeing me hauling this sack of shit with me, "Oh, hey! There you two are! I was wondering where you got off to."

"Please, man. I don't know what's happening! This guy is a fucking *monster!* That shit's not supposed to be real," he starts blubbering to Fritz, seemingly believing him to be my mortal puppet master. After a few minutes, he ends his nonsensical rant with, "I got money. You want money?"

"No. Shut your mouth," I order, "Is anyone in that house?" I nod towards it, asking Fritz.

He shakes his head, looking over our guest, "He sure doesn't seem so tough when there's not someone smaller than him around, does he? Seems like a little bitch boy to me."

Finally, the man has a backbone for half a moment, his fury overpowering his fear, screaming, "I'll fucking kill you! You think I'm scared of two fucking freaks?" He lunges toward Fritz but stops instantly as I grip him by the hair and yank him back, ripping out a handful of the greasy, thin strands. He looses a pained groan, falling to the ground, clutching his head in pain.

Fritz's eyes glitter with malice as he looks to me, "Come on, let's get inside before the real Neighborhood Watch catches us." He opens the door into the dark house, holding it open for me to pull the soon-to-be-dead fucker across the threshold.

I find a chair from the nearly empty kitchen and place him on it before crouching down to his level, "Now, listen here, friend," I say as I drag a claw not so gently down his cheek. "I have two days to play with you before I must return home, and I can't have you dying until I'm done with my fun," I explain.

He starts crying and begging, and I hold up a hand, standing, "I wasn't *finished,* Sam." I hear Fritz tsk out *no manners* behind me, "As I was saying, I need you to tell me if you have any medical conditions that could cause this little game to end too quickly."

"Oh, god. No, don't kill me. Please. I'll do anything. I'll pay you. I'll give you whatever you want. Insider trading? I have all the inside scoops. Ummm-" I look at Fritz, who is wearing a similarly unimpressed expression.

"What's insider trading?" I ask Fritz, ignoring the babbling man for the moment.

"It's just like... rich assholes having knowledge they shouldn't have and using it to make more money," he explains. *Huh.* I shrug, folding my arms over my chest and staring down at our victim.

"Okay, buddy. I'll tell you what I want," I tell him jovially, "I want... every fucking drop of your blood to paint this home red. I want you to be severed so thoroughly that no one will be able to recognize your body as human. I want the police and coroners to weep at the desecration and defilement of you they find."

"Do you have a will?" Fritz asks suddenly, and the man nods, "Who's in it?"

"My- my kids, they get everything when they turn 18."

"Nothing for the mother of your children?" Fritz pries, the derision in his voice palpable.

"Why should that bitch get a fucking p-" Fritz suddenly flares into his demonic form and punches him across the face, causing spittle and blood to fly from his mouth, "Fuck!"

Fritz smiles at the bloody drool spilling from the corner of the man's mouth, wiping his fist against Sam's shirt, "Watch your fucking language, Sammy. I won't be so nice next time."

The man sobs, losing his tough facade. He wipes the back of his hand against his mouth before answering, "Is that what this is about? My fucking wife? You crazy assho- you guys can have her."

I don't bother to tell him we are quite happy with the woman we have. He doesn't deserve even a mention of her. I roam around the kitchen, hoping for ropes or something to keep him secure, but no such luck. The only thing I find is a collection of butcher's knives. I pick the longest, thinnest one, serrated and *oh-so sharp.* I twirl it in the light, letting Fritz and the man watch as it reflects the small amount of light coming from the lamps outside.

The man starts whimpering in fear, and Fritz is buzzing with energy from the malevolence rolling off of me. "Would you like to do the honors, or should I?"

He thinks on it before responding, "Be my guest, I have a few tricks up my sleeve that won't work until he's bleeding a fuck of a lot more."

As I slowly walk back over, I consider all the places I could jam this knife. It's close to the length of his forearm, and I consider severing his arm at the elbow altogether just to compare. But that would be too much blood loss too soon.

I stare down at the man before me, cowering with his eyes closed. He's praying quietly, and I wonder aloud, "Did your wife ever pray for mercy from you?"

"Yes," he sniffles.

"Hmm. And did you grant it?" As he opens his mouth to tell me a lie, I slam the knife through his right shoulder, straight through to the chair behind him, securing them together. He screams in agony and tries to move, but the knife has him held perfectly still against the chair. Each wiggle he makes causes the serrated steel to slice him open a bit further. His blood slowly begins to soak his shirt, causing the material to stick to the wound and the coppery scent of it to soak the air.

Fritz leans around to see the back of the chair, commenting, "Aw, man. You ruined a perfectly good chair, Cas. The knife went straight through."

"Apologies. Couldn't find any other way to secure him," I shrug.

"I swear, I'll never hurt another person again. Please, please don't kill me," the man begs again. Part of me thinks it would be wise to gag him; to prevent others from overhearing. But I will not deny myself the symphony of his pain and suffering.

"I think his tongue should go next. He's annoying the shit out of me." Fritz suggests. He begins humming that same tune from earlier, so upbeat it doesn't seem to have a place in this moment.

I raise my brows in consideration of this compromise before nodding, "I'll need a smaller knife. Excuse me, boys." As I rifle through the discarded collection of weapons I hear the man scream out in agony again, so I turn to see what's happened. Fritz has his hand on the wound, eyes closed in concentration.

Curiously, I make my way over with my finds, watching Fritz work. *Is he... is he freezing it?*

He looks at me with a manic gleam in his eyes, "Freezing works the same as cauterizing. Well, for a while, 'til it melts. But it hurts *so much more*. Then you can freeze the blood over and over again. It'll slow down the whole *dying* thing, but won't stop it."

I stare at the crystalized blood, the bastardization of natural coagulation Fritz has created, "Huh." I reach out to poke it before Fritz slaps my hand away.

"Don't touch it, it'll melt faster," he says before adding, "Well, fuck, he passed out already.

With a sigh, I lightly slap Sam's face a few times, trying to wake him to no avail. "This guy's a big baby," Fritz adds, "One stab wound and a little frozen blood? Please." He rolls his eyes before he walks toward the next room. "Lemme know when he wakes up, Bachelor starts in five," then much quieter, he sings to himself, "*It turns out he was a missing person who nobody missed at all.*"

27

Wrong

Caspian

50 hours of glorious torture later, we finally call it a day.

"Hmm. Not the longest session I've seen, but definitely the most satisfying." Fritz comments, eating something he found in the pantry.

The piece of shit before us is covered in bruises and slices, has only one eye left as the other was shish-kabobbed by a *fondue stick*, and has tiny little paper cuts between each of his toes and fingers. I found that to be my favorite part.

The irony of Bel's tiny injury that brought me here being one of the ways I tormented the human who dared harm her brings a grin to my face. She's going to be angry when she discovers our deception in getting here, but surely she'll understand.

With a pleased sigh, I turn to Fritz, "You ready for the finale?"

"Fuck yeah. I need to shower, sleep, and go see our girl," his excitement is contagious, leaking into my bloodstream. Now that this weight over her head will be gone, we can just have more fun. *So much fucking fun.* I'm daydreaming over the events we'll enjoy with her once we get home. Fritz will likely die of excitement upon seeing her toy closet.

He sets his hand upon the man's lolling head, him being unable to do much more than groan in agony, seeing as his tongue is on the floor... *somewhere,* as is nearly three liters of blood. It's been frozen over several times, and it's caused the texture of it to become utterly vile. Even I won't touch it.

With a small breath of concentration, Fritz sucks the final drops of life from the man's body. As his magic works, it's like watching an entire life sped up in time. He goes from looking like your average— okay, severely under average— late 20's man, then through the stages of his 40's to his 60's. Until he looks like someone decided to dig up a mummy and desecrate their grave.

"Do we want them to find his body? They won't know what to make of it," I ask him.

He runs his hands through his hair, taming the wild waves, contemplating before answering, "Yeah, they'll need to be able to identify him in order for his family to receive life insurance or whatever he left behind." I nod, not fully understanding. But that's why he's here. I couldn't navigate this kind of thing without him.

I spend another second just staring at this Sam person. His ending was earned, and I will not spend another fucking second worrying about him. His family, and mine, are all free from his poison now.

"Let's get the fuck out of here," Fritz finally says, equally sick of seeing what's left of him. After we both snap back to our human bodies we leave the house and the corpse behind. Traipsing back to where we parked his car, he continues to whistle that same fucking song the whole way.

"Can you stop that?" I finally snap.

He gives me a mischievous smirk before singing *very* loudly and horribly, "*They sell Tennessee ham and strawberry jam and they don't lose any sleep at night.*" Then sliding into the driver's seat, waiting for me to sit in mine.

He's been singing that god's damned song to himself for two days now, and I'm ready to kill him, too, just to stop hearing it.

Despite my annoyance at my friend, I feel immensely better. A little dismemberment and torture to those who deserve it brings me peace. The only thing better than this is obviously my sweet Bel's perfect body. Two days is two too many to go without feeling her, all wet and hot, clenching around me as she comes.

After you shower and rest. I didn't use much of my magic on this trip, but I also didn't eat him. The idea of using that filth to fuel me didn't sit right. His death was as useless as his life, as it should be. Now he's nothing. Not even rotting flesh anymore, thanks to Fritz. Fully decomposed, barely recognizable.

The drive to the hotel we were supposed to sleep in for the last two nights drags on, the horrific smell of death and decay covering us both. We could use magic to clean it all away, but I'm exhausted and want to do it the lazy way.

When we finally climb out of the car and walk towards our room, I get hit with overwhelming dizziness again, causing me to stumble. I lean against the wall to get my bearings, waiting for it to pass. *Perhaps I'm more drained than I thought.*

"Hey, man, you good?" Fritz asks, concern filling his features.

"I'm alright, I think perhaps I'm just tired from all this. I'm not sure I've adjusted to being back yet," I assure him.

"Okay, I just texted Bel to check-in. She hasn't responded yet but it's late so we'll probably hear from her in the morning." He unlocks the door, and we pour ourselves inside. I try to drop onto the bed, but he grabs my arm to lift me back up, "Hell no, you need to shower first. I'm pretty sure you got eyeball juice on your chest," he mimics gagging, and shoves me toward the bathroom.

After a very long shower, I flop face down on the bed and think about reaching out to Bel. But Fritz already did, and she's probably asleep by now. I should have messaged her while we've been away, as I know Fritz has. But communicating so frequently is a new thing to me. It wasn't even close to possible in my day, and I'm not sure what the social protocols are for it.

There's also the matter of fact that had I reached out, it would have ruined the illusion that we were having some kind of romantic getaway. Fritz didn't think it would, and perhaps from him, it did not. This is all just so... infuriatingly confusing for me still.

On his way to the bathroom, Fritz calls out, "Bel texted. She said she was out with Isla all night, just got home, and can't wait to see us tomorrow." *Oh, good.* I was concerned that maybe she had been alone while we've been away.

If she's been going out with Isla every night, she'll be sleeping all day tomorrow. We could get a few hours of sleep, be on the road before dawn, and make it back before she wakes. I tell Fritz as much, and he sets an alarm to wake us in four hours.

Tomorrow. We will be back with our sweet sacrifice in less than 12 hours.

* * *

Of all the car rides I've had in the last weeks, this one is by far the longest. *Traffic.* How do the mortals have international communication and interplanetary travel, yet cannot conquer this thing called traffic? It is utterly absurd, and I tell Fritz as much. Several times.

As we move at a snail's pace across the asphalt, Fritz tells me a little more about his time over the last few centuries. He was an actor in plays for a while, which makes perfect sense. He fucked a king so hard that he killed him and had to cover it up. That story made me laugh out loud, seeing as the only possible way to do that would be on purpose.

Fritz's craving for violence is wholly different than mine, less conspicuous, but it's still there, simmering under the surface. He scares me sometimes because his inventiveness far outweighs my own. I once watched him order the quarter and drawing of a man, using his powers to keep him alive as long as physically possible to ensure he felt every second of his body tearing into pieces.

And he watched the entire thing with his cock buried inside someone's mouth.

He likes to be tortured almost equally as much. I've used a branding iron on him more than once due to him asking *very* nicely, of course. Idly, I wonder if he'd be more inclined to give or receive pain from our little dove.

"Bro, are you hard right now?" he asks suddenly, breaking me out of my trance.

I glance down at the very obvious proof, "I'm thinking about all the ways I'm going to have Bel cause you pain," I answer honestly.

"Oooooh," he reaches to turn the dial and make the music filling the car fall to near silence, "What have you come up with thus far? I can't tell you how many times I've rubbed one out thinking about her fucking me with a strap on."

There's an idea. Definitely one we should explore, once she's comfortable. "I was thinking about the times I branded you," he groans, "but she'd probably be too scared for something that extreme. She can watch, but I'd bet she wants to keep it simple. Flogging, maybe. Let her slap you around a bit while you beg to have her."

"I like all of those ideas," he palms himself through his pants, "I've wondered if she'd like to tie me up and use candle wax to burn me. A softer version of branding, I suppose. Still leaving a mark." The ideas he's sharing has me biting back a moan. She'd look so good, wrapped in some of those strappy, lacy underthings, painting a picture on his pale skin. She'd be rocking her hips against his hard cock as she does so, drawing soft groans from him while he struggles against the bindings.

"Fuck, hurry up, Fritz. We need to get home, now." She is our home, whether she knows it already or not.

Finally, *finally*, we pull into the parking lot, spotting Bel's car in its designated spot. Fritz is as antsy as I am, and we plot to sneak into her room and tackle her right into her bed. I'm so ready to have her in my arms again, with her sweet cries and animalistic groans.

Fritz hasn't had the privilege of enjoying her yet, and I can't wait to witness that, too. They're going to be so gorgeous together, and I'm going to teach her exactly how to tame him when he acts up.

Silently, I unlock her front door and sneak in behind Fritz. Her purse is on the "drop pile" table she designated right inside the door, along with a pair of sky-high heels tossed beside it. There's an unfamiliar human smell, but I think nothing of it, knowing Isla was here and they likely ordered delivery.

I point up the stairs and start climbing them. Fritz follows a few steps behind me, the only sound our quiet breathing. I open up her bedroom door, hoping it doesn't creak as it sometimes does.

It creaks so fucking loud I'm sure it would wake the dead, but that's not the most upsetting thing I notice.

"Where is she?" Fritz asks, echoing my silent question. Her bed is completely empty, disheveled and still smells like her. Like *us*. No one but her and I have been in this room, but something isn't right. The smell is stale and faint.

"She didn't sleep here at all." *Where is she?* "You said she was out with Isla all night? Did she spend the night at her home?" I'm trying not to panic, sure there's some explanation. The two of them are attached at the hip, so it wouldn't be a stretch to assume she slept there.

Fritz frantically pulls out his phone, showing me the message that says she's home. The idea that she's lied to me crosses my mind for only a moment, but I know she wouldn't do that. She is many things, but dishonest is not one of them.

A few moments later, I hear the ring of a phone from downstairs. Fritz and I look at each other before making our way toward the sound. On the kitchen table lies Bel's phone, right next to its charging station. Fritz disconnects his phone call, and the pinging stops.

I pick it up and type in the code Bel told me last week when she allowed me access. When it unlocks, there's a whole list of notifications.

10 missed calls - Isla Parker

17 texts - Isla, Mom, Dad, Fritzy

3 Voicemails - Isla Parker

The texts from Isla are the most concerning, reading:

Yesterday, 12:31 PM: **You lied to me.**

Yesterday, 4:43 PM: **Are you still coming?**

Yesterday, 8:03 PM: **Look, I'm mad about this whole thing since you lied over something so stupid, but you're my best friend. I'm sure you have your reasons. Just fucking call me back.**

Today, 10:30 AM: **You're starting to scare me. Your mom just called me asking for you.**

Today, 1:12 PM: **If you're so busy getting dicked down you're willing to scare the shit out of all of us, I'm going to be pissed.**

Today, 1:43 PM: **I'm coming over. Right now. You'd better be dead or**

dying.

Reading over my shoulder, Fritz's fear becomes palpable. When I close the message screen, my own panic doubles.

The background of Bel's phone has been changed. She's holding yesterday's newspaper, tears and snot running down her face. She's bruised and bleeding from a small cut on her neck, dribbling blood. The knife pressed to her throat has insignia that I know I've seen before.

"Sanctus Scultis." Fritz curses, "Those fuckers have her, Cas! They're going to kill her!" He spirals, muttering about how they're going to torture her like we just did Sam and–

"Stop," I tell him, "Call your Ammon friend." I have to remain calm or I'm going to kill every person between here and wherever they've taken Bel.

"Eamon!" he snaps his fingers, "Eamon! Yes. Okay, okay, okay, I'll call him right now." I can't tear my eyes away from the phone, the terrified look on Belissendas face. *I'm going to kill every one of them.*

I overhear Fritz telling someone, presumably this Eamon person, what we've just found. He repeats when the last time we heard from her was, and I open the text exchange she supposedly had with Fritz.

Her last text to us was last night, but she hasn't been responding to anyone else. Her last message besides that one was to Isla a few nights ago, reiterating that she definitely wasn't sleeping with both of us. *Technically, not a lie.* But I don't think the semantics matter here.

Bel told Isla nothing is going on with Fritz, and somehow she found out that's not true. But how? What the fuck is going on?

"Thursday," I say out loud.

"What?" Fritz covers the phone with his hand to hear me more clearly.

"Her last text to anyone else was Thursday night. She's ignored her parents and Isla for two days?" I don't believe that for a second. They had her. They had her *here* in this apartment the entire time we were gone.

"They only knew when we would be back because I texted her last night. *FUCK!*" he corrects his story to his contact while I continue to search through her phone for any useful information.

Two days they had her here, preparing for my return. But why leave then?

As Fritz hangs up the phone, I have so many questions. I know how they knew we were coming, but how did they get into her phone? They had to have tortured her to unlock it. How did Isla find out about Fritz and Bel? Why hold her here for two days? Why the picture? They didn't leave any kind of clue as to where they'd taken her or what they wanted.

What the fuck am I supposed to do?

"How would Isla have found out you and Bel were also seeing each other?" I show him the proof in the texts, still trying to piece the puzzle together. It shouldn't matter, and I'm sure it wouldn't to Isla, but the betrayal of your closest friend lying would hurt anyone's feelings.

He looks sheepish for a moment before quietly admitting, "I... I posted a picture of us on Instagram." *What the fuck is Instagram?* "It's like an online place where people share photos with others."

"What kind of photo, Fritz?" I'm going to kill him.

"Hey!" he warns, backing up, "It wasn't anything salacious. I got a selfie of us together at dinner, remember?" I nod, and he continues, "I was feeling... amorous between torture rounds and posted it. I honestly haven't even thought about it since then."

So Isla saw the picture and got mad. Bel's going to be heartbroken, and she's going to kill Fritz. Correction, she's going to make *me* kill him. We have to fix this. All of it. After we get her back.

Gods damn this stupid modern world and its stupid fucking inventions.

"You're going to fix this," I tell him, pointing a finger at his chest in warning. "Isla finding out about you, and *them* finding out about you is completely due to your incessant need for attention." If they had kept her here, waiting for just me, and we both showed up, this wouldn't have been an issue. But instead, any element of surprise we had vanished, and they took her somewhere else.

"Hey, dickhead, we wouldn't be in this situation at all if you hadn't wanted to go exact your fucking revenge and leave her here, completely unprotected," he argues back, shoving my hand away. His demon form starts to leak black into his eyes, fingers turning into claws.

"Do *not* blame me. You needed that as much as I did," I try to keep myself contained, but I know the smoke is rising from my shoulders.

"But *I* did not want to hide it from her. She could have come with us, remained safely by our sides had she known," he shouts, growing in size and shoving me with both hands. "But *noooo, you* wanted to keep it from her, pretend we were going away for a fuckfest so you wouldn't have to step away from your torturing to touch base with her."

"*I* did not *know* there was a risk of danger for her here!" I yell, allowing the monster inside me to take over.

"*Neither. Did. I,*" he shoves me again, and I'm preparing to punch him right in his gods damned face. Before I can, he sighs in annoyance and softens his voice, "That's the whole fucking point. There's no use placing blame, Cas. *We didn't know.* There was no warning, no reason to believe she was in danger."

He shrinks back into his human body before plopping on the couch and burying his face in his hands, "One of us should have just claimed her. We both knew she was ours, we were just stalling so we didn't scare her." *He's not wrong there.* "Eamon will be here within the hour," he adds.

"The hour? Does he live in the city, too?" I ask. That would be quite the coincidence.

"No, he can travel through the Aether," he answers, and my jaw drops in disbelief. "Trust me, I don't understand it either. I know it's fairly simple to push things through time and space, but pushing yourself through it? I thought that was impossible."

"Well, we've done all we can for now," I tell him, dropping onto the couch that still smells of her and her fear. I contemplate all the ways I'm going to kill the people who took her to pass the time. We sit and wait in bated silence for what feels like hours when there's finally a loud knock at the door.

28

By the Way, I'm Going Out Tonight

Bel

"Are you sleeping with both of them?" Isla asks halfway through drink number three. *Shit.*

"No," I answer, probably too quickly since she's giving me that knowing smile.

"Hmmm," she swirls her straw around her drink, considering, "Maybe you should be, they're both fine as all hell."

I mean, she's definitely not wrong. Fritz looked so fucking handsome today, it was all I could do not to wrap my arms around his neck and plant one on his cute face. His big, nearly black eyes were like a kicked puppy dog when he didn't get to touch me. I could tell right away he put Isla on edge though, and if she gets through drink number four before she's had enough, I'll ask her about it.

"They are both very handsome." I agree, just to say something. *Christ,* she's too perceptive. I have to play this cool. If I tell her about him, I have to tell her about Vegas. And if I tell her about Vegas, I have to give her a good reason why she wasn't invited. Not to mention the absolute scolding I would get for going on vacation with a man I just met.

There would be no way to justify that without telling her everything. Nothing less than end-of-the-world type shit would be a good enough reason for doing something so reckless.

"Maybe I'll make a pass at that one," she blatantly lies. He's too soft for her. "We could double," she adds, but I can hear the disdain in her voice at that idea.

I cackle before responding, "Isla, you would eat that poor boy alive."

Her thoughtful expression breaks instantly, quiet laughter spilling out. "Okay, you're right," she tells me between giggles, "But you know, if you wanted them both, there wouldn't be anything wrong with that."

"I know," I assure her.

"Lots of people do the whole polyamory thing now. As long as you're all openly communicating, it could be fun." She playfully pushes my shoulder, gushing, "Could you *imagine* being between those two gorgeous men?"

I do, frequently, I want to tell her, but I refrain. I feel the warmth rising in my cheeks and hope that doesn't give me away.

"You little minx! You *have* thought about it." She stops our conversation to thank Ash for bringing her drink number four before turning back to me, "Spill!"

My drinks have made me a little loud-mouthed, and if I just tell her *something*, maybe she'll let it drop for now. If she knows I'm at least thinking about it, she won't push on whether I'm actually *doing* the... doing.

"Ugh," I groan, "Fine. *Maybe* once or twice I've considered what it would be like to be with both of them. Together. At the same time," I give as little as possible.

She gives me her best *no fucking shit* look and waves her hand in my direction, wordlessly asking for more. We never hide anything from each other, even our strangest fantasies. After one of her favorite reads— *that I recommended, of course*— she called me to spill about gaining a blood kink. She had said *It's highly impractical due to all the risks and how sick the blood could make you but like... it would be hot as fuck.*

I completely disagree, but I'm fucking a man who would have to literally feed me his flesh to claim me forever, so who am I to yuck someone's yum? Thinking about the acts I would have to commit to live forever with Caspian makes me sick to my stomach, nearly ruining the night altogether.

Shaking my head clear of its errant thoughts, I give her something, "I've thought about... making a trip to Paris."

"Yes!" she all but squeals, "That would be hot. I've never been one for group play, but that could be way fun for you. The two of them look at you like they'd do anything to have you, even if it meant sharing." *Too god damn perceptive.*

"I don't know about all that. I mean... I hardly even know Fritz," I say, trying to stop myself from telling her anything else. I definitely don't need to tell her that he smells like cinnamon, sandalwood, and sex or that he whines when he needs to come.

Her whole demeanor changes with the mention of his name. "How do they know each other, by the way? And why did he pick up Caspian from *your* apartment instead of his own?" she asks, leaving the naughty ideas behind for more intrusive questions.

"I'm not really sure how they know each other, I just know they have for years and years," I shrug, "And I guess my place was closer to the main highway than Cas's? Or he wanted to say goodbye properly?" I'm rambling. "I don't actually know, I didn't ask."

"I love you, but you're not being very cautious. You should ask more questions. Especially about that smaller one-" Isla begins lecturing me again.

"Fritz," I say, "That's this name."

"Right. Fritz," she repeats, "you need to ask more questions about him. He gives me weird vibes."

"Like bad?" I ask, wondering if it's because he basically let himself into my house when he'd never been there before, or because he called me a strange nickname, or did a double take and practically glared at Isla when he saw her.

"Not *bad*," she clarifies, "Just... off. Like something about his features and demeanor didn't add up."

"Uncanny valley," I mutter to myself, thinking about how I thought the same thing when the two of them stood side by side. Having one inhumanly handsome man in a room can be explained, but two of them, who just happen to be friends? It feels... like you're being hunted, which I guess *is* 100%

accurate.

She snaps her fingers at me in excitement, "Yes! That's exactly it. They're *too* good looking, too symmetrical and their eyes are too bright, and they don't act like your usual hot guys who have no redeeming qualities and too much confidence. They act like... I don't know. But *not* like normal guys."

I nod, completely agreeing but needing this conversation to end. Right now. I can't keep talking about this, or she's going to figure out there's something wrong about them. I hate changing the subject like this, but I have to.

"Hey, speaking of not normal, have you responded to your parents about them pushing you to visit?" I internally cringe at the dejected look I've caused on her face. She chugs down the last of her drink before responding with a single syllable, "No."

I just nod, knowing she can't be pushed into talking about this. If she wants to, she will. I know I'm the worst friend in the world for bringing this up, but keeping her safe from her own questions is the most important thing.

"I think I'll just refund the tickets and call it a day. Once mother sees it on her statement, she'll get the message," she rolls her eyes, "How much longer will I have to do this?"

I wish I had an answer for her, but all I can do is purse my lips and shrug.

"I don't wanna talk about them anymore. They're dead and gone, as far as I'm concerned. Much like this drink." She asks Ash for a water, deciding she's had enough liquid courage. I get the sentiment, I'm about at my limit before my loose lips start to sink ships.

"What about work? What's happening at work?" I need her to keep talking, so I don't have to.

"Work is boring, same as always. Lots of reading, lots of pointing out the obvious." Isla's job does not make a lick of sense to me, honestly. She's a research analyst, which tracks since she's the smartest person I know. But she does it from home, barely interacting with her clients at all. She makes her own hours, chooses which jobs she takes on, and basically does it all.

And she makes incredible money doing it. She's said that lots of people can *do* research well, but it's the making sense of it that screws them. Apparently, being an outside source lets her look at the numbers and patterns without the biases the researchers have.

Fuck if I know what she's talking about, but she's happy doing it, and she doesn't have to work face-to-face with people. Honestly, it's the perfect setup for her. She gives people million-dollar advice wearing footie pajamas with a spiked coffee in hand.

"Are you listening to me?" she asks with a laugh in her voice, "Or were you dreaming about getting DP'd by *The Wonder Boys* again?"

"Isla!" I snort, "No, I was honestly thinking about how perfect your job is for you. Even if it's boring as all hell." She smiles, obviously pleased with herself for making me snort with laughter.

"It is great. Boring, but great. Speaking of," Isla glances at her watch, "I need to head home to get some rest. I *do* have to get some work done tomorrow morning."

I'll never admit it, but I'm grateful to call it a night. I'm exhausted from all the sex marathons Caspian has put me through, and my body is begging me to bathe and rest for the next few days until they return. I also have, like, 12 hours' worth of recording to catch up on and a few emails waiting for responses.

We order our cars, pay the tab and start walking out into the frigid air. With one last hug and one last attempt from Isla for me to tell her more about the guys, we part ways.

As soon as I walk in the front door, I kick my shoes off and set my stuff down. After plugging in my phone and shooting a text off to Fritz, I make my way upstairs to shower, taking my sweet time to let the hot water relax me and admiring the countless love bites peppering my skin.

I can't help but wonder what the guys are doing right now. Did they skip straight to the fucking? Or are they doing romantic stuff? I can't imagine they're the types to wine and dine each other, but what do I know? Maybe they're having a few drinks, chatting, and catching up on all the years they've been separated.

As I throw on pj's and braid my hair back, I find myself wondering if they're in love. Or were? After a few centuries apart, they'd have to basically start over. Fritz has had several lifetimes to move on, find new lovers, be happy.

They seemed pleased to see each other, but both of them were more excited to have me, so maybe they weren't *that* close.

There's a small part of me that *is* jealous I was excluded, but if this is going to work, they'll want to have their own time as much as I want one on one time. Though *more* parts of me wish they'd call so I could see what they're doing without me. Or send naughty pictures. I'd take a text full of filthy details, just to help my imagination out a bit.

With thoughts of them and their long, muscular limbs tangled in each other, groaning and sighing in pleasure, I meander over to my office, hoping to find a toy that will almost make up for missing out on this experience with them. I'm so tired, I should just go to bed, but I am who I am. And who I am right now is a horny, needy bitch, so I'm gonna go with it.

Before I can make my choice, I hear a knocking sound. *Who could be at the door? It's almost ten.* I start towards the sound, and halfway down the stairs, I hear, "Miss Hart, it's Officer Taylor... from last week?"

Fuck.

I make my way toward the door and crack it open, seeing the youngest of the officers who checked up on me. I think again that this kid can't be more than 20 years old, with nearly white blonde hair, blue eyes, and cheeks so round and sweet he looks like a little cherub. "Hi! What can I do for you, officer?" I ask through the slight opening in the door.

"Ma'am, I'm sorry to bother you so late, but we've had some developments about the strange occurrences around your home last week." He pulls at his uniform uncomfortably, wiggling his shoulders, adding, "May I come in? I'd rather not discuss this in the hallway."

I consider turning him away, but I'm not sure I can afford the kind of attention he would bring if I did. He might show up with a search warrant, and that would absolutely land me in the big house. *Are there guts in my freezer? No. There's not. Right?* If I let him in now, I can at least guide him away from the kitchen.

I open the door, moving out of the way so he can enter. He walks in and places his gun holster next to my purse, "I don't need that here, do I?" he laughs, "This is just a friendly check up."

Him not having his gun on him does help me breathe easier. I walk towards the couch, hoping he'll follow, ignoring the comment about needing a firearm here. It wouldn't help if the guys were here anyway, but that's probably not something that needs to be said aloud.

I'm still feeling a bit of a buzz, so keeping my mouth shut against my thoughts is probably the safest bet.

"You said there were developments?" I ask, hoping to let him fill the silence.

"Well, it would appear that some of your neighbors reported an unfamiliar man coming in and out of your apartment around the same time as the disappearing officers and strange noises." He begins wandering around the living room, looking over my sparse decor.

"Oh?" Of course, people saw Caspian, he's impossible to miss. But those nosy fucks have *unfamiliar* guests all the time, and I'm not spilling their business to a twelve-year-old cop.

"Yes, but most of them... amended their stories a little when we were touching base again since then." That could be very good or very bad. "They've all said that as it turns out, *strange* noises leave this apartment every time they see him come and go." I begin to blush, and he chuckles, "See, that's what I figured. Nosy neighbors inserting themselves into someone's dating life."

"This is so humiliating," I mutter. Our sex life is so loud that my neighbors are reporting it to the cops? I'm going to have to install soundproofing walls on every surface. "Everyone in the building..." I cover my face with my hands, refusing to even finish that sentence.

I think about what he's said for another minute, asking, "But you also mentioned the missing officers? What's the update on them?" Though I'm unsure if I want to know.

"Well... They- I probably shouldn't be telling you this, but I want to assure you that you and your neighbors are safe. There were remains found in a dumpster a few blocks down. Two men, wearing police uniforms. It would appear that they were parading as officers, so it can only be assumed that they stole those uniforms from the missing men."

"*Jesus.*" He flinches at my use of the curse. *Oops, religious type.* In a small voice, I add, "Sorry. Didn't mean to offend."

He turns toward me and shrugs nonchalantly, but I can still see barely concealed fury across his features. Through gritted teeth, he states, "My faith is not everyone's, so I cannot expect you to abide by not using His name in vain. Though I would *appreciate* it if you tried while in my presence."

I nod, standing. Goosebumps break out along my skin at the officer's reaction to something as small as a curse word, and I know I need to get rid of him immediately, "Of course. Now, if that's all, officer, it's late and I was just about to go to sleep." As I start walking towards the exit, he follows behind me. Right as I'm about to reach out and open the door, I realize he left a huge part of the story out, and I ask, "How did the guys posing as officers die?"

"Well, from my understanding, your little demon pet got ahold of them," then, with a small pinch in my neck, everything goes dark.

29

My Fucking Head

Bel

I wake up with the worst headache I've ever had. I slowly blink my sandpaper eyelids to adjust to the bright light shining in through the windows. *How much did I drink last night?*

"Oh, good. You're awake." I look to my left where the voice came from and see officer Taylor, sitting ramrod straight on the couch. I finally piece together the events from last night, him showing up and then me blacking out. He mentioned Caspian, then knocked me out. He's one of them... The.. the sanctimonious... *fuck, I can't remember their stupid name.*

"You drugged me." I say aloud finally, hoping that's the worst of what he did while I was unconscious.

"I did. It was... a necessary evil, I'm afraid," he responds, "The flesh eater was supposed to be here when I arrived- as he is most nights I'm told- so I could take care of this quickly and quietly." Well, if his disgust is any indication, he has *no* interest in touching me or my apparently filthy body. Small victories, I guess.

"A necessary evil? *You. Fucking. Drugged Me!*" I scream, trying my damnedest to direct it towards him, even though I'm bound with my arms behind my back and my legs tied to the legs of a dining room chair.

"I will ask you again to refrain from using such language," he says, "I truly did not want to do things this way. However, to hear that not only are you harboring the demon, but in fact, you've been seduced by him... it makes things unpleasant."

Seduced? He thinks I'm just some dumbass the demon tricked into fucking him. I roll my eyes, hoping the holier-than-thou child playing cop doesn't see it.

"Fuck you, dude," I mutter. He stands and storms toward me before stopping himself. Maybe I shouldn't poke this particular bear, seeing how I'm restrained and he seems very sure that he's doing the right thing here. He also seems like he's seconds away from snapping and I have no desire to be the target of his aggression.

With his fists and teeth clenched, he asks, "Where is the demon, Belissenda?"

I shrug, noticing he's said *demon* twice now and has no clue that there are in fact two of them. I don't think he could take on Caspian alone, much less with Fritz there to help. I'm keeping my fucking mouth shut about that, not telling this little asshole anything.

"Vacation," I utter one word, hoping it signifies the extent of my cooperation.

"When will it return?" he continues and I shrug again, telling him I don't know. "When. Will it. *Return?*" he repeats through clenched teeth.

"I. Don't. Fucking. *Know.*" I mimic his cadence. Before I can take a breath in, his fist smashes against my cheek and I cry out in pain.

I've never been punched before.

That shit *sucks.*

"I do not enjoy doing this. You could have told me what I needed and made this simple," he comments, "I've heard that demon apologists exist, but I never believed someone could let a demon... defile them as you have."

Rather than try to think or talk through whatever monologue he's gearing up for, I focus on my breathing and think of happier times, as I've learned to do whenever reality becomes too much. Cas and Fritz dancing with me, my spa day with Fritz, all the simple, quiet dinners between me and Cas. I hardly hear what the not-cop is saying until he mentions the compass.

"I'm sorry, what?" I ask him to repeat. Maybe if I use manners, he'll go easy on me. Though somehow I doubt it. I think this dickhead has been looking for any reason to beat the hell out of someone. His red face just screams repressed rage.

"I *said*, tell me where the compass is," he gestures around the apartment, "I searched every corner while you were out and it's nowhere to be found."

"That thing? I haven't got a clue. Caspian probably took-" he punches me square on the nose, causing it to immediately start pissing blood.

"Do not utter that *monster's* name. It is filth, a creature of nightmares, and you will not use its chosen name amongst the Sanctus Scultis." He seethes down at me, and I'm nearly choking on the blood running into my mouth with no way to stem the flow. He shouts in frustration, "Look at what you've caused! I didn't come here to hurt you, yet now look at you."

"Please," I choke out, "I don't know anything. He just left, didn't say where or what he was doing. You can check my phone if you don't believe me." I try to nod towards my bag on the table where my phone should still be.

He walks over and grabs it, bringing it back to unlock it with my face. He grips me by the nape of my neck to hold my head in the frame, definitely leaving fingerprint-shaped bruises. After three unsuccessful tries due to the bruising and blood splatters, he orders, "What's the passcode?"

"Two, eight, six, eight." *Just like you, bitch.*

After a few tense moments of him scrolling, muttering to himself, and tap, tap, tapping away, he tosses my phone aside. I get the feeling he's seconds away from ripping his hair out of his head.

He pulls out a knife and points it at me, seething before he starts to pace back and forth, muttering, "It's not supposed to go like this. I have *God* on my side, this is supposed to be *easy*." I don't think this is actually supposed to be a two-sided conversation so I don't add anything.

He brings the knife closer to me, pointing it at my face in his fury and I fail to hold in a whimper. I'll admit it, I'm fucking terrified. Cas and Fritz are going to find me here like this, sliced up like some piece of trash. They're going to be devastated.

And *Isla.* I'm the only family she has left. Everyone else she's ever cared for treated her like she was expendable if she didn't abide by their demands. She won't have anyone when I die. She's going to be so fucking alone. That thought is the one that finally causes the dam to break.

I start weeping and just repeating the same things over and over again, begging for mercy, "Please. I don't know anything. I don't wanna die like this."

He scoffs, "Stop crying. I'm not going to kill you. *You* are not the target and *I* am not the monster." Somehow I don't think it'd be helpful to point out that from where I'm sitting, he absolutely is the bad guy here. But he said he wouldn't kill me, so I won't argue. He pulls his knife from my face, looking at it like it jabbed itself at me, instead of him being the driving force behind it.

"We'll just have to sit here and wait for him together," he finally decides, "I don't want to hurt you, so please don't provoke me."

I'm going to cheer them on when they find you and rip you to fucking shreds I think to myself. I'm not going to give him any more reason to hurt me so I'll just sit here like the good little prisoner I am until my demons come to get me.

Fuck. "I have to pee."

He grunts in frustration before wandering over and using his knife to release me. He slides it back into his belt and I notice he's put the gun back on. My eyes are glued to it, hoping he doesn't pull that out. A firearm and an unhinged zealot can only end in disaster for me.

"Any funny business and you'll end up with more than a few bruises," he warns me, not that he needed to. I just nod and hold my hands up, walking a weird backward scootch to the powder room.

I'm suddenly struck with how much I feel like I did that night so long ago. The violation, the angry blue eyes, the insistence that this is all my own fault. With that thought, my body forces all the bile to exit my stomach. I barely make it to my knees in front of the toilet before everything in me is forcibly ejected. The guilt and shame invading my body cause me to shake and pushes fresh tears from my eyes. How can I feel so guilty, *again,* when I'm the victim?

I don't care what this psycho says, I don't deserve this treatment. Caspian and Fritz don't deserve to be hunted down like animals just because of what they are. They didn't choose this life.

After wiping the corner of my mouth with my hand and finally relieving myself, I dare a quick glance in the mirror.

I look horrible. Bruises are starting to form on my face, and dried blood under my nose is mixing with some still running to create a horrible crusty waterfall of it. My hair is the least of my concerns, as are the small remnants of black makeup around my eyes. *How the fuck am I going to get out of here?*

"I also need to change. For both of our sakes, I think." When he's not putting his hands on me, he seems scared to even look at my scantily clad body, so we're both clearly uncomfortable about how much of it he's seen.

"Fine. Make it quick." He has my phone and a gun, so he must not see me as much of a threat now. To be fair, he's not wrong. Is the one I shot Caspian with still in there somewhere?

After I sprint up the stairs with him one step behind me and let myself into my bedroom, I quietly look in the places I would normally stash it, thinking maybe Caspian returned it to its home. I'm putting on a big pair of sweats and a sweater while I rifle through my things. *God damn it, where is it??*

I hear a tap on the door before my captor says, "I have what you're looking for. Did you really think I would not look to see if you have weapons?" I nearly claw my eyes out in frustration at his condescension. I flip the bird at him through the wall with both hands, hoping it'll help me feel better. It doesn't, but the thought of his crazed face if he saw it does a little bit.

"Get out here, you've had enough time to change and if you haven't, that's your own fault," he barks.

I leave the room and make my way back down the stairs, trailing behind him like a naughty school kid who's been scolded. He points at the couch, not bothering with words. He knows I'll follow his silent command.

He plants himself against the wall, leaning against it with his head tilted back, clearly as unhappy with this situation as I am.

"I cannot keep you here by myself indefinitely," he sighs and my heart soars at the possibility of him leaving, "so I'll have to call in back up to stay here and keep you under control until your demon arrives." All the hope drains from me instantly.

Another one of them in here? The only thing worse than one crazy religious fanatic is *two* of them. He pulls out his own phone and shoots off what I'm assuming is a text to someone before he comes to sit near me.

I look at him, glaring with all my might before he holds up both hands in supplication, "Look, Miss Hart, I know you're not a fan of me right now, but I promise we're the heroes here-"

"Tell that to my fucked up face, asshole," I regret it the moment I say it, but for once he doesn't strike me. He clenches his fists like he wants to but only releases his white-knuckled grip a moment later.

"As I was *saying*, I do not want to hurt you. I truly think you're an innocent in all this. Stupid, but innocent." I glare, holding my tongue and he continues, "But my higher ups are not as willing to empathize with those who have been tricked by the devils wicked sons."

I'm not sure I understand what he's saying, but it can't be good.

"If you use continue using this foul language, disrespecting us, and refusing to be helpful, they will not be as merciful as I have been," he adds. "They've killed many whose only sin was being tempted by demons."

"What is the point of your little club? Hmm?" I ask, hoping to start some kind of open dialogue so he sees the craziness he's supporting.

"To send all of demon kind back to Vankhala," he answers, intoning like it's some kind of oath, which I guess it probably is.

"So, it's *not* to save humans, or to save anyone, really. Just to kill?" I push, probably stupidly but I can't help it.

"Saving all of mankind sometimes requires the sacrifice of a few," he tells me as if I'm the dumbass here.

"And *you* are the one who gets to decide whose life is less important?" I ask him, accusation coming out in my tone.

He stands and shouts, "Stop talking!" Pacing, he points at me as he walks, "I'm trying to do the right thing here by warning you the kind of measures my leaders are willing to take to ensure they cleanse this world of demons. I do not want you getting caught in the crossfire."

"Then let me go," I plead, "You have my phone, my apartment where you know he'll be returning. Probably sooner if I stop responding to phone calls and texts."

He considers me for a second and I think he might actually do it, but then the doorbell rings and he straightens up, fixing his hair and uniform back to rights. *Well, there went that idea.*

He answers the door and lets in another man, similarly dressed but infinitely more comfortable in the get-up. *He looks so familiar.* I can't quite put my finger on where I think I've seen him before. His tan skin and ashy brown hair are screaming at me for recognition, but maybe I've just seen him around town?

The newcomer sees me and grins, "Hello, demon slut" I just raise my brows in equal parts fury and amused disbelief because any other reaction might earn me a bullet or a punch, "or do you prefer Bel? How about Red?"

"Bel is fine, thank you." I tell him, trying to match his cavalier attitude and failing terribly.

"Red it is." He looks at his compatriot and laughs, a terrible, vicious sound, adding, "Well, *Red* and *Officer* Taylor, we are going to be getting pretty up close and personal while we wait for this demon scum to return. As long as you behave," he says, peering at me, "we won't have any problems. Got it?"

I nod once, refusing to dignify this fuckhead with any more responses.

"Good," he chirps before turning and heading toward the kitchen, "Got any coffee?"

He digs through my coffee mugs and grabs the monster fudger one, causing a new flare of rage to course through my body. He must see my reaction since he just keeps grinning as he prepares himself a cup like he owns the fucking place.

Taking a sip from Caspian's designated mug, he looks over at me, his stupid smug face full of cruel mirth, "Name's Alastor, by the way, but you can just call me Al."

* * *

Two horrific days later I'm sitting on the couch without so much as changing out of my sweats. No shower, haven't brushed my hair, and barely managed to brush my teeth before one— or both of them peeked into the bathroom, instructing I return to the TV room.

I suppose it could be worse. They've kept me fed and caffeinated, and let me sleep on the couch. But having two grown men with weapons overseeing you while you eat, sleep and piss is humiliating.

Alastor plops down onto the couch beside me, one of my jalapeño bagels in hand, and whispers to me conspiratorially, "How you holding up, Red? You must be feening for a hit by now." He widens his eyes comically, and I just roll mine. He scoots closer and tries again, cruelly pretending we can be buddies while he's holding me hostage, "Listen. I'm sorry Taylor slapped you around like that. It wasn't supposed to be part of the deal."

I just *hmm* in acknowledgment and he continues, pointing his chin at his colleague, "You know he's got a nickname back at the compound?" This finally gets my attention and I look at him with my eyes narrowed. He chuckles quietly and says, "They call him the Rabid Pup. Wanna know why?"

"No."

He wraps an arm around me, pulling me closer, lowering his voice, "Based on the state of your face, you've already seen it." I start to push him away but he squeezes my shoulder painfully, all while keeping his relaxed disposition, "He's like a little puppy, all wide eyed and naive with the best intentions. But push him just a little bit and... well, you know," he pointedly looks at my face before releasing me with a laugh.

"Oh, no," the boy in question utters, "Oh, no. Al, this is bad."

Al sighs and stands, heading toward the kitchen. They're both looking at my phone when Alastor releases a humorless laugh, "Well, well, well. You have been a busy girl. Two of them?" *Fuck.* "What have you got between your legs that has them both so smitten?"

Taylor nudges Alastor, "Demons aren't usually known for..." he swallows, "*sharing.* You don't think they could possibly be-"

"Do not say another word, Taylor," he commands, eyes locked on his subordinate. I note the weird exchange, wondering what Taylor was about to ask him. "She's nothing special," he turns to me, "are you? Just a willing body for not one, but two monsters."

I sniff, ignoring the jab. The only advantage I had was them not knowing about Fritz and now apparently that's gone. *I'm not going to react.* I'm not going to give them that satisfaction.

"Your *bestie*, Isla, is quite upset about all the lies you've been telling," he keeps prodding, amusement written across his face with every word. *I will not cry, not in front of this prick.* "Ooh, I wonder what *mommy* would have to say about all of this."

I grit my teeth, fighting back frustrated tears when Taylor grips Alastor's arm lightly, whispering something to him. Alastor looks down at the point of contact with disgust, showing how he truly feels about his little errand boy.

He looks back up at me and sighs, "I suppose you're right. Things *have* changed. She'll have to come back to the compound with us." Then a vindictive smile graces his face and chills run down my spine, "We'll just have to leave a little message behind for her demons to find."

The look on his face coupled with his words send me off the couch, trying to run for the first time since they've been here. If I can even buy myself a few minutes, maybe that'll be enough time for Caspian and Fritz to get here. I don't know when they're supposed to be back, maybe I can get upstairs and lock myself in–

The click of a gun stops me in my tracks, "I'd rather not kill you, but I have no issue at all sending a bullet through one of your legs," Alastor warns. I get the feeling he'd love doing just that, so I take a calming breath and turn around with my hands up. "Now that's a good little slut," he coos, and I want to vomit. He points the gun from me to the couch, gesturing for me to sit.

As I do, he whistles to himself, waltzing toward the front door, "You get the paper here?" *Paper?*

"The newspaper? No one gets the newspaper anymore," I answer.

He hums in thought, then says, "BRB," and walks out the door, slamming it behind him.

For a few tense minutes, I sit in agonized thought, wondering what he needs a newspaper for. *A little message* he had said. I don't dare even look at where the other guy is standing watching me, lest I inadvertently trigger his punch-happy hands. I just sit and touch the bruises on my face, testing for their tenderness.

When Alastor returns, newspaper tucked under his arm, he drags the dining room chair to the middle of the room, ordering me to sit. I slowly make my way over and plop into the chair.

He gestures for his friend to join us before telling him, "Her bruises look a little... faded. I think she needs a fresh one. For incentive, you understand," he adds in my direction.

"No! No, ple-" That little shit gets me right on the cheekbone over the top of my already throbbing previous injury, and I scream in agony.

The grin splitting Alastor's face tells me he enjoys using his little pet against me immensely, and I wipe away my tears before forcing my expression back to its stony facade. He hands me the newspaper to hold up and stands back with my phone, "Say cheese," he says, aiming the camera at me before pausing, "Hmmm. Something's missing. Here, you take this," he throws it to Taylor.

Standing behind me, I feel him grip the back of my neck with one hand, and something cold presses against the front of it. I choke back a sob as a sluice of warmth trickles down my throat, coupled with the coppery scent I've quickly become accustomed to in their presence.

"Smile pretty," he tells me, pressing the knife against me slightly harder, causing fresh tears to fall. I try to remain calm and not let the terror show on my face, but I'm pretty sure I fail miserably.

Once they're done with the picture and doing whatever it is they've decided to do with it, Alastor turns to me again, pulling a syringe out of his pocket. "I hate doing this, you know. I think it would be more fun to drag you kicking and screaming. *But* I don't think we would get very far before someone stopped us and asked too many questions."

"I won't fight. Please don't drug me again," I beg. Pathetically, I'll admit.

"Yeah..." he waves the syringe around, "here's the thing. I don't believe you." He doesn't give me another warning before jamming the motherfucker into my neck, far harder than the other guy did it, and I'm lost to oblivion again.

30

That's it. I'm Coming In.

Caspian

"Shit," I say.

"Shit," Fritz repeats.

"Belissenda Hart, you open this door *right fucking now!*" Isla yells from the other side of said door.

"What do we do?" Fritz whispers to me.

"I don't fucking know." I whisper back, debating on just letting her in. If her friend is missing, I think she has a right to know.

"Bel, I swear to fuck, you better answer this door. We are all worried *sick* about you." Fritz's eyes widen, staring at the thin slab of wood separating her from us.

"We should just open it, right?" he asks me, "Isla is harmless, she's just worried about her friend."

Before either of us can make our way toward the door to answer, there's the sound of a key turning, and Isla slams it open, looking at us with narrowed eyes, "Where's Bel?" she asks with false calmness.

How are we supposed to explain to her that her friend was kidnapped, and we are just standing around here, not calling the authorities?

"I can explain," I start. "Bel–" I pause, "Bel is…"

"Bel is *what*, Caspian? She's sleeping off the epic threesome you've had?

She's comatose from an overdose of orgasms? Those are the only fucking answers I wanna hear," her voice wobbles.

I hold my hands up, placatingly, "Someone... took her," I try, "I'm so sorry. It's my fault."

"Someone. Took her," Isla repeats back, eyes watering, "What the fuck does that mean?"

"She was kidnapped," Fritz adds unhelpfully, gaining her instant ire, "But if it makes you feel better, they were after Cas."

"Where. Is. She?" she looks back at me, "Why aren't you doing anything if you know who has her? Where are the police? Her parents? Someone, anyone?"

"Look, I swear we can explain," Fritz starts, "and we *are* doing something. We called an expert who will be here any minute."

"Oh, thank God, an *expert*." she laughs without humor, "You two assholes got my friend kidnapped, but you've called in an *expert* to get her back. Fuck you, I'm calling the cops."

Before she can do just that, I snatch her phone with my power and bring it to me, "I'm truly sorry, Isla, but you can't do that. For all we know, the authorities are in their pocket." I hate doing this to her, and Bel would be furious if she were here.

She looks at her phone in my hand, then back at her hand, muttering to herself, "How..." looking back up at me, she questions, "How did you do that?"

"Magic," I think Fritz might enjoy riling her up, as there's no way he's just this dense. "We," he gestures between us, "are demons, we can do magic."

At this, she starts laughing hysterically, doubled over, hands on her knees. Then she stands and wipes her eyes, "You got me, I almost shit myself being so scared," she looks around, raising her voice again, "Come on out, Bel, you got me! Hardy har."

At the lack of humor on our faces, she says, "No. That shit's not real. It's not real." I allow myself to grow to my true form because we don't have time to ease her into this. Bel didn't want her to know, but it's a little late for that. She screams bloody murder before shaking her head, falling into true hysteria. "No, no, no, no no nononono *no*," she mumbles, "It *can't* be real."

I change back into my human form, righting my clothes before we continue this conversation. At this point, Isla cannot so much as look at me, and the last thing I want is to cause her more discomfort than necessary.

"Look, I. We-" Fritz starts.

"Don't call me that," she jams a finger in his direction, "You don't fucking know me, you don't get to call me that."

"My apologies. Isla. Honestly, I am truly sorry. We had hoped you didn't need to find out, as did Bel, but-"

"She knew?" *Shit.* I shoot Fritz a look, and he shrinks back in shame.

The pain written on her face turns the knife in my heart. We are destroying their friendship, one lie at a time, just by being here. I'm not entirely sure if Isla's tears are from her friend's deception or her disappearance. Likely both.

Suddenly, she blurts, "Who?! You said *someone* and *they*, but who the fuck is *they*?" she screams, voice cracking at the final word, tears falling freely.

"Sanctus Scutulis," I answer, "Demon hunters."

"And I suppose Bel is a fucking demon, too?" she deadpans, likely plotting our death herself. I can't say I blame her.

"No, just... us."

"And they took her because you're both fucking her?" I cringe, unsure how much to tell her. Maybe full honesty is what she needs right now, but fuck, I'm not good at this.

"Technically, I have not had sex with Bel. Yet." Isla narrows her eyes at him, and I fully understand the idiom *if looks could kill.*

"Well, *technically*," she mocks, "that little detail doesn't really fucking matter, does it? She's gone because of her *involvement* with the two of you. Am I right?"

I nod, head hung with guilt. I walk over to where Bel left her phone, knowing I'm going to cause a new wave of tears. But no one knows our girl better than Isla, and she's far more clever than most mortals. Honestly, we are lucky she's here. If anyone can find Bel, it's her.

"I'm so, so sorry," I tell her, my own voice thickening with the tears threatening to appear, "I didn't know she was in danger." I hand her the phone, ignoring Fritz's protests about what she will find.

She sobs aloud as she looks at the photo on the main screen, crying out for her friend, giving voice to the sentiment we all feel.

"We are going to do everything in our power to find her," Fritz says solemnly, "She's the only thing that matters to us."

"Where were you, then?" she asks in a small voice, "What was more important than being right here if you care so much about her?"

"Killing Bel's rapist," Fritz answers proudly, and her head snaps to him so quickly I fear it caused her whiplash.

"You *what?*" Looking back to me, she reiterates, "You killed him?" I nod, "And it took you two days?"

"I would have preferred it take longer, to be honest." Fritz continues to run his mouth, "I think he should have suffered more."

She considers his thoughts for a minute, before looking back and forth between us. "You tortured him to death for two days, over a crime he committed nearly a decade ago? Because he hurt Bel?" she asks with disbelief in her voice.

"Yes," we say in unison before I add, "And I would do it again. *Anyone* who hurts her dies slowly and in exquisite agony."

Through her tears, she starts to grin, "These fuckers are so toast."

I sigh a breath of relief until she adds, "I'm still pissed. And you three have *so much* explaining to do. She lied about you," she gestures to Fritz, "a trip to Vegas *without me*, and apparently knowing about the supernatural. The supernatural that I was convinced wasn't real until just now."

Distantly I wonder about her verbiage. She seems like she's heard about these things before and brushed them off. But now she's been forced to face the evidence, and she's taking it in stride. I'll have to ask her more about that later, but for now, we need to get Bel back.

But where do we even begin? From what Fritz said, his contact will know what to do, being the one who has built a whole team fighting against them.

Suddenly I feel a scorching pain running down my arm, and I scream in agony.

"Cas, what the fuck?" I look down and see a red line on my arm, like someone ran a claw down it, barely not breaking the skin. But it burns like someone ran a scalding sword across my flesh. Fritz examines it as I breathe through gritted teeth.

"They're hurting her." I seethe, "They're fucking *torturing* her, Fritz." The photograph of her has a few bruises and a teeny cut, but whatever they're doing now must be causing her unimaginable anguish. As soon as it came, the pain is gone, the red line disappearing from my arm.

Instantly, my other arm begins to feel the same, only much worse. Like someone is running a needle dipped in acid along my skin in intricate patterns.

"Well," Fritz clears his throat, "That's one way to send a message." I open my subconsciously squeezed-shut eyes and peer down at my forearm. Beneath the smoke starting to rise, there are rough letters scratched into my skin.

H D

E E

L M

L O

O N

Written in twin columns down my left arm, crude and misshapen, like the canvas was shaking, and I'm certain she was. I'm shaking from the pain, and I can only imagine it's so much worse for her.

"They're dead. All of them, fucking dead." Fritz begins to pace, fighting to keep his mortal form. I feel the same, only remaining in this skin, making it easier to read the horrific message they're leaving across Bel's body.

I'm offered a slight reprieve and try to take deep breaths. Of all the agony I've endured, being ripped to shreds and sent through the Aether to Vankhala, then back, this might be the worst of it all. Knowing Bel is suffering because of me, having a glimpse of the torment she's enduring, it's a worse fate than anything I've felt in all my centuries.

Isla watches my arm, her sharp nails digging into it as silent, angry tears stream down her face. She looks up at me, determination in her eyes, "I'll fucking end them. Whoever is doing this to Bel is going to wish they'd never been born."

"That's a lovely sentiment, Isla, but these are trained hunters. They've been doing this shit since they were born," Fritz tries to explain, "They have weapons and magic, and we've just got us."

"Just got us?" she asks incredulously. "You two are fucking demons with power and have the determination to torture a man for two whole days without killing him. And I'm... well, I'm motivated and fucking pissed."

Truly, she is something to be feared. Mortals rarely have the courage to stand amongst demons, much less dare to stand *with* us as allies. Bel is fortunate to have a friend willing to look death in the eyes and spit venom rather than cower in fear.

I scream as more words appear, this time across my collarbone, so I tear my shirt open at the neckline to see the message,

C O M E A L O N E

Come where??

Without even a moment's break, I start to feel the same tearing, burning sensation across my back. I rip the shirt over my head, frantically freeing myself from it so someone can tell me what the message contains.

"Nice," Bel and Fritz say in unison, glancing at my abs before they look at each other, revulsion at their common ground evident. *Not the fucking time.*

I turn around so they can read the script across my shoulder blades.

"Jesus, that's disturbing." Isla comments, "They drew some strange symbols, before writing some shit in like Latin or something. I haven't got a clue what it says."

"Fritz?" I ask.

He heaves out a breath, "Dolor ducit te." *Pain leads you.*

"What does that mean?" I ask. *Pain leads you?*

We all stand in silence, considering the message. Fritz continues his pacing, Isla sits on the couch with her face buried in her hands, and I stand there, frozen. The only thing I know this means for certain is that Bel will suffer much further before I get to her.

31

That's a Big Motherfucker

Fritz

She's gone. She's fucking gone, and they took her, and it's my fault. I can argue with Cas 'til we're blue in the face, but the fact of the matter is that *I'm* the one who had to brag for the whole world— okay, more like 17,000 people on Insta- to see about my girl. *I* had to reach out while we were away for a scrap of her affection.

But what was I supposed to do? Cas doesn't get it. He doesn't understand that in this world where we can communicate across miles and miles within seconds, it's a choice not to. A choice that sends the message, *I'm not thinking about you*, and I refused to let Bel feel that way for even a second.

I wouldn't let her think we ghosted her, I couldn't stand even letting her think we were fucking without her. I don't want Cas without Bel. Do I want Bel without Cas? I mean, yeah sometimes. She's mine, too. Not just *ours*.

But none of that shit fucking matters because right now, she's *gone*. And I know Cas feels the loss as deeply as I do. I've never seen that guy fucking cry, and I fear one more little *message* from our hunter friends is gonna push him right over the edge.

I'm wearing a trail into the carpet, and I know it, but I don't care. If I stop moving for even a second, I'll start draining the life from every goddamn mortal between here and wherever they've stashed Bel.

"How long ago would they have moved her?" Isla asks suddenly. She stands and grabs the phone, releasing another sob at the picture before she quickly opens the message app.

"I texted her late last night, and she- they- texted me back from her phone. That was maybe like one? Two AM?" I turn to Cas suddenly, "Right around the time you got all dizzy and shit."

"You think they drugged her to move her?" Isla clarifies my thought process.

"Oh, they'd have to. She'd go kicking and screaming and biting otherwise," Cas answers, causing a small smile between all of us. Damn *right*, she'd go apeshit the whole way. Lost in thought, Caspian adds, "I had another lightheaded moment when we were watching that piece of shit manhandle his wife. It was so mild I thought it was in revulsion to the scene before me."

"Why didn't you say anything?" I accuse. We're fucking demons, a dizzy spell isn't something you can just chum up to nothing. I internally facepalm. We should have known something was wrong immediately.

"I didn't know," he shrugs, and *fuck,* I wanna punch him in his stupid, handsome face. There is nothing that would please me more than to slap that sad, mopey look off his face. He doesn't get to be fucking sad right now. We caused this, and we have to fix it. He can whine about it later, once we have our Bel back in one piece.

Two days. Whoever has her held Bel captive in her home for two whole days while Caspian and I were playing vigilante. There's no telling what those religious zealots would do to her, thinking her to be filth since she *laid with* one of us. The "cleansing" rituals those sick fucks used to do to impure women... I can't think about it because if I do and picture Bel's sweet face, I'm going to accidentally drain Isla dry before she can take her next breath.

The hunters just don't get it. We didn't choose to be what we are. We didn't choose to be suddenly ripped into existence, into sentience, full of power, and without any kind of guide or manual on how to use it. Usually to just wake up surrounded by men with weapons who have just bled out a child or very young adult. We have no say in the bloodthirst we feel in the vicinity of the wicked.

This shit isn't fucking fair. Caspian and I finally find a slice of happiness, and because of our violent tendencies, someone fucking *took her*. What can we possibly do in the face of our evolution, the hunters, and the entire fucking world trying to keep us apart? We *need* her, and she needs us. I'll be damned if I let some sanctimonious douchebags take her from us.

Cas's face continues to fall, and I wanna tell him to stop fucking sulking, but it wouldn't help and I'm doing the same shit, so I keep my mouth shut.

Isla does the math, "So they probably moved her in the middle of the night, nearly 13 hours ago." That's so long ago. They could be halfway across the country by now. Across the border into Mexico, deep in bumfuck nowhere Texas, *anywhere*.

And what the fuck is "the pain leads" anyway? The pain leads what? Sacrifices are never alive long enough for us to know anything about them. *God damn it, when is Eamon going to be here?*

Moments later, I sense a huge force shifting into our vicinity.

"What the hell is that?" Cas must feel it the same moment I do.

"Eamon," Fucking *finally*.

Even Isla must feel it, goosebumps rising along her flesh as she looks around in discomfort. As he finally solidifies, looking as though he's just finished walking through a doorway instead of the Aether, I realize I'd forgotten just how fucking *massive* he is in his demon form.

"That's a big motherfucker," Isla mutters in disbelief. I nod in agreement because what else can you do when an eight feet tall monster with our signature blue-black skin and giant-ass moose antlers suddenly appears in your living room?

He looks at us, one by one, giant blood-red eyes swirling as he assesses each of us before landing on Isla. He narrows his eyes in accusation before asking in his deep tremor of a voice, "Why is there a hunter in your home?"

Acknowledgments

Holy shit.

If you're actually reading this, that means you read my book. How are you feeling? A little mad, probably. I get it. I also want to throttle authors who leave cliffhangers. But I am nothing if not a hypocrite.

So first of all, let me thank you. Thank you for taking a chance on a debut author and reading the beginning of Bel, Caspian and Fritz's story. As an avid reader and reviewer, I know it can be daunting to branch outside of our favorite storytellers, so I appreciate you more than you know.

Next, my amazing husband, Andy. First he let me turn an entire room in our house into a reading sanctuary, paint and decorate it however I want. Then, when I decided it was time to start creating my own books, he let me take over the house with my madness. If I needed a hand *visualizing* something *ahem* yes, like that, he was always willing to do whatever I asked of him and offer advice and a different perspective. He helped me brainstorm ideas, had google translate ready to go for me whenever I needed to name something, etc.

Then, we have to talk about my amazing beta readers. Karolina Wilde, author of House of Pain and upcoming House of Ruin, was one of the catalysts into my author journey. I loved her book and her dedication ignited something inside of me to also spin my trauma and hurt into a beautiful story of love in unexpected places. She then was kind enough to beta read while writing her own book and offer me incredibly helpful feedback. Addie Gray was another amazing beta reader, she left me super specific line notes on things I hadn't even thought of and she 100% made Albatross better than I ever could have by myself.

About the Author

Karlee Berrios is a full-time mom and part-time daydreamer. She lives in Arizona with her husband and daughter and spends all her free time lost in a book or creating her own. Albatross is her debut novel, the beginning to the Birds of Prey series, and she's currently plotting approximately 49027 other fantasy/ paranormal novels.

You can connect with me on:

🔗 https://linktr.ee/authorkarleeberrios

Subscribe to my newsletter:

✉ https://mailchi.mp/ca36010e0a1e/eqcfg49ihw

www.ingramcontent.com/pod-product-compliance
Lightning Source LLC
Chambersburg PA
CBHW020321160726
47992CB00004B/1632